Praise for Juli Zeh's

DECOMPRESSION

"A mesmerizing and disturbing psychological thriller. . . . Fantasy and reality entwine in . . . contrapuntal narratives. . . . Zeh's talent pulls this morally murky tale up from the depths and toward a redeeming light."

—*The Wall Street Journal*

"A tale that unfolds at a high level of psychological excitement."

—*Der Spiegel*

"This is phenomenal. . . . A nightmarish, furious, cold thriller. . . . Juli Zeh is at her literary best when she's describing underwater silence, when she's describing situations in which isolation is total and the world as it exists above water is bidden farewell."

—*Frankfurter Allgemeine Sonntagszeitung*

"Juli Zeh's love-triangle drama easily bears comparison with the work of Patricia Highsmith, doyenne of the conspicuously amoral."

—*Brigitte*

Juli Zeh

DECOMPRESSION

Juli Zeh's novels include *Eagles and Angels*, winner of numerous prizes including the German Book Prize; *Gaming Instinct*; *In Free Fall*; and *The Method*. She has worked at the United Nations in New York, taught at the German Institute for Literature in Leipzig, and currently lives in Brandenburg. In 2013 she was awarded the Thomas Mann Prize.

ALSO BY JULI ZEH

Published in English

Eagles and Angels

In Free Fall

DECOMPRESSION

Anchor Books

A Division of Penguin Random House LLC

New York

DECOMPRESSION

A Novel

Juli Zeh

Translated from the German by John Cullen

FIRST ANCHOR BOOKS EDITION, JUNE 2015

The Library of Congress has cataloged the Nan A. Talese/Doubleday edition as follows:
Zeh, Juli.
[Nullzeit. English]
Decompression : a novel / Juli Zeh ; translated from the German by John Cullen.—First American edition.
pages cm
1. Man-woman relationships—Fiction. I. Cullen, John, 1942– translator. II. Title.
PT2688.E28N8513 2014 833'.92—dc23 2013034654

Anchor Books Trade Paperback ISBN: 978-1-101-91050-4
eBook ISBN: 978-0-385-53759-9

Book design by Maria Carella

www.anchorbooks.com

146122990

For Nelson

DECOMPRESSION

1

We discussed wind directions and sea swells and speculated about what kind of weather the rest of November would bring. Although the daytime temperature seldom dropped below sixty-eight degrees, the island had its seasons too; you just needed to pay closer attention. Then our conversation moved from meteorology to the European economic situation. Bernie, the Scot, argued in favor of controlled bankruptcy for Greece. Laura, who was from Switzerland, believed that smaller countries should get international support. I had no interest in politics. If I'd wanted to spend the whole day surfing the Internet for news, I wouldn't have had to leave the Federal Republic of Germany. Laura and Bernie agreed that Germany was the new economic policeman of Europe—powerful, but unloved. The two of them looked at me expectantly. Every German abroad is Angela Merkel's press spokesperson.

I said, "As far as we're concerned, the crisis has been over for a long time." Germans and Brits were going on vacations again. We were doing better, and some of us were even thriving.

We kept our cardboard signs wedged under our arms. The clients listed on Bernie's sign were the EVANS FAMILY and the NORRIS FAMILY. Laura's sign said ANNETTE, FRANK, BASTI, and SUSANNE. My sign bore only two names that day—THEODOR HAST and JOLANTHE AUGUSTA SOPHIE VON DER PAHLEN—but they went on so long that they barely fit. The signs had to be small enough that we could make them disappear under our jackets at a moment's notice. An island law designed to protect taxi drivers forbade us to pick up clients at the airport. If we were caught doing so, the fine was three hundred euros. The taxi drivers stood just outside the glass doors of the arrivals terminal and kept an eye on us. Because of them, we usually greeted our baffled clients by hugging them like old friends. On the board above our heads, the display flipped: *20 minutes delayed.* Bernie raised his eyebrows in an unspoken question. We nodded.

"With much milk," I said.

"Lots of," Laura said.

Laura had been trying for years to teach me English, but I'd never even learned Spanish very well. Bernie didn't care about my bad English as long as he could understand what I meant. He stuck his hands in the pockets of his shorts and strolled over to the coffee stand. His five-day beard and swaying gait always made him look like a man walking on the deck of a ship.

We'd finished our coffee by the time the first passengers came out into the arrivals area. Some of Bernie's people immediately surrounded him. Five so far—he'd make good money. I pictured the two members of my group as an elegant older lady and a white-haired man, the latter pushing a cart piled high with an assortment of different-colored suitcases. That was the only way I could imagine a Theo and a Jolanthe. The deal we'd agreed on gave them exclusive rights to my services, at a price that could be paid only by people who already had a large part of their lives behind them.

It was always exciting to pick up new clients at the airport. You never knew who you were going to get, who had taken it into their head to give sport diving a try. Because Antje handled all the office work, I usually hadn't even spoken to clients by telephone when I met them for the first time. What would they look like? How old would they be? What preferences, occupations, life stories would they have? Being near the ocean was something like being on a train; in a very short time, you came to know other people amazingly well. As I was in the habit of never judging anyone, I got along just fine with everybody.

The Air Berlin passengers came through the gate at the same time as passengers deplaning from a Madrid flight—shorter people, less warmly dressed, and not so pale. I'd had a lot of practice at guessing nationalities, and when it came to identifying Germans, I guessed right almost 100 percent of the time. A couple was coming my way. I glanced at them briefly, thought *father and daughter*, and kept looking past them for Theodor and Jolanthe. The couple stopped in front of me, but only when the woman pointed to the sign in my hand did I realize that my new clients had found me.

"I'm Jolante, but without an *H*," the woman said.

"Are you Herr Fiedler?" the man asked.

A taxi driver was observing us through the revolving door. I spread my arms and embraced Theodor Hast.

"I'm Sven," I said. "Welcome to the island."

Theodor tensed up while I kissed the air to the left and right of his face. A faint scent of lavender and red wine. Then I grabbed the woman. She was as yielding as a stuffed animal. For a moment I was afraid she'd fall to the floor as soon as I let her go.

"Wow," Theodor said. "What a greeting."

I'd explain the effusive welcome in the car. "I'm parked right outside," I said.

By then, Bernie had gathered his second family around him, and Laura was standing in the middle of a group of young Germans. They all fell silent and stared over at us. I looked back at them and shrugged. Antje would have laughed at me and pointed out, once again, that I was "slow on the uptake." Theodor and Jolante casually guided their wheeled suitcases toward the exit. He had on a tailored suit, but neither a dress shirt nor a tie; his open jacket revealed a light-colored T-shirt. She was wearing combat boots and a sleeveless gray linen dress with a knee-length skirt. Her long black hair glistened on her back like crow feathers. She and Theodor bumped shoulders together, laughing about something. Then they stopped and turned around to me. And now I saw it too: They didn't come across as tourists. They looked more like models in a travel ad, and Jolante seemed somehow familiar. Half the people in the arrivals terminal were gaping at her. The words *magnificent specimen* crossed my mind.

"Well, have a great time," Laura said, her eyes on Frau von der Pahlen's legs.

"*Canalla,*" Bernie said in Spanish, grinning and slapping me on the shoulder. *You rascal.* His new clients—two families—were all redheads. That meant sunburn and nervous children.

❖

Outside in the parking area, I opened the side door of my Volkswagen van and invited my clients to get in, but they thought it would be more fun to sit in the front with me. The front seat had room for three; Theodor sat squashed in the middle. I was wearing shorts, and my bare leg looked uncouth next to his suit pants. When I put the van in gear, my hand brushed his left thigh. He kept his knees pressed together for the rest of the trip.

"We go by first names here," I said. "If that's all right with you."

"Theo."

"Jola."

We proffered hands. Theo's fingers, warm but limp, lay briefly in my own. Jola had a man's firm handshake, but her hand felt amazingly cold. She rolled the window partly down and stuck her nose into the wind. Her sunglasses made her look like an insect. A really cute insect, I must admit.

Arrecife was a concentration of various kinds of unpleasantness. Government offices, law courts, police stations, hotel complexes, hospitals. Antje used to say you didn't drive to Arrecife unless you had a problem. I had one on the day in question, but I didn't know it yet. I was just happy to be leaving the city. I stepped on the gas, turned onto the arterial road, and reached escape velocity. The landscape opened up: a couple of bearded palms standing beside the road, and everything beyond them black, all the way to the horizon. The island was no beauty, not in the classical sense. Looked at from an airplane, it resembled a gigantic granite quarry, with what seemed to be the remains of snow lying in the valleys between the brown-gray hills. During the final descent, the snowy patches revealed themselves as villages of white houses standing close together. A landscape without any vegetation is like a woman with nothing suitable to put on—they both have a hard time being admired. The island's lack of vanity was the precise reason why I'd fallen in love with it from the very start.

How was your flight, how's the weather in Germany?

How big is the island, how many people live here?

I chose the route through the wine-growing region. Innumerable funnel-shaped ditches, in each of which a vine found protection and fertile soil. That there were people who gouged out a one-yard-deep hole in the lapilli layer for every single plant, reinforced the borders of each ditch with a little stone wall, and thus perforated an area of twelve thousand acres like a Swiss cheese—that fact never ceased to fascinate me. In the distance the craters of the Timanfaya glowed red and yellow and purple and green from the lichen covering the volcanic rock. The only plant growing anywhere around us was a mushroom. I waited to see which of my companions would be the first to say, "Like being on the moon."

"Like being on the moon," said Jola.

"Sublime," said Theo.

When Antje and I arrived in Lanzarote fourteen years ago, equipped with two backpacks and a plan to spend the largest-possible portion of our future on the island, though not necessarily together, she was the one who'd said, "Like being on the moon," when she first saw the Timanfaya. I'd thought something along the lines of *Sublime* but hadn't found the right word.

"If you like rubble," Jola said.

"You have no feeling for the aesthetics of the austere," Theo replied.

"And you're just glad to be back on solid ground."

Jola took off her boots and socks and cast a questioning glance in my direction before bracing her bare feet against the windshield. I nodded in approval. I always liked it when my clients relaxed as quickly as possible. They were *not* supposed to feel at home.

"So you don't like to fly either?" I asked Theo.

He gave me a scathing look.

"He pretends to be asleep," said Jola. She'd taken out her telephone and was tapping in a text message. "Like all men when they're afraid."

"I get drunk as fast as I can," I said.

"Theo takes care of that before boarding."

A cell phone chirped. Theo reached into the inside pocket of his suit jacket, read the caller's number, and answered.

"Do you go back to Germany often?" Jola asked me.

"Not if I can help it," I said.

Jola's cell phone chirped. She read the screen and poked Theo in the side. When she laughed, she curled up her nose like a little girl. Theo looked out the window.

"I like this landscape," he said. "It leaves you in peace. It doesn't require you to marvel at it and admire it all the time."

I understood exactly what he meant.

"For the next two weeks, I'm only interested in what's underwater," Jola said. "The world above the surface can go to hell as far as I'm concerned."

I understood that too.

We reached Tinajo, a small town of white houses with little oriental-looking towers rising from the corners of their flat roofs. At the bookstore, which looked as though it had been renovated and then closed, we turned off to the left. After a few hundred yards, the last of the well-tended front gardens were behind us. They were followed by terraced fields wrested from the rubble. Here and there a couple of zucchini lay on the black soil. A flat-topped shed with a German shepherd tied up on the roof in the blazing sun was the last sign of civilization. The road turned into a gravel track that was marked off by whitewashed stones and wound like a ribbon through the volcanic field. This was the stretch where most clients would begin to get excited. They'd cry out jokingly, "Where are you taking us?" and "We're at the ends of the earth!"

Jola said, "Wow."

Theo said, "Awesome."

I abstained from historical and geological tourist tips. I said nothing about the volcanic eruptions that had buried a quarter of the island between 1730 and 1736. I held my tongue and left my clients to their astonishment. All around us was nothing but rocks in various bizarre shapes. The silence of the minerals. There wasn't even a bird in sight. The wind shook the van as though it wanted to get in.

We rounded the last volcanic cone and suddenly the Atlantic was spread out before us, dark blue, flecked with white foam, and a bit implausible after so much rock. The breakers exploded against the cliffs and sent up high clouds of spray that rose and fell as though filmed in slow motion. The sky, gray-blue and white and windblown, was a continuation of the sea by other means.

"Oh man," said Jola.

"Do you know the story about the two writers walking along a beach? One of them complains that all the good books have already been written. The other writer shouts, 'Look!' and points out to sea. 'Here comes the last wave!' "

Jola laughed briefly, I not at all. The silence of the minerals always wins out. A few more minutes' drive brought us to Lahora. The entrance was marked by an unfinished building, a concrete cube on a foundation of natural stone. The building's empty window openings looked out over the sea. The gravel track now turned into a strip of slippery sand that climbed steeply up to the village, if *village* was the right word for a group of thirty uninhabited houses.

While I'm thinking about the best way to describe Lahora, it occurs to me that I've been using the past tense to talk about the island and everything on it. The first time I drove Theo and Jola to Lahora was barely three months ago. As usual, I hugged the cliff at the upper end of the village so my clients could enjoy the view. I explained that contrary to what you could read in many travel guides, Lahora was by no means an old fishing village. It was rather a collection of weekend houses built by wealthy Spaniards who already owned estates in Tinajo, handsome properties but utterly lacking in ocean views. The government of the island, I went on, had granted title to the building site, which lay in the middle of the biggest volcanic area, but hadn't bothered to provide any infrastructure. Lahora had no building plan, I told them. No street names. No sewer system. All in all, except for Antje and me, Lahora didn't have any inhabitants either. Lahora was a mixture of abandoned building site and ghost town, a variation on the blurry boundary between not-yet-finished and falling-into-ruin.

In fact, the Spaniards had long since given up tinkering around on their half-finished houses; instead they would sit on their driftwood-fenced roof terraces while the salty wind gnawed the plaster off their walls. Wooden cable spools served as tables, stacked construction pallets as benches. Lahora was a terminus. A place where everything came to a halt. Furnished with objects that would have landed on the rubbish pile long ago if they were anywhere else. The ends of the earth.

We sat in the van and looked out over the flat roofs, with their accumulations of water tanks and solar panels and satellite dishes, and then down to the first row of houses, which practically stood in water at high tide. I promised my clients they'd find the place uniquely silent. The owners of the houses came, if at all, only on weekends.

I ended my little discourse by announcing two rules for their stay in Lahora: no swimming, and no going for walks. The little cove was a seething cauldron in any weather, I said, and the volcanic fields regularly broke headstrong hikers' bones. In Lahora you could sit around, look out over the sea, and contemplate the smaller islands to the north, which crouched like sleeping animals in the haze between the water and the sky. Besides, when all was said and done, they were here for diving. Every day we'd drive to the best diving spots the island offered, and if in addition they wanted to do a little sightseeing, then, as arranged, I'd be available to act as their chauffeur and guide.

They weren't listening to me. They seemed completely absorbed, holding hands and gazing at the village and the ocean. They didn't ask, as other clients did, why I'd settled in such a remote place. They didn't prattle on about former diving adventures. When Jola turned her face to me and took off her sunglasses, her eyes were moist—from the wind, I thought, the breeze blowing through the open window on her side.

"It's absolutely beautiful here," she said.

I shivered and turned the ignition key.

Today it seems to me as if that first meeting took place half an eternity ago, in another century or in an alien universe. Although I can still see the Atlantic through my window as I write, the island's no longer in the present tense. I'm literally living out of suitcases. Down at the port in Arrecife, a container holding all my equipment is awaiting shipment to Thailand, where a German from Stuttgart wants to open a dive center on some palmy island with white beaches. A second container with my personal stuff is almost empty. When I was considering what I could use in Germany, hardly anything occurred to me. What would shorts, sandals, portholes from sunken ships, and a swordfish I caught and mounted myself be doing in the Ruhr? The only suitable place for all that is the past.

◆

We coasted slowly down the dirt road and turned left at the touchingly hubristic little wall that divided the Atlantic from the dry land. My property constituted the end of the village. Standing at oblique angles and a stone's throw from each other on the edge of a large sandlot were the two houses: the two-story, generously roof-terraced "Residencia" where Antje and I lived, and the "Casa Raya," the somewhat smaller guesthouse. The area both houses occupied had been blasted into the black rock overlooking the sea. They stood raised up on natural stone foundations the sea spray couldn't hurt. I'd acquired the houses for a good price and renovated them lavishly, and Antje had worked real miracles in the gardens around them. She'd fought with the contractor for days on end about how much excavation would be required, she'd drawn up irrigation plans, she'd insisted on bringing in special soil. She'd conscientiously investigated wind load and sun angles and the direction of root spread. With the passage of the years, there had sprung up on the edge of the rocky wasteland an oasis it cost me a fortune to keep watered. Royal Poinciana, hibiscus, and oleander bloomed all year round. Masses of bougainvillea threw their cascades of color over the walls, and above them two Norfolk Island pines stretched their thick-fingered needle leaves to the sky. The bloom of flowers on Lahora's outermost edge burned a bright hole in the bare surroundings.

"No, not possible," said Theo, shaking his head and laughing softly, as if he couldn't believe his eyes. Jola had her sunglasses back on and remained silent.

There were clients who didn't care for Lahora, but everybody liked the Casa Raya. The house, a simple white cube with blue shutters on its windows, contained only a bedroom, a living room, a bathroom, and a cooking niche, but in spite of its small size, there was something majestic about the place. Under the steps that led up to the front door, the lava rocks were battered by the Atlantic, which seemed not so much raging as experienced; it's been throwing itself against them in the same way for a couple of million years. Every two minutes the water in the cove surged up and spewed skyward a huge fountain sixty feet high. It was incredible that such a drama had nothing, not the smallest thing, to do with us humans. After guests left the Casa, they'd go back to Germany and write us to say that the fabled roar of the surf had stayed in their ears for days. It was a sound that inhabited you.

Antje was already sitting on the Casa's steps, waiting for us. Todd, her cocker spaniel, was asleep on the hood of her white Citroën. The only dog in the universe that would voluntarily lie on hot sheet metal in blazing sunlight. This was his way of making sure Antje wouldn't drive away without him. Or so she believed. When she saw us coming, she jumped up and waved; her dress was a big, shiny spot. She owned an entire collection of vivid cotton dresses, each in a different pattern. She'd accessorize from a range of flip-flops in various matching colors. On this particular day, little green horses on a red background galloped over her body. When she extended her hand to Jola, it looked for a few seconds as though someone had taken still shots of two different women in two different films and artfully spliced them together. Theo gazed at the ocean with his hands in his trouser pockets.

I set the luggage on the dusty ground. Antje raised her hand in thanks. We'd greeted each other rather scantily. I didn't like her to touch me in the presence of other people. Even though we'd lived together for many years, it always struck me as funny that we were a couple. In public, at any rate.

While I lugged the empty scuba tanks from the morning dive

into the Residencia's garage, where the fill station was located, Antje showed our guests around their vacation home. Getting clients settled in was one of her responsibilities. In addition to the Casa Raya, she also managed a few holiday apartments in Puerto del Carmen for their owners. My diving students made up the majority of the guests. Antje did bookings, turned over keys, settled up, cleaned up, tended the garden, supervised workers. At the same time, she ran the business end of my diving school—took care of the office, updated the website, did all the paperwork required by the various diving organizations. It had taken her less than two years after our arrival to make herself indispensable. She even knew how to cope with the *mañana* mentality of the Spanish islanders.

I threw the used diving suits into the washing shed in the yard and went into the house. I was suddenly thirsty for an aperitif. Campari over ice. Ordinarily I drank only when I had to: in airplanes, at weddings, or on New Year's Eve. The Campari I wanted at the moment was somehow related to Jola and Theo. I could smell and taste it before I knew whether Antje had any on hand. I found a bottle in the refrigerator, poured myself a large glass, and listened with pleasure to the crackling ice cubes. Glass in hand, I stepped out onto the lower terrace. If you put your chair right up against the railing, you could look across the sandlot and into the Casa's living room. Just then the curtains were opened. Antje's colorful dress was visible through the window. I could see Jola and Theo in the background, contemplating the cooking alcove. They were probably used to much better kitchen arrangements. Or maybe they were wondering how they could get anything to cook anyway, seeing that there wasn't so much as a chewing-gum machine in Lahora. On this, their first evening, Antje would invite them to dinner, and tomorrow after the morning dive, she'd take them shopping for supplies. That was what we always did with the guests who came to the Casa.

Across the way, Antje was explaining stove, microwave, and washing machine. Theo appeared to be listening, while Jola let herself drop onto the sofa. Her head bounced up and down in the window; she was probably testing the sofa for springiness. I was tempted to imagine Theo throwing her onto the dining table and pushing up her dress—but I deleted the image at once. Female clients were taboo. In my profession, your work clothes were a pair of swimming trunks.

JOLA'S DIARY, FIRST DAY

Saturday, November 12. Afternoon.

Incredible place. White facades and barred shutters. Blazing sun and black sand. Zorro might come around the corner at any minute, rushing to prevent a duel. The air tastes salty. I find it fabulous here, but since Theo likes it too, I naturally have to take the opposite side. The sublime aesthetics of the austere! All right, old man. Why not just give it a rest? The world doesn't become any more beautiful because you dump your poetry on it. Not bigger either, or more important or better. All you do is crash into the world and bounce off. Like the sea hitting the rocks, your words burst into spray and flow back into you. If you had ten thousand years, maybe you'd be able to round off a little corner, but you won't live that long. You least of all.

As for me, I'm keeping my mouth shut. I'm not talking about literature, I'm not talking about dying. We're both making an effort. This is going to be a lovely vacation. I won't provoke him, and he won't let himself be provoked. Armistice.

Well, maybe vacation *isn't the word. The real reason why I'm here is the part. The part I want. The part I need. Lotte's my last chance. I tore her picture out of the book and pinned it to the wall over the bed. I could look at her and look at her. Charlotte Hass, Lotte Hass. The Girl on the Ocean Floor. She's wearing a red swimsuit and old-fashioned diving equipment and holding on to part of a sunken vessel. Her eyes are heavily made-up behind her diving goggles, and her long hair is spread out like a water plant around her head. She's so beautiful. And strong. A female warrior. Home and children weren't enough for her. She went looking for danger. Her diary's as thrilling as a crime novel. In the 1950s diving wasn't a sport, it was pioneer work. A test of courage for men, not for women. Lotte was the first girl who insisted on swimming with the fish. When Theo noticed the photograph over the bed, he bit his tongue.*

Sven's a beamish boy. Only two years younger than Theo, but built differently. With webbed feet and gills behind his ears. He doesn't look at me. Doesn't even see me. Probably because I'm not a fish. Which is what he's supposed to turn me into. That's what he's being paid for, and he doesn't come cheap.

Sven comes with Antje, who's his—what? Assistant? Wife? Sister? Secretary? She introduced herself as "Sven's Antje," as though giving both her job title and her family status in one go. Sven, meanwhile, was staring into space. Antje apparently embarrasses him. She's a little thing but quite a looker, she talks a lot, and she smells like Nivea. Blond as a Swede. She stays out of the water. She made us aware of that right from the start. The water, she said, is Sven's "state of matter." I think she probably meant "element" or maybe "business." Something like that goes through the old man like a burning knife. If you can't talk right keep your trap shut, that's his motto. He can't stand to be around people he thinks sound like children. On the other hand, he seems quite happy to gaze upon Sven's Antje.

Lahora. The Spanish textbook in school had some strange sample sentences: My dogs are under the bed. I hear myself scream. Te llegó la hora—Your hour has come. *Not another soul for miles. No automobile except for Antje's, the car with the dog on the hood. Without a car, there's no getting out of here. In short, except for us, the place is deserted. The old man liked that right away: "Somebody ought to set a story here," he said. Go right ahead. Set a story. Write something instead of always just talking about writing something. I didn't say anything.*

The old man let his eyes rest on Antje's Swedish bosom and listened to her attentively. Used toilet paper should be thrown not in the toilet but in the bucket next to the toilet, because otherwise the pipes get blocked. Electrical appliances are to be turned off whenever we leave the house. If we want warm showers, don't take one right after another. Don't drink from the taps. Don't put any garden furniture on any of the watering hoses. When we want to log on to the Internet, tell Sven so he can adjust the satellite dish. No swimming, and no going for walks—but we knew that already.

Then I stood in the garden for a long time and watched the sea playing with itself. All at once the old man was behind me with a glass of red wine in his hand. He put an arm around my shoulders, pulled me to him, and kissed the crown of my head. "Little Jola," he said, nothing more.

My eyes got damp. I held him tight. When he's in the mood, it can be a great thing to touch him. It's always this way: you travel thousands of miles to sleep less comfortably and understand yourself better.

2

A typical evening. All the windows were open. Warm air flowed through the house and eliminated the difference between inside and outside. Antje was banging around in the kitchen. A sound as pleasant as rain on a tent roof. I was glad to sit at the computer in our tiny office while she busied herself around the stove.

Three hundred and eighty-four thousand hits on Google. That was a shock. Even though I didn't know exactly why it frightened me. In the background, a software program was uploading data from my dive computer. If Antje appeared in the doorway, I could click onto the other screen in a flash. I didn't feel like explaining what I was doing and why. Googling clients wasn't really my style.

It looked like half the Internet consisted of Jola. Wikipedia entry, fan pages, Facebook profile, Twitter, press reports, YouTube. Hundreds of photographs. How many faces could one person have? The longer I looked, the faster they seemed to multiply. From page to page, from link to link. It was fascinating. And somehow offensive.

> Jolante Augusta Sophie von der Pahlen (stage name: Jola Pahlen), born 5 October 1981 in Hanover, is a German actress. Von der Pahlen comes from a Baltic German noble family. At the age of eleven, she recorded a CD of children's songs and performed a singing role in a production of *Woyzeck* at the Staatstheater in Hanover. She gained her first television experience (1995–1997) in the children's program *Toggo*, which was broadcast on the Super RTL network. Since December 4, 2003, von der Pahlen has played the role of Bella Schweig in SAT.1's daytime drama *Up and Down*. Jolante von der Pahlen lives with the writer Theodor Hast.
> • *See "Jola Pahlen" in the Internet Movie Database (German and English versions)*

A chirping sound came from the ceiling. The gecko had left his sleeping quarters behind the curtain rod and was preparing himself for his nightly insect hunt. Years ago, when I saw him for the first time, he was approximately three centimeters long, practically transparent, and clueless about life. Now he was longer than my index finger, and he knew he had nothing to fear from me. I'd baptized him Emile, even though Antje declared he was a female. She claimed that this particular gecko species includes no males whatsoever; the females reproduce by self-cloning, she said. Then she grinned at me, as though she was talking about some masterstroke on Nature's part. None of that bothered me. I liked Emile.

He had the most beautiful feet, and he used nanotechnology to run upside down across the ceiling.

"Frau Pahlen, you come from a noble family. In what ways has your family background shaped your character?"

"Everybody's shaped by their origins. I've learned from my family to protect and preserve beautiful things. It causes me physical pain to see someone put a water glass without a coaster on the bare wood of a Biedermeier table. Carelessness is beauty's worst enemy."

"Your father is a successful film producer. Your family is rich. Do you sometimes feel a desire to do something independently?"

"Everything I do I do independently. My father doesn't stand in front of the *Up and Down* cameras, and neither does anyone else in my family. That's me."

"But people say, don't they, that your father got you the part in *Up and Down*?"

"Success always requires a combination of luck, hard work, and talent."

"Frau Pahlen, you turned thirty last week. Isn't it time to leave *Up and Down*?"

"Why? Do you think thirty's too old for soap operas?"

"Not for soap operas, but maybe for a first real film role."

"I'm looking at a serious project right now."

"Then we wish you good luck, Frau Pahlen."

The delicate scampering of soft feet. Emile appeared on the computer monitor, whose illuminated surface attracted little flies. He walked across the screen and sat in the middle of Jola's face. Then he looked at me with his black button eyes and stuck out his tongue. In the movies, if a reptile sits on a character's picture, that character will go crazy before the end.

Theodor Hast racked up 12,400 links on Google. Most of them referred to his relationship with Jola Pahlen. His Wikipedia entry consisted of two lines, with no accompanying photograph: "German writer, born 1969 in Reutlingen. His first novel, *Flying Buildings*, was published in 2001. He lives in Berlin, Stuttgart, and New York."

The triple residence awakened unpleasant memories. In law school we were taught to cite all the publishing offices when quoting from the technical literature: "Volker Schlön, *Securities Law, with Special Emphasis on the Securities Trading Act.* Berlin, Heidelberg, New York, 6th edition." A book like that cost 129 deutschmarks, and the copy in the university library was notoriously unavailable whenever a paper relating to securities law actually had to be written. In Theo's case it wasn't his book but he himself who apparently lived in three places at the same time.

"An irritating gem."

"A clear harbinger of future masterpieces."

"'There are many people who like me, but only one has to live with me. And that one's myself.' (Theodor Hass, *Flying Buildings*, p. 23.)"

According to the jacket copy posted on the publishing house's home page, the novel was about a character named Martin and the search for identity. It sounded complicated. I scrolled down and came to an excerpt from the text:

> He asked himself how it could be that God created the world in six days and gave himself the seventh day off. Were there already days before the earth took its first twenty-four-hour spin around the sun? And how was it that God opted for the seven-day week? That must mean God had held down a job somewhere. Martin would have very much liked to know where. He set his glass down and looked up. The tattered sky was hurrying eastward, as if it had something urgent to do there. *Emigrate*, he thought. But that would make sense only if the country we escape to weren't always and only ourselves.

Antje read a lot. Whenever I tried to read a novel, it would put me to sleep.

A pan started sizzling. I smelled rabbit. I got up but left the computer on. The monitor was a fabulous hunting reserve for Emile.

Antje had set the table for four. Two glasses per person, one for water and one for wine. I noticed that the glasses were standing on the bare wood of the teak dining table. I started searching the sideboard for coasters.

⁂

Jola talked a great deal. Her hands flailed the air as though she was shooing away insects. Her long hair seemed to be in her way. She was constantly swiping it from one side to the other. Antje served salt-crusted Canary potatoes, mushrooms in olive oil, and three different *mojo* sauces. The conversation revolved around Jola's movie project. She was reading a book about Lotte Hass, and she had romantic notions about the adventure of diving: you put on a chic bathing suit, jumped into the water, and quickly emptied your breathing tank, preferably while eye to eye with a whale shark. Theo ate potatoes. In a steady rhythm, one after the other, like a man doing a job.

I said I was going to instruct them strictly by the book. Caution and security would be primary concerns in every situation. It wasn't about having an adventure, it was about knowledge of the subject and mastery of technique.

Jola stuck out her lower lip and played the little girl. Couldn't she make friends with a whale shark?

I said we'd see angel sharks. Six feet long at most, and generally lying flat on the seafloor. At this the little girl turned into a strategist with narrow eyes and a dangerous smile. "Just as long as I can tell Casting I've had experience with sharks."

I thought it wasn't at all necessary for her to act that way. A cute little space between her upper incisors compelled me to keep looking at her mouth. Suddenly her hand was lying on my arm. The way she batted her eyelashes revealed practice. Didn't I think she'd make a good Lotte?

Theo looked up from his plate. "Get ahold of yourself," he said.

It sounded like a slap. Antje flinched as though it had been meant for her. The wind moved the curtains on the open windows; the air had become slightly cool. The clock on the wall gave the time as shortly before seven. The night was already creeping out of the corners of the rooms. I stood up to turn on the lights and close the windows.

"Don't you like the potatoes?" Antje asked.

"Oh yes," said Jola, quickly snatching the smallest one off her plate with her hand and stuffing the little morsel in her mouth. "But I'm not really hungry."

"Eating disorder," Theo explained. He emptied his second glass of wine and poured himself some more. "She's already too old for the part. If she gets fat to boot, she won't have a chance."

He laughed as though he'd told a very good joke. Antje disappeared into the kitchen to fetch the rabbit dish. Jola stared at her unsoiled plate. Clients were like family members; you didn't get to pick them. While we were waiting for the main course, I broke the silence to clarify once again what we could expect from one another. They would get exclusive rights to my services for two weeks, twenty-four hours a day, with an unlimited number of dives, completion of the Advanced Open Water Diver course, and nitrox certification, in addition to lodgings in the Casa Raya, the loan of all equipment, and chauffeur service to all the diving spots and places of interest on the island. I would get fourteen thousand euros. Ordinarily I had several clients, whom I would divide into groups. Jola and Theo were paying for the fact that I hadn't accepted any other requests for the coming fourteen days. It wasn't cheap, but in return I belonged to them alone. We shook hands. Jola's telephone chirped. She read the display, smiled, and tapped in a reply. Antje came back, carrying a steaming stewpot between two kitchen towels.

"*Conejo en salmorejo*," she said.

Bones were sticking out of the ragout. Theo's telephone chirped. He smiled and put his hand on Jola's thigh. They were actually sending each other text messages while in the same room. Antje served out rabbit pieces. Her cocker spaniel, Todd, came out of the kitchen, where he'd been worshipping the stove, assessed the situation, and took up a position next to Jola. He apparently considered her the weakest link in the chain. I tasted the food, praised it, and reminded my clients of my single condition: on the Wednesday after next, November 23, I would have a day off. Theo wanted to know why they would be obliged to do without my services on that particular Wednesday. He liked the rabbit. He also liked the wine, which he was drinking practically alone. With a quick look, I stopped Antje from getting a second bottle. Jola saw us exchange glances and laughed; for the first time that evening, her laughter was completely unaffected.

"What?" asked Theo.

"Nothing," said Jola.

You're not right for each other, I thought, and once again I forbade myself to think like that. The private lives of my clients had nothing to do with me. I explained what was up on November 23. Late that past summer, I'd been out deep-sea fishing and started to get an unusually strong sonar signal. There was an object about one hundred meters down, an object more than eighty meters long. Maybe it was only a heap of stones with an unusual shape. Or maybe it was a sensational find. For years there had been hardly any new discoveries of sunken ships anywhere in the world, and certainly none in divable waters. I marked the coordinates on my GPS device; finding the right place again wouldn't present much of a problem. But diving into a wreck for the first time at a depth of one hundred meters wasn't exactly child's play—especially if you did it alone. I'd spent weeks preparing for the dive, calculating gas mixtures, racking my brains to figure out how I could lengthen my stay on the bottom by twenty minutes and yet avoid needing more than three hours' worth of decompression stops before I could surface. In addition, I'd ordered some specially made dry gloves, and I was working on a heating system to install in my diving suit. Bernie had promised that he and his equally Scottish pal Dave would man the *Aberdeen* to provide my floating base. These were all professional requirements for a professional undertaking.

Jola listened as though the word of God were coming out of my mouth. Her big eyes began to reflect my own enthusiasm. I found it hard to come to the end.

On November 23 I'd be forty years old, and I wanted to celebrate my birthday one hundred meters below the surface of the ocean. Alone. Or better yet: in the company of a World War II freighter that went missing seventy years ago.

"I want to go too," Jola said. "I can help the boat crew."

"This is an expedition, not an excursion," I said. "Every move the crew makes has to be exactly right."

She looked at me insistently. "I grew up on ships."

"Her father owns a Benetti Classic," Theo said.

I had to pause and digest this information. A used Benetti cost about as much as a luxury penthouse. And in Manhattan, at that.

"Nevertheless," I said. "I'm sorry."

"Or you could train me for that depth and then I could dive with you. Lotte would have liked that."

Against my will, I laughed.

"Please!" Jola cried out. "We have two whole weeks!"

"You'd need at least two years," I said. "If I tried to take you down there with me, I'd wind up in prison."

"For how long?" asked Theo, without taking his eyes off Jola's pleading face.

"For life," I said. "Convicted of murder."

"That's enough," said Antje, who didn't like the conversation. "Only professional divers can survive those kinds of expeditions. Would anyone like some cactus pear sorbet?"

"I'd be more than happy to spend a couple of years in prison," Theo said in the tone of a man who wants to change the subject. "Then I'd finally have enough peace to write."

Antje drew back the hand that was reaching for his plate. She said, "But in exchange for that, you'd have to harm another person."

"That's the advantage, isn't it?" Theo turned the wine bottle upside down and shook the last drops into his glass. "If someone already wants to go to jail, he gets a free shot. Then all he has to do is pick his target."

Jola was scraping rabbit pieces off her plate with the back of her knife. Todd caught them on the fly. "Don't listen to Theo," Jola said. "Shocking his audience is part of his job. Unfortunately, for the past few years he's preferred to be shocking at the dinner table rather than the computer keyboard."

"Which is still better," Theo said, "than making a fool of yourself by standing in front of a camera and spouting idiotic lines."

Jola stood up abruptly and walked over to the window. "My idiotic lines," she said with her back turned to us, "pay our rent."

Humming and sizzling inside the wall lamp, a moth was burning itself to death. The rabbit fibers between my teeth gave me an uncomfortable feeling that spread through my whole body. Antje raised her head and gave Theo a sympathetic look. "So why don't you write anymore?" she asked.

Sometimes I could kill her.

JOLA'S DIARY, FIRST DAY

Saturday, November 12. Night.

They're so cute, both of them. Blond, friendly, down-to-earth. Serving potatoes and bunny stew in their little white house. Normal and . . . yes, that's it: healthy somehow. So what does that make us*? Abnormal and sick? We didn't even thank them properly for dinner. All of a sudden the old man was in this big hurry to leave. At first he didn't even want to wait for dessert. Cactus pear sorbet. Difficulty level: complicated. Time required: two hours. According to my iPhone. Poor Antje. Now I'm waiting for the old man to fall asleep. He doesn't like me to be lying next to him while he's trying to doze off. I sleep well, he doesn't. Sleep turns you into a corpse, he tells me. How am I supposed to relax with a dead person next to me?*

I text him: "Sleep well, Theo. I love you."

His phone chirps in the bedroom. I can hear the sound through the thin wall. No answer. It's pitch-dark outside. Every now and then a dog howls. Our first night here and already I'm alone on the living-room sofa. This is how it begins, our very last serious attempt to get things straightened out.

3

"They're sort of funny."

This was the prelude to what I called the "postgame analysis." Scarcely had a person left the room when he or she became the subject of instantaneous, diagnostic discussion. Assessments were compared, details of judgments mutually corrected, and speculations transformed into a consistent psychological profile. Antje and her girlfriends practiced this discipline at the expert level. As for me, when it came to postgame analysis, I was the worst partner imaginable. If Antje gave it a try all the same, she must have felt some real sense of urgency.

I stood at the sink, scraping food remnants from the plates and trying to ignore Todd while he stared a hole in me. Right from the start, it had seemed creepy to me that he not only had the same name as my parents' now-deceased dog but also looked exactly like him. Antje firmly believed that we'd killed the first Todd by leaving him behind in Germany. I was afraid she believed just as firmly that the second Todd was a reincarnation of the first, whom she'd called back into life by recycling his name.

"Don't you think?"

I turned my back to her and the dog. I hated it when people judged one another. It was an obsession, a curse. I had left Germany because I couldn't stand living any longer in an all-encompassing net of reciprocal judgments. Judgers and judged found themselves in a permanent state of war, and everybody, depending on the situation, played one of the two parts. Everything my clients from back home told me was a report from the judgment front. What they thought about their boss. What their colleagues thought about them. What they thought about the chancellor. What they thought about the other divers. Then, after the first three beers some evening, what they thought about how their wives performed. And at the end of their dive holiday, they'd log on to a diving website and post what they thought about how I'd performed. It was as though people were afraid they'd fall silent forever if they stopped passing judgments.

"Sometimes Jola just stares into space," Antje said. "Like she's miles away. And she eats nothing. Did that strike you too?"

There was a reason for my aversion to judgments. Before I left Germany on New Year's Eve in 1997, I had studied law for five years. I belonged to a generation of students who didn't want school to come to an end. For us, high school graduation was by no means a happy event. It scared us. Most of us had no idea what to start doing with our lives. In school everything had been simple. You knew how to do things right and how much rebellion you could permit yourself. If something went wrong and there was any doubt, it was the teacher's fault. I did my compulsory military service, extended it for a year with the Army Engineer Divers, and then decided to go for a law degree, because it was said that such a degree left all possibilities open. It wasn't long before I really began to love my studies. Once again I'd found a field in which I could do everything right. As long as I took notes during lectures and spent three evenings a week in the library, I could enjoy the pleasant feeling that I was on the safe side. As a rule, I passed my exams with grades of 90 or higher. My fellow students' envy relieved me of the necessity of having any doubts at all.

After five years of study, my scores on the final written examinations were so good they made the impending oral exam seem like a mere formality. I bought a new pair of shoes, shopped around for the most appropriate aftershave lotion, and visited the barber. On the day of the exam I felt slightly nervous, but a sense of impending triumph buoyed me up on the way to the Justice Ministry.

Four professors seated behind a long desk. In front of it, me and another examinee, whose bad preliminary marks were stinking up the whole room. The longer the professors put him through the wringer, the more restlessly I shifted in my chair. I sat on my hands so I wouldn't forget myself and start waving one like a geek in German class. I tried to establish eye contact with the examiners and to indicate by movements of my eyebrows that I knew the answer to every single question. In short, I behaved like a complete jackass.

At last, Professor Brunsberg, an expert in constitutional law, addressed himself to me. Notorious for his halitosis, Brunsberg had a reputation for speaking directly in students' faces, knowing that his victims, fearful of bad grades, wouldn't turn their heads.

"Herr Fiedler," said Professor Brunsberg, "as you are obviously a very knowledgeable man, you're surely familiar with the name Montesquieu."

As if he'd pressed a button, I broke out in instantaneous perspiration. Political theory had played no part in my five years of legal studies. We were supposed to learn, for example, what constitutes an *Erlaubnistatbestandsirrtum*, a "permission facts mistake," and not what dead philosophers had said about the functioning of the state. I had no choice but to nod slowly.

"Good, Herr Fiedler. Then spell it, please."

"I beg your pardon?"

"Am I not speaking clearly? Spell *Montesquieu*!"

A row of blurred letters appeared before my mind's eye: a *Q*, a couple of *U*s, some *E*s. I got the "Montes" part right away, I knew it was followed by "qu," but everything thereafter lay in God's hands.

"M-o-n-t-e-s-q-u-e-u-e," I said.

Brunsberg slapped the table in delight. "*Queue* like 'cue stick,' right, Herr Fiedler? Is that what you've been doing the past few years? Playing pool?"

It became clear he wasn't going to let it rest. He was out to get me.

"You get a second attempt, Herr Fiedler. We're not inhuman."

Under my jacket, my shirt was stuck to my back. A spot on my behind itched so unbearably that my brain stopped working. I produced an alphabet salad that didn't have very much to do with

Montesquieu. Brunsberg's mood abruptly darkened. His bored colleagues looked toward the window. Outside, a couple of sparrows were fighting for the best spot on the ledge.

"Good, Herr Fiedler, or rather, not good. The question about Montesquieu has a second part. You'd like to get at least fifty percent in this examination, wouldn't you? Then tell me—quickly—the great father of constitutional doctrine's first name."

I took my time. I'd learned by heart examination presentations for fourteen different forms of legal action. I was thoroughly familiar with the Maastricht Judgment of the German Federal Constitutional Court. While the sparrows' dispute got louder, I wondered why it was that neither Montesquieu nor Voltaire seemed to have had a first name. You included the first names quite naturally when you referred to Thomas Hobbes or John Locke.

I felt at peace when I said, loudly and clearly, "Friedrich." That was Brunsberg's first name. The rest of the examination disappeared into fog.

When, two hours later, we were called back into the room to be given our results, I had become a different person. I couldn't understand myself anymore. Had I really paid four thousand marks for tutorial courses, spent eight hours daily in the library, and sat for a six-hour mock exam every week just so I could be inducted into the Asshole Club? The thought that I could spend the rest of my life in an occupation where people like Brunsberg called the shots nauseated me.

Maybe life would simply have gone on all the same if they had subtracted half a point from my total exam score because of that wretched oral. I would have gotten angry, done better in the next state examination, and landed a decent job in a law office. But in fact my average was even slightly improved by the oral. Brunsberg himself gave me almost a perfect score. When he shook my hand, he bared his teeth with joy. "You're a good lawyer, Herr Fiedler," he said. "If you do a bit of delving into the philosophical underpinnings of the law, you'll get even better."

Seeing that he no doubt meant well, on top of everything else, made the interior light in my head switch on. Everything in me was radiant with realization. My friends gathered around to congratulate me. The other candidate had failed the exam; he stood alone at the window, weeping. I stopped hearing what was being said. In my mind, I'd already left the country.

Charles-Louis de Secondat, Baron de La Brède et de Montesquieu. From that time on, there was no problem that formula couldn't solve. "Montesquieu" prevented me from passing judgments on other people, meddling in their lives, or even just handing out well-meant advice. I wanted nothing more to do with Germany, which I've thought of as "the war zone" ever since. When I began my new life on the island not long afterward, the fundamental expression of my worldview was "Stay out of it."

◆

"Maybe she's a drug addict," Antje said. "Lots of actresses have drug problems." I slammed the dishwasher door and inadvertently stepped on Todd's paw. "Don't talk nonsense," I said.

It sounded harsher than I meant it to. If I didn't want to show that my tone of voice had been a mistake, the next thing I said had to be spoken just as sharply. "You're not allowed to take drugs and dive. If she's using, she's obligated to tell me."

Antje shared with Todd a bad habit of looking utterly innocent when you fussed at her. "You want to know what I think?" she asked. "I think Jola's the kind of woman who needs to have a child. It would do her good. Think about Luisa. Or Valentina. Remember how nervous they always were? And they're super calm now that they have children."

Antje had a great many Spanish girlfriends who envied her blond hair and who were all raising children or expecting children or both. It irritated me exceedingly that she let pass no opportunity, however far-fetched, to present me with her own desire to have kids.

"Don't you think a child would be a good idea for her?"

I said, "As you well know, I don't want children. So stop with this shit."

Antje's head sank. I left her standing next to the dishwasher and went to bed, where a bad feeling kept me awake. When Antje quietly crept into the bed, I closed my eyes tight and turned to the wall.

4

The sea was quiet, the air still and for eight o'clock in the morning unusually warm. The dead calm made me uneasy. Whoever's that quiet is up to something.

I could see the two of them from our roof terrace, where I was gathering up my sandals and a couple of towels. They were standing in front of Casa Raya, waiting for me. Theo reached out a hand to Jola and with two fingers grabbed the soft skin on the back of her upper arm. When she tried to pull away, he pinched her harder; I could see the pain on her face. He kept those two fingers clamped on her arm, stroked her cheek with his other hand, and talked at her. I could hear his voice, but I didn't understand what he was saying.

Once I'd caught Antje with her arms raised in front of the bathroom mirror, scowling as she appraised her triceps: problem area.

Theo let Jola's arm go and dug his fingers instead into the flesh above her hip bone, where all women who aren't anorexic have a little pad of fat. He squeezed her twice and released her to light a cigarette.

*

In the van, I asked them what no-decompression time was. Jola said it was the number of minutes a person could stay underwater. Theo added that it had something to do with nitrogen.

As always before the first diving session, Antje had briefed me at breakfast about our new clients' level of experience. In the course of a trip to Vietnam some years earlier, Theo and Jola had taken a diving course and obtained entry-level certification—the "Open Water Diver"—and that was it. Their logbooks documented no more than ten dives. So in their case, a bit of theory couldn't hurt. Basically, diving wasn't a dangerous sport as long as you internalized a couple of rules. For their diving-license exam, most beginners learned a few sentences and set phrases by heart and forgot them immediately afterward. Maybe they could define *no-decompression time*, correctly, as the length of time a diver can remain at a given depth and still ascend rapidly to the surface without exposing himself to grave health risks. But only a few inexperienced divers had the ability to visualize the reality behind that definition. Most beginners were particularly unwilling to accept that their lives could depend on accurately calculating their no-decompression time. I was rather proud to think of myself as a conscientious teacher in this regard.

While we drove to Puerto del Carmen, I rolled out my standard explanation. The high pressure underwater, I said, causes nitrogen to build up in the body, in blood, tissue, and bones. You can imagine it as similar to carbon dioxide in a fizzy drink. As long as the bottle remains closed and under pressure, there's no problem. But what happens when you open the bottle too fast? Something similar happens in your body when you stay underwater past your decompression time and then ascend to the surface too quickly. It's not pretty.

Suddenly Jola cried out, "Stop!"

I slammed on the brakes. Jola had risen halfway from the passenger seat. "Did you see what was on the road?" she asked.

I leaned far out of the window on my side and looked back. "Nobody's there!" I yelled.

"'Everything is will,'" Jola said. "In giant letters, sprayed across the asphalt."

I exhaled, put my hands on the steering wheel, and concentrated on letting my shoulders drop. "Are you crazy, scaring me like that?"

A car overtook and passed us, its horn blaring.

"A message," Jola said. "A message for me. Written in German, even!"

"Sounds like a very German idea," said Theo. He was writing in a notebook balanced on his knee. "Good title."

"I can do it. I can do Lotte," said Jola. "It's only a matter of will."

"Only if you know what no-decompression time is," I said. "You have until Puerto del Carmen to understand it."

I put the van in gear and stepped on the gas.

For starters, we walked down the little road to Playa Chica without any equipment. I pointed to a buoy in the water about seventy meters offshore.

"Swim there and back, is that it?" Jola asked.

"At a comfortable pace," I said.

"But we're not beginners," Theo protested. "We have diving experience."

"I just want to get an idea of what kind of shape you're in," I said.

Jola, who'd already pulled her sleeveless shirt over her head, stepped out of her jeans and stood there in a bikini. Theo looked around as though searching for his valet. Or at least a changing room. I helped him out of his linen suit jacket.

While he hopped around on one leg, trying to get his pants off, I observed his girlfriend. In my line of work, I had a great deal to do with bodies. Most clients chose to change into their swim clothes while badly hidden behind the back of my VW van. They'd stand there in gray socks and shabby underwear, looking at the ground because they were ashamed of their hollows and folds and spots. Jola, on the other hand, was not hiding herself. She stood in the middle of the quay, narrowed her eyes, and gazed at the horizon. She was perfect, a living statue. Thoroughly fit, toned, and yet soft. I assured myself that this was not a judgment on my part. It was simply a fact. I knew what a body like that required. Not only time, money, and discipline, but also a sense for the correct measure of things. The knowledge that beauty is to be found not in the extreme, but in balance. Jola had shaped her body like an artist. I frankly admired the result. I would have liked to offer her a word of praise, from one expert to another, but the danger of a misunderstanding was too great.

"Get out of the sun," Theo said to her. "We can see your cellulite."

Jola crouched and sprang headfirst from the quay wall into the water before I could call her to order. I considered whether I should break off this practice session and deliver a lecture on security. It was possible that Jola, as a sailor, could estimate how deep the water in front of a landing place was. Nevertheless, checking water depth before jumping in was normal routine. I decided against chewing her out; it was her first day. With one hand on the rail, Theo carefully walked down the steps to the sea.

While Jola swam a crawl, calmly propelling herself through the water, Theo practiced a mixture of breaststrokes and sidestrokes. Jola was already halfway back when he reached the buoy. She turned over on her back to float and wait for him.

"What a slowpoke!" she shouted, kicking out when he got close and splashing seawater in his face. Then she swam away laughing, not back to the quay, but a bit farther off, in the direction of the beach. He didn't catch up with her until they reached shallow water. She defended herself, squealed, flailed; he clung to her waist. I didn't intervene. They might as well have been tussling children. I thought I heard them laughing. Then Theo lifted his girlfriend high in the air and flung her away. Jola screamed. There were rocks in the shallows, and those rocks were thickly covered with sea urchins. Theo came out of the water, put his linen jacket back on, wet as he was, and ran across the boardwalk to the public toilets.

I was alarmed to see that Jola was limping. As she came

toward me, she raised one reassuring hand. We sat on a bench on the quay, and I put her foot on my knee. One of the sea urchin's spines had penetrated the sole of her foot and broken off. I took out my pocketknife and did my best to think of her foot as an object. I worked until I could take hold of the spine, and as I drew it out, she stared into my eyes.

"So that's it now," I said. "No more fooling around. Accidents can happen too easily."

"Believe me," she said, rubbing her foot. "He meant to do it."

❋

The parking spots around the Playa Chica were assigned according to an unwritten law. Bernie's white minibus with WONDERDIVE written on its sides was parked in the no-parking area near the steps leading to the boardwalk; he and his people were already in the water. As always, my vehicle was in the entrance to the old Spaniard's place; once a day, he came out of the house to remind me of what he planned to do to me if I damaged his fence. Theo was leaning against my VW van, waiting for us. He took the cigarette out of his mouth to kiss Jola on the forehead, and she snuggled against him. "No more antics from now on," I admonished, and both of them nodded as if they understood. I spread the canvas on the ground and set out wet suits, buoyancy compensators, diving cylinders, fins, and masks. I took off my shorts and slipped my feet into my sandals. Jola's eyes strayed briefly over my swimming trunks.

"Take a look," she said to Theo. "*That's* what I call equipment."

The way she stressed the *that* had the power to bury a man's ego, but Theo just kept gazing with furrowed brow at the diving regulators and inflator hoses and trying to remember how such things worked. With his big, loose swimming shorts, which covered him almost entirely from the belly on down, he was going to have a hard time getting into a neoprene suit.

To refresh their knowledge, I put them through the whole beginners' program. I showed them how they could use the inflator to pump air into their buoyancy compensators or let it out again; how to hook up the diving regulators they'd breathe through, which adjusted the high-pressure scuba-tank air to the ambient pressure; how to fasten a tank to a buoyancy compensator and get the whole thing onto your back. I laid special emphasis on fundamental principles: caution, prudence, and cooperation between diving partners. They listened, asked questions, and helped each other with their equipment.

One hour later, they were floating in their inflated buoyancy compensators like two corks on the water. I showed them how to read the pressure gauge to determine the fill level of their tanks, explained the hand signals, and gave tips about blowing water out of the diving masks. We practiced supplying one another with air in an emergency by means of passing the so-called octopus, a second diving regulator through which one could breathe air from a diving partner's tank. My two clients acquitted themselves well. We swam some distance out into the bay. I made a circle of my thumb and forefinger, the signal for "okay." They repeated the gesture to show that everything was in order. We dove down.

After descending barely three meters, we were kneeling on the ocean floor. They were both breathing a bit too fast and holding on to their regulators with one hand, as if they might fall out of their mouths. But this was normal for beginners. Most clients suffered a mild shock when they breathed underwater for the first time. After that, reactions differed. Some would feel incredible euphoria, a kind of mental orgasm triggered by the fact that with the aid of technology they had been able to put one over on a hostile element; totally enclosed in water, guests in a strange environment, they could nonetheless breathe as freely as fish. Others didn't feel so good. They sensed they didn't belong in this world, didn't trust the apparatus that was supplying them with oxygen, and were tormented by the impression that they must go back up to the surface at once. Such persons couldn't relax underwater. Only a lot of practice could make good divers out of them.

It was immediately clear to me which of my clients belonged in which category. Despite Theo's mask, I could discern a beaming smile on his face. His knees only lightly touched the sea bottom; he was already on the point of giving himself over to weightlessness. The parrot fish he was following with his eyes came closer, looked us over, peered inquisitively into Theo's goggles, and finally moved off in the direction of the solidified lava stream. I knew what Theo was experiencing: one of the happiest moments of his life.

Jola, by contrast, turned her head frantically right and left, as if an attack could come from any direction. The sand she was swirling up with her fins obstructed her vision. She kept one hand clamped to her regulator and waggled the other to maintain her balance. I swam close to her and showed her the "okay" signal. She stared at me uncomprehendingly for a few seconds before responding in kind. By way of distracting her, I gave her some little tasks. She had to swim a few meters, use her inflator, check her pressure and depth gauges. I demonstrated how she could balance herself by consciously inhaling and exhaling and pointed out a couple of sardines that were flashing through the water like lightning bolts some distance away. We moved deeper almost imperceptibly. At last, she smiled and nodded.

I waved to Theo to join us and take part in the exercises. We began with "hovering," trying to remain motionless in the water for a minute or longer. Theo and Jola hovered close to each other, their arms folded, and concentrated on breathing so smoothly that the amount of air in their lungs caused them neither to float up nor to sink down. I looked at my watch to see if the prescribed minute was up, and then suddenly Theo grabbed his diving regulator and made a few frantic turning movements. He tore the octopus out of its holder, clapped it to his mouth, and threw it away again at once. Although he was too unfamiliar with the routine to give the correct sign, I nevertheless understood that he wasn't getting any air through either of his mouthpieces. Before I could reach him and offer him my octopus—as we'd discussed doing in emergencies—he pushed off the bottom and shot toward the surface. I had no chance of holding him back. At a depth of eight meters, that presented no problem. At greater depths, such a move could in the worst case cost a diver his or her life.

I quickly followed him to the surface, indicating to Jola that she should also come up. It took some force to keep Theo from swallowing more water as he coughed. With eight kilos of lead in his belt, he lay in my arms like a concrete pier. When I tried in vain to fill his buoyancy compensator with air, I guessed what had happened. Jola, who was shaking with laughter, made any further explanation superfluous. While they were hovering, she'd reached behind him and shut off his valve.

By the time we reached the beach, I was so furious I had to clench my teeth to keep from screaming. We were barely ashore when the rage burst out of me. I told them I had something I needed to make crystal clear. I told them they'd had their last chance. I told them that if one of them dared to pull any such shit again, any such childish and moreover dangerous stunt, their training would be at an end, and it wouldn't make any difference who they were, who they thought they were, or how much they paid. On land they could bash each other's head in for all I cared, but underwater they had to follow my rules. When they were down there, they had to behave like adults. Underwater they were partners, I said, their lives were in each other's hands.

There was a stunned silence. Even Theo looked aghast. Apparently they hadn't thought me capable of such an outburst. I announced that I was going to get a cup of coffee. During my absence, I said, they could consider whether they wanted to stick to the rules or whether our working relationship should cease at once. And with that, I left them where they stood. The Wunder Bar café had German cheesecake. Just what I needed sometimes. My rage calmed down, but only very slowly.

JOLA'S DIARY, SECOND DAY

Sunday, November 13. Afternoon.

He blew his top. Right after we came back. I barely had time to put down the bags and hang up the wet towels before he grabbed my arm and threw me across the room. Not because of the prank with his air valve. Not because of my "equipment" remark. But because I showed him up when we were swimming. Well, what was I supposed to do, old man? Swim clumsily on purpose? So you wouldn't seem like such a slowpoke? He said we both know I miss no opportunity to make him look ridiculous. I had to apologize, he said, or he was going to slug me. I said, You'll slug me anyway, sooner or later. He grabbed my hair. I get anxious about my hair. My hair is part of my capital. I said, I apologize. He let me go but kept that look on his face.

It was totally idiotic of me to think a vacation trip could change anything. The old man himself said it best years ago: "Emigration would make sense only if the country we were running from wasn't ourselves." How I love him when he writes like that. And that's precisely why he doesn't let me read his stuff anymore. It's his way of taking himself away from me. He pretends he's not working. He deletes his things. Hides them. Publishes nothing. And tells me lies. Because he thinks living with a writer is too good for me. A failure is what I deserve, a failure and nothing more.

It's so quiet here. The absence of people in Lahora is like breathing underwater—wonderful, but a little scary. If I had to make a quick getaway, I wouldn't even have a car. Rilke: Who, if I cried out, would hear me then . . . ? *Answer: Sven, at best. I'll make sure he's always nearby. I felt really sorry for him, sorry that he had to get so upset over us. He stood there amid the trappings of his little diving-instructor world, trembling with rage. I was shocked by how shocked he was. Because I understood that he doesn't understand us. No one would ever turn off Sven's valve—he's not the type. He didn't even know there were people who did that sort of thing. All at once I felt a strange kind of longing. I'm going to make an effort for his sake. And for Lotte's sake. Underwater, I was so close to her. As alert and nimble as a fish. While Theo was bobbing around like a sack of potatoes.*

We don't have to be on vacation. The old man could get to work on writing a book about the island. I can train for Lotte. That's the beauty of being in the arts. You can call everything work, and then you can realize it's shit without being disappointed.

5

The Lobster's Paradise was an insider's place. The kind you had to reserve a few days in advance. At least, if you weren't Geoffrey's friend. Geoffrey was a Northern Irishman who at some point had had his fill of constant war and left his homeland. His companion, Sasha, had been a professional handball player, a member of Yugoslavia's national team. When war broke out in Yugoslavia twenty years ago, Sasha signed with a Spanish handball club. Now he ran a paragliding school near Famara during the day and in the evenings helped at the restaurant. Immigrants ran half the businesses on the island. Most of us stuck together, which was why I could always get a table at the Lobster's.

Geoffrey's business model was making him a fortune. The Lobster's Paradise was in the middle of nowhere, that is, in the middle of a rugged field of solidified lava on the Famara massif. No signs marked the way; customers had to cover the last three hundred meters on foot. Inside, the place was always too crowded and too hot. There were two dishes on the menu: lobster and rabbit. Nobody ordered rabbit.

Theo and Jola insisted on inviting me to share their meal. The incident that morning was still fresh and I didn't much feel like letting them take me out, but it was a part of our agreement that I must be available for any free-time activities they chose, twenty-four hours a day. After driving them to the Lobster's and accompanying them to the entrance, I could hardly decline their invitation and wait outside.

They made a genuine effort. Theo held the door open and then held Jola's chair for her. She was wearing a blue band in her hair that made her look sweet and a little old-fashioned. Delighted to be able to discuss the wine list with a connoisseur like Theo, Geoffrey brought us the bottle he ordered along with a second bottle for us to try. Despite my protests, Theo poured me a glass, and I had to confess that the wine tasted remarkably good.

Then they started to talk about things back home. Or rather, Theo talked while Jola looked at him attentively with both hands on the table, like a well-behaved spouse. The wine and her gaze combined to set him off; he talked like a waterfall.

As a writer, Theo said, he was basically a sort of big businessman. Thousands of people lived off his work. Publishing-house employees, booksellers, librarians, copy editors, critics, translators, printers, cultural program directors for television and radio, to say nothing of the entire dramatic profession, including actors, dramaturges, directors, and stage technicians, as well as anyone involved in the movie business—all those occupations existed solely for the commercial exploitation of texts. And what's the author? A nothing. The weakest link in the food chain. Despised, ridiculed, rarely acclaimed, mostly ignored. A nobody who tortures himself at his writing desk in the dead of night, only to be derided in the end as a loser by the artistically impotent.

Jola laid a hand on his arm and remarked that many reviewers referred to him not as a loser but as a writer of great promise.

Theo insisted that it was a matter of principle. How does a man who has no artistic accomplishments get the right to judge someone else's work? Even a critic who hands down a positive judgment thinks himself more important than the author he's assessing, Theo said. It's an upside-down world, and it teaches you repugnance as a form of being.

I knew the feeling. When I imagined the life Theo lived as a cog in the gears of the big judgment machine, the thought made the hairs on the back of my neck stand up.

Basically, Jola said, Theo was right. Her case was similar, she said. Every moron who cowered in fear at the very thought of having to get up on a stage felt perfectly entitled to go on the Internet and criticize her ability.

"We need a law!" Theo cried out. "Anyone who criticizes someone else without exposing himself to criticism is to be prohibited from speaking for a period of not less than two years."

They shared a confidential laugh. I was happy to listen when clients bad-mouthed Germany. In my ears they sounded like soldiers on leave from the battlefront, reporting on conditions in the war zone. They reminded me of what I'd run away from and made me feel I'd been right to do so. When Theo tried to refill my glass, I put my hand over it and switched to mineral water. The food came. We spurned the side dishes and plunged up to the elbows in lobster juice.

Jola asked why I'd left Germany. I told my story about Brunsberg and Montesquieu. Theo and Jola laughed hard, holding their sides. While I was gazing at Jola—who didn't look like an actress anymore, but simply like a high-spirited young woman—I thought about that morning. The incident with the closed valve suddenly seemed less dramatic.

Still laughing, I asked them why they didn't just stay on the island, like all those who'd grown tired of living with pointless stress and lousy weather. Theo dipped his hands in lemon water and answered me seriously. He said he envied and pitied me at the same time. Then he cracked open another lobster tail, removed a bit of intestine, took the choicest piece from the middle, and gave it to Jola.

"Jola could buy a luxury *finca* with her family's money," said Theo. "On the prettiest basalt hill. Boat included."

Jola made a face. You could physically feel the mood capsize. She said, "I'm not my family."

"I can live off her here or in Berlin, it makes no difference at all to me. Then again, maybe here *would* be better. Less humiliating." Theo laughed as though he'd just made a joke. When he tried to kiss Jola, she shoved him away. The first bottle of white wine was empty.

"But I can't leave the battlefield without putting up a fight," said Theo. "Jola and I, we're born fighters. Isn't that right?"

Jola looked in another direction. Geoffrey broke into the ensuing silence with a second bottle, which we hadn't ordered, asked us what we thought about the American government's debt policy, and left the table before anyone could answer his question. He always did that. Jola began to talk about the United States, which she believed she knew well because of a theater workshop she'd attended in New York. I was used to thinking I couldn't save people, so I leaned back and listened. After all, it was better that way. A paradise stops being a paradise if half the world moves there. And that goes especially for islands.

After dinner a windstorm came up, a predictable sequel to the morning's calm. On the way back to the van, the blow whipped our pants legs and bit our faces. We laughed, bracing ourselves against it. As they walked, Theo kept one arm around Jola's waist. "So you don't fly away!" he shouted before kissing her hair.

They insisted on visiting the Mirador del Río, the famous café and viewing platform that the island artist César Manrique built out of the lava rock on the highest point of the Famara massif. Antje used to call Manrique a poor man's Hundertwasser. The whole island was filled with the bulky, large-scale trash he created. But tourists loved his naive figures, stood in long lines outside his buildings, and bought postcards featuring his "toilet people," male and female restroom symbols with outsize sexual parts. Manrique had fortunately died before he could turn the whole island into a multimedia artwork.

My objection, namely that there was nothing to see from the Mirador at ten o'clock in the evening—the café was closed and protected by walls on all sides—was judged inadequate. In that case we'll just take a nice digestive walk, they said. Jola dissembled the fact that she'd already purchased my acquiescence by making a pretty-please face.

We walked on the road that ran along the cliff coast. On the sea side was a knee-high wall. Behind it lay a stretch of bare earth, beyond that the edge of the steep cliff. Five hundred meters of perpendicular rock, and below it the raging sea. A half-moon inside a wreath of white light shone in the sky. Scraps of black cloud rushed past. It was as though we were watching the earth hurtle through space.

All of a sudden, Jola reached out a hand and drew me to her side. The three of us walked along in a close embrace. Jola, warm and safe in the middle, looked up to each of us in turn. I felt her fingers on my hip and couldn't avoid contact between my arm and Theo's. It was absurd and beautiful.

Then my cell phone rang. I knew it was Antje, wanting to know how the evening had gone, when we were coming home, and what preparations, if any, she should make for tomorrow. It was a habit of hers to call me several times a day, no matter whether there were things that needed coordinating or not. Normally I had nothing against that; after all, the logistics of our business required a lot of cooperative effort. At that moment, however, it seemed like she was disturbing us on purpose. I detached myself from Jola and ran back a few steps, looking for the lee of the wind in the Mirador's gateway. I shouted into the phone that everything was fine and we'd be heading home soon. I could barely understand what Antje said.

When I got back to the road, Theo and Jola had disappeared. For a while I ran back and forth, calling out their names, as distraught as a ewe that's lost her lambs. Then I stopped, stood in one place, and considered. In the moonlight, I could see over to the rocky cliff, several hundred meters away. I'd been on the phone two minutes at most, so they couldn't have gone very far. The terrain was flat, with good visibility in all directions. Except for the part occupied by the Mirador.

I jumped over the roadside barrier and followed the Mirador's outer wall to the edge of the cliff. Through the pales of the locked gate at the end of the wall, you could see the café's terrace, which served as a viewing platform. By day, sweaty tourists struggling with high-tech equipment would photograph their wives standing beside the balustrade ("But not against the sun, Robert!"), with the stunning view of the neighboring island, La Graciosa, in the background.

I saw them right away. They'd climbed over the gate and were standing on the terrace. Or, more precisely, on the balustrade of the terrace. They were stepping one behind the other, holding their arms out like tightrope walkers. To their left was a free fall of half a kilometer. The onshore wind was playing its usual tricks, blowing harder and harder and then suddenly dying down, causing the two bodies on the balustrade to stagger. I forbade myself to climb over the gate and run after them; the danger of scaring them was too great. I thought about the wine bottles in the Lobster's Paradise. My arms were trembling; I'd pulled myself halfway over the gate, and both fists were clamped around the metal struts. I didn't even dare to call out. Theo caught up with Jola at the end of the balustrade and embraced her with both arms. At first I thought they were kissing, but then I realized I was witnessing a struggle. I heard a scream and in the same moment perceived that I was the screamer. Jola heard me. She spun around, dragging Theo with her. For a few seconds it wasn't clear which side they were going to fall toward. Then they landed almost simultaneously on the tiled floor of the viewing platform.

I didn't wait for them to get up. I ran back to the van alone in the dark. Only after I got in did I realize that I was soaking wet. It had begun to rain, the moon had vanished, and the high plateau was crosshatched as though by a draftsman's hand. I felt a mighty urge to simply drive away. Instead of doing that, I sat motionless behind the steering wheel, shivering and staring into the rain until Theo and Jola came running up. They yanked the side door open and climbed in. I started the engine without a word.

During the drive I tried hard not to look into the rearview mirror. In the backseat, Theo and Jola were kissing each other hungrily. I didn't want to know what their hands were doing. I kept my eyes fixed on the road and considered what should happen next. The nitrox compressor in the garage wasn't paid off yet, and the Casa Raya was in urgent need of new windows. But were things so desperate that I had to let myself be bought? As a rule, I didn't have to worry very much about my diving students' reliability. The Atlantic instilled respect. Normally. However, I reflected, the very last thing I required of people was that they should fit the normal case. Admittedly, a big part of my job was making sure that nobody died. But underwater. On land, they could bash each other's heads in, as I'd already told them. Whatever they did above water was no concern of mine. *Stay out of it.* I felt myself growing calmer.

The windshield wipers fought frantically against the torrents of water. The headlights barely reached fifty meters ahead. A drenched fox crouched on the roadside. He looked pathetic. As far as I know, there are no foxes on the island.

JOLA'S DIARY, THIRD DAY

Monday, November 14. Two A.M.

I had to get out. I couldn't breathe inside. The storm has shredded all the clouds, and it's not raining anymore. I'm thinking it's been seven years since we met for the first time. It was the traditional summer party at the country house. Three hundred guests, lots of them familiar faces: the brightest stars in the German acting firmament. Daddy risked muscle cramps from spreading out his arms so much. The smile on his face stretched from the east wing to the west wing. Not long before, he'd gotten me the part in Up and Down, *I'd promised to make a real effort, and I'd come through the first couple of episodes with flying colors, which made me suppose I was at the beginning of a brilliant career. I was twenty-three years old, and I had on a high-necked dress with a leopard-skin pattern. The other actresses' eyes tickled the back of my neck. To this day I can feel how beautiful I was that evening.*

Daddy appeared on the stage in the garden, opened his arms wide, and said something about celebrating someone's debut. A writer went up onto the stage. Not a handsome man. He stationed himself behind the lectern, swaying awkwardly as he shifted his weight from one leg to the other. He gave a reading. Sentences like neurotoxins. I stood there, unable to move.

"There are days when I'd like to answer all questions with my own name."

"I sense mortality everywhere in my body."

I love those sentences to this day. It makes no difference what an asshole their author is.

When I expressed my enthusiasm, he grimaced. Then he leaned on a bar table and stared at the dance floor but didn't participate. In anything at all. He was twelve years older than me, I learned. He explained that actors had to be stupid so that there would be room in their empty heads for their characters' identities. He said that actors inherently admired writers, because writers provided the texts that they—actors—parroted every day. I danced with a couple of my U & D *colleagues and wandered through the rooms of the house and kept going back to the writer leaning on the bar table. As if he were a fixed star and I had slipped into orbit around him. The next thing he told me was that he'd been impotent ever since his publisher started calling him regularly to ask about his progress on his new manuscript. By two* A.M.*, we were screwing in my parents' bathroom. While we were at it we broke a perfume bottle, and so for the rest of the night we smelled like Mama's Chanel No. 5.*

Seven years later we're sitting in a restaurant, eating lobster and drinking a Meursault Premier Cru and crying over the wicked world and dreaming of emigrating. Because living in a penthouse apartment with a roof terrace in Berlin is a total nightmare. Because we'd be much happier with floppy hats on our heads and garden soil under our fingernails. The old man would sit on a simple wooden bench, his back against the sun-warmed wall of the house, and spend the livelong day musing. I'd make pottery, earthenware vessels he'd drink his wine out of. Once a minute, we'd look up and smile at each other. We'd be nice to each other from morn till night. He'd never again, just for fun, try to push me over a cliff.

I thought he wanted to apologize. To blame it all on the wine. To say he didn't know what had gotten into him, he could have killed us both. Very softly, he came up to the sofa. I lay there with my eyes closed, enjoying the way he was stroking my cheek with one warm finger. He does that so damned seldom. The wind rattled the shutters, which Antje had closed while we were out. When I opened my eyes, it wasn't a finger, it was his dick.

What would Lotte have done? When I tried to get up, he put his hands around my throat. I told him to let me go. He tried to shove himself into my mouth. I clenched my teeth. He pressed on my windpipe. My lips opened and I gasped for air. It felt like he was choking off my hearing as well as my breathing. The sound of the wind vanished. Absolute silence. It was dark in the room. I could see his face, far away, and his moving mouth. He was looking at me the whole time. I thought I'd better not vomit, it would suffocate me. I wondered how long this could go on. Sometimes he needs a good while. I thought everything would go black soon. Then everything went black.

The thing Lotte and I have in common is that she could take a lot and so can I. I keep thinking about her time on the El Chadra*, the hundred-year-old Arab pearl-fishing boat Hans Hass used as an improvised expedition ship. There was Lotte Hass, afloat on the Red Sea off the Sudanese coast, huddled together with ten men on the* *boat's vermin-infested planks. I think about how she wrote her diary at night when the heat prevented her from sleeping. "August 12. People who see this in a movie theater will sit back in their plush chairs, offer one another candies, and think, 'Oh, how nice! I'd love to sail on a ship like that. How romantic!' In the future, I believe I'll look at expedition documentaries with different eyes, and when I see our film, I'll ask myself, 'Is that really me?'"*

I lay in his arms. He was holding me the way he should always hold me, good and tight. He stroked my back, my hair, my face. I could hear again. He was crying. He told me what a brave, good girl I was. Said how much he loves me, loves me more than anything in the world, loves me to distraction. Said what a bad person he is. Nevertheless, he said, I can't leave him. Because he needs me, because I'm his angel. He started crying louder. I sucked in his nearness like a drug. My jaw hurt. I began to comfort him. I told him everything would be all right. Said we just had to try a little harder. He was clinging to me like a child. He thanked me as though I'd saved his life. I smiled. I'm absolutely sure we can do it, I said. I put him to bed.

Not long afterward, he started snoring. The bedroom door was ajar. I took my notebook and came to sit out here in front of the house. Now I imagine I'm on the deck of a ship, and the heat is the reason I can't sleep.

6

She's asleep. Her lips are slightly parted, revealing the adorable space between her front teeth. I feel a mighty urge to stroke her head, and I consider whether I dare do such a thing. When my fingers touch her forehead, she opens her eyes. I say her name: Jola. We look at each other for a few seconds, and then her jaws spring open. Like a moray eel, she has a second pair of jaws in her throat and launches them into her mouth. With the teeth of a predatory fish, she snaps at my fingers.

I flinched away from her and sat up in the bed. It was pitch-dark; the digital alarm clock read 4:00 A.M. Very gradually, I came to the realization that the woman beside me was not Jola but Antje. She was sleeping on her back with outstretched arms, her head tilted down to one side, in an attitude of crucifixion.

My revved-up heart slowly calmed down. Now I understood the unnatural darkness: Antje had closed the shutters. The wind was still blowing around the corners of the house, though not howling as hungrily as a few hours earlier. I hated dreams that seemed like the inventions of a psychologist. There was no question of my going back to sleep. I figured I might as well get up and go out to my workshop.

I stood briefly in front of the house, looking over at the Casa Raya, the only bright spot in the midst of black darkness. For a moment I thought something long-haired and human-shaped was crouching on the garden wall, but it turned out to be nothing but a cactus pear whose paddles were moving in the wind.

The package had come the previous day, and Antje had put it on my workbench. For the first time, I'd decided to equip a dry suit with a heating system. At a depth of one hundred meters, seawater's cold. The helium in the gas mixture promotes the loss of body heat, and the long decompression times are an additional factor. The package I'd received contained twenty meters of monopolar wire—the kind also used in heating car seats—a heating unit, electric cable, a couple of E/O cords, and a twelve-volt battery. I spread my undersuit on the table, threaded a needle, and got to work. In an instant, I forgot everything else. When Antje came to get me, it was already broad daylight outside and almost time to set out.

❋

The weather had turned cooler. Theo had exchanged his linen suit for jeans and an anorak, which made him more simpatico. Although the wind had died away, experience told me the sea wouldn't calm down until late in the afternoon. My suggestion that we spend the day sightseeing on land was rejected. My references to the waves we'd encounter when entering the water and the bad visibility below the surface also fell on deaf ears. I spoke sentences in which the phrases *difficult conditions* and *at your own risk* occurred. Jola smiled at me and climbed into the van. I was glad to see that her teeth were in fine shape. We started to drive across the island—I thought it would be best to try our luck on the leeward side.

There was something strange about my two clients that morning. We were in Teguise before I realized what was different about them: they were behaving like perfectly normal people. Theo asked, "Sweetheart, can you reach in the backpack and get the water bottle?" Jola answered, "Sure," and handed him the mineral water. They were both sitting up front with me, swaying a little with the movements of the van and holding their hands on their knees. When a phone rang, it was mine, with a text message from Jola: "Looking forward to the dive. J."

◆

The dive site near Mala was a lonely spot, not easy to reach. Level places for entering the water were nonexistent. You had to clamber down barefoot over slippery rocks with the heavy scuba tank on your back and the fins and mask under your arm until you were close enough to the bay to jump. I left the van on the edge of the gravel road; we stood in black sand and changed into our diving gear. Slowly, step by step, reaching for each other's hand to get over the hard parts, Jola and Theo climbed down. The sea was rougher than I'd hoped it would be. I decided to hurry up so they wouldn't have too much time to stare down into the waves. I quickly demonstrated how they should jump into the water, with one hand on their weight belt and the other in front of their face. Theo stroked Jola's shoulder before launching himself. He surfaced near me and made the "okay" sign.

Jola was still standing on the rocks; her body language was the picture of a struggle. Apparently she was giving her legs orders they had no wish to carry out. At last she leaped forward, a little too forcefully, and dropped right on top of me. I softened her impact, held on to her, fully inflated her buoyancy compensator, made sure her head remained above water. She'd temporarily lost her diving regulator, and she was coughing. I wanted to get under as quickly as possible, because it was dangerous to stay so close to the rocks. Under the water, calmness would reign. I gave the sign to submerge, and down we went.

Immediately, a great quiet surrounded us. The special silence of the sea. Movements slowed down and communication became a dance, a choreography of signs and gestures. Underwater, relationships were simple, requirements unequivocal, and responses radical. If you dove down ten meters, you simultaneously traveled back ten million years in the history of evolution—or back to the beginning of your own biography. You were in the water where life began, floating and mute. Without speech, no concepts. Without concepts, no justifications. Without justifications, no war. Without war, no fear. Not even the fish were afraid of us. Some curious ones came close and accompanied us for a while. If we kept still, they'd cast intense glances into our diving goggles. In exotic worlds, the tourist doubled as an attraction. I was fascinated by the peace that prevailed underwater, where hunter and prey lived together, courteously avoiding one another—a peace interrupted only by the brief cravings of hunger, which was no treachery but rather a generally accepted process of selection.

Despite the swells, subaqueous visibility was amazingly good. One of the most beautiful dive sites on Lanzarote stretched out before our eyes. The island's bizarre volcanic landscape continued underwater, forming a stone city with towers, columns, archways, and battlements. When the sun broke through the clouds above, we found ourselves floating inside a dome of rising air bubbles and light. I felt happiness like a fist in my stomach. Theo lay in the water next to me and looked up too.

Something wasn't right with Jola. In order to get around a lava stream that reached well out into the sea, I'd led my two clients close to the rim of the ledge, where the seafloor dropped straight down. Two groupers, as long as grown men, lay on the rim as though enjoying the view. Jola had swum out over the ledge, emitting air bubbles far too frequently. Like a bird unsure of whether it could really fly, she was staring into the deep. Fear of heights presented a serious problem underwater. With a couple of fin strokes, I moved beside her and grasped her arm. She flinched away. For a second I thought she was going to strike at me.

Over the years, I'd developed an automatic reaction: the more frantic a diver was, the calmer I became. I slowed my movements down to the point where I hardly knew whether I was actually doing something or merely present. Behind her diving goggles, Jola stared at me with wide-open eyes. Her chest rose and fell much too fast; she was already hyperventilating. I squeezed her forearm several times, trying to get her to focus her attention. When her eyelids stopped fluttering and she began to concentrate on me, I nodded approval and signaled, *Good.* I moved one hand slowly away from my mouth and closed my eyes: *Exhale. Wait.* I opened my eyes: *Now you.* She exhaled but immediately filled her lungs again, shot panicked glances left and right, and even looked upward, considering whether she should simply go back up to the surface. I tightened my grip on her arm and shook my head emphatically: *No. Look at me. Exhale. Wait. Inhale slowly.* Now she was following my instructions, but her eyes were still too wide. We found a common rhythm. *Exhale. Wait. Inhale slowly.* She calmed down. I let go of her arm, took her hand, and shook it: *Congratulations, well done.* She sheepishly returned my "okay" sign. When I tried to withdraw my hand, she clung to me hard: *Don't leave me!* Peering through her mask, I could see she was crying. The sensation of suffocating is among the worst a person can experience. At that moment, Jola needed only one thing in the world: me.

The reading on her pressure gauge was under 100 bar; she'd breathed her tank half empty in two minutes. I was determined to proceed with the dive, and it was essential to do so in an orderly fashion. One of the most important principles beginners must grasp is that diving problems have to be solved underwater. Emergency surfacing isn't an option. I signaled to her that we were going to share my air supply. We'd practiced this—two divers breathing from one tank—in shallow water. Now I showed her my octopus, my spare demand valve, and made sure she understood me. *Inhale. Take your own regulator out of your mouth and switch to the octopus. Breathe again.* She did everything right.

We took each other by the hand. From that point on, we were joined together like Siamese twins, connected to the same air supply by two different hoses. We swam away slowly. I could feel her trembling; hyperventilation leads to poor blood circulation. She probably felt she was on the verge of freezing. As well as our equipment would allow, I put an arm around her waist and drew her close to me. Naturally, my body heat couldn't warm her underwater, but freezing, like most things in life, is primarily a matter of attitude.

Theo had observed the scene with interest. Instead of looking out for rays, he'd kept his eyes on us, as though he'd discovered the two most fascinating marine animals in the Atlantic Ocean. I guided Jola close to the coastal rocks and showed her some bright yellow snails and the shrimp that were hiding in crevices between stones and groping toward us with their long feelers. I shone my pocket flashlight on a starfish to bring out its red color. Jola turned her head and smiled at me, and then something happened. I suddenly realized that I liked holding her in my arms. I didn't want to let her go. I wanted to stay down there with her, I wanted us to observe the creatures of the sea together until the last trumpet. Jola felt how hard I recoiled and pressed herself closer to me. I gently pushed her away and signaled that she should switch back to her own air supply before we started to ascend. The exchange was flawless. We detached ourselves from each other. It felt like an amputation.

❁

When I knocked on the Casa Raya's door that evening, intending to pick up Theo and Jola and drive them somewhere for dinner, Jola didn't want to come. She declared that she had to study for her nitrox certification. Then she looked away and drummed her fingers on the tabletop. Nothing to be done. After the unsuccessful dive a few hours earlier, she'd stood off to one side, wrapped in a towel, with the volcanic panorama in the background. I could still see her like that: shivering piteously and looking small, as if the coldness of the water had shrunk her, with hunched shoulders and blue lips and strands of wet hair stuck to her cheeks and neck. Theo had carried her equipment to the van. Now he glanced over at me with a new, thoughtful look on his face.

Theo and I left Jola in the Casa Raya and drove away. While we rumbled down the gravel road in the direction of Tinajo, I reproached myself. I shouldn't have expected Jola to execute the difficult water entry at Mala. Instead I ought to have insisted on taking a day off and chalking it up to bad weather. At the very least, I should have kept Jola away from the brink of the ledge. After all, I knew she lacked Theo's fundamental confidence in uncertainty. I also knew she had a strong will, which caused her to make bad decisions in moments of doubt. In all probability, she'd felt fearful of the sheer ledge and for precisely that reason she'd swum out past it. That wasn't her fault. Judging how much I could expect of clients was part of my job. If my assessment was wrong, the responsibility was mine and mine alone.

After a panic attack like that, some people never went diving again. That's why it would have been important for Jola to recompose herself a little more. I would have gladly told her that such a thing could happen to anyone. I knew experienced divers who went out one fine day and for no apparent reason began to hyperventilate. We could have discussed my theory that it was particularly hard for women to feel safe while diving, because unlike men, women didn't readily make their lives dependent on technical apparatus. Women liked to maintain control. It was the same reason why they viewed automobiles, computers, and airplanes with mistrust. Above all I wanted to tell Jola that she would become a good diver, more than good enough for the role of Lotte Hass. It was harder to overcome fear than not to be afraid. We would have had so many things to talk about. If she didn't want to see me, it probably meant she was angry.

At this point I forced myself to stop brooding. It wasn't my style to try to think my way into other people's heads. I'd accept their behavior, and in that way I'd get along with them quite well. Now it was a question of winning back a diving student's confidence. I stopped the van on the side of the road, asked Theo to excuse me for a moment, and got out. While I positioned myself beside a large rock as if I had to pee, I took my cell phone out of my pocket and wrote, "Good luck with your studies. You're in our thoughts. S." Because I rarely sent text messages, I needed a long time to tap out those few words. The answer came back so fast it made me jump. It was brief and it hit me like an open hand, delivering either a blow or a caress; I couldn't tell: "It's not because of you. J."

Giselle made a fish soup that was one of a kind, a recipe handed down from her French great-grandmother. Giselle was French-Canadian; her husband came from the Congo. On the walls of their little restaurant, African masks hung beside photographs of Notre-Dame de Québec. We were the only guests. Theo let me talk, and I talked as though I'd been wound up. One diving story after another. About manta rays, dolphins, and whale sharks. About the wrecked ship I was going to dive down to in the following week and how this exploit would make me famous in diving circles. Along the way I praised his and Jola's talent and stressed how enjoyable it was to dive with sensible people.

He asked, "You find us sensible?"

Aside from that he sat there in silence, smiling thoughtfully and drinking apple juice. After the meal he suggested we go for a walk.

As a general rule, Tinajo's streets were lively, but that evening the temperature had dropped below sixty degrees—unusually cool—and there was barely a soul in sight. Theo walked down the middle of the street, swinging his arms and watching his feet. For the moment, he seemed to have forgotten my presence. In the village square, we sat on one of the whitewashed benches near the little church. The dragon trees screened the light from the streetlamps. At regular intervals, the end of Theo's cigarette glowed in front of his face. Now that we'd come this far, I found myself wishing we had simply walked back to the van after dinner.

He said, "You've got the hots for her, don't you?"

I started to make some reply to this, but he waved me off. "Forget about it. It's what she does. It's like an addiction with her." He offered me a cigarette, which I declined. "Basically, I just want to warn you."

It would have been easier for me to listen to him that evening if he'd been drinking. Unfortunately, I knew he was cold sober.

"Jola comes from an old family. They got rich by exploiting other people and managed to preserve their fortune through two world wars. A woman like Jola has no idea what it means to work for something. She expects to be given what she wants. The only thing she's never been able to get is recognition. And that's precisely what makes her dangerous."

I wasn't remotely interested in anything he was telling me. Nevertheless, I suddenly wanted him to go on talking.

"Basically, she's still just a little girl, trying her best to win her father's respect. Hartmut von der Pahlen. Does that name mean anything to you?"

I shook my head.

"Film producer. One of the most important in the business. Also an asshole. Whatever."

Theo stubbed out his cigarette and lit himself another one before going on: "I'm a substitute father for her. She's still looking for paternal love, and that's where I come in. As long as I don't give it to her, she stays with me. And exacts her revenge a thousand times a day."

"Only child?"

I bit my lip. Listening was bad enough. Asking questions was even worse. Normally in such situations, I changed the subject.

"She has two older brothers, one a doctor and the other a banker. Jola's father never gets tired of enthusing about how successful they are. Whatever."

A motor scooter drove by. The young woman sitting behind the driver yelled something in his ear. They both laughed.

"I'll tell you a story," Theo said. "It'll help you understand how Jola grew up. When she was a child, she desperately wanted a pet. A guinea pig, a bunny, something she could cuddle with, something she could love. When she got a kitten for a Christmas present, she was overjoyed. She tended to the little animal night and day and carried it around with her wherever she went. Two weeks after Christmas, the heating in her house went on the blink. So the kitten wouldn't freeze, Jola took it to bed with her and covered it with her pillow. The next morning she found the kitten under her pillow, cold and stiff as a piece of wood. Jola's mother threw the kitten into the trash can, and from then on she told the story at parties. She'd pull Jola's braid and laugh and say, 'My little murderess.'" Theo looked around the square with narrowed eyes. "Whatever," he said. It seemed that this was becoming his favorite expression. We fell silent for a while.

"Maybe you're asking yourself what I'm doing with her in the first place," Theo said at last. "It's quite simple. I love her. Besides, I can't get it up with other women. I've tried. With assistant directors in theaters, with culture-hungry housewives after readings, with street hookers. Total disaster."

He turned to me and pointed his index finger at the tip of my nose. "The first rule in dealing with Frau von der Pahlen: never believe what she says. Particularly if it's anything to do with me. She tells the whole world I'm a man of leisure, a layabout. Whereas the truth is I'm working on a big social novel. It'll appear in three or four volumes, I'm not sure yet."

He marked a pause and stretched his back as if we were in the middle of some physically demanding job. Then he went on: "For years I've watched colleagues slogging through the quagmire of their own mental states, wearing themselves out in the effort to make sculptures out of sludge. Not me. I'm after the big picture. I can wait. Jola calls it writer's block; I call it patience."

Theo moved his fingers in the air as if he were playing piano.

"In the meantime," he said, "I write short stories. Finger exercises." He looked at me sideways. "Would you like to read something?"

I cleared my throat. "Unfortunately, where literature is concerned, I don't get it," I said.

"So much the better. The enemies of literature are the best readers. Remind me to give you something of mine when we get back."

He stood up and slapped his pants as though we'd been sitting in the worst kind of filth.

"This is what I really wanted to say: If you're hot for Jola, I have no problem with that. I would just advise you to be careful. At the moment I don't know what she's planning to do. But she's surely planning something. Shows like the one she put on when we were diving are typical of her."

I hid my smile behind a yawn. What was really typical was the logic of the war zone: some dark plan lay behind every sort of behavior. You asked a lot of questions, and as a punishment you got the answers. Theo sneezed three times on the way to the car and then lit another cigarette. "Shit," he said. "I probably caught something on that cliff last night."

•

Light shone through the Casa Raya's closed shutters. Apparently Jola was still awake, studying her nitrox materials. Theo and I bade each other good night with great warmth. I liked him. He was suspicious, but he couldn't help it. All the inhabitants of the war zone were like that. Suspicion was a natural result of their lifestyle. I felt satisfied. In the course of our conversation, it had become clear to me that the three of us were going to get along just fine for the remainder of their stay. I'd earn a pile of money, they'd learn how to dive and maybe along the way even how to have a normal relationship. They wouldn't be the first to figure out what really mattered while underwater.

Antje was standing in the hall. She looked as though she'd been waiting for me for hours. When I kissed her forehead, I held her by the shoulders so she couldn't cling to me.

"How was it?" she asked.

"Nice," I said. "Really very nice."

"How about a nightcap?"

"I'd rather not."

"Come on, stay up another thirty minutes. We've got something to talk about."

"I've had a hard day."

"It's only ten o'clock!"

She knew I hated to go to bed after ten o'clock. I needed to feel I could lie awake for two hours and still get six hours' sleep. And if I stayed up past midnight, the fear of not being able to fall asleep would keep me awake all night long.

"Please," Antje said. "Fifteen minutes, no more. Please!"

*

I'd known Antje since before she was even born. The Berger family lived two streets away from mine. Antje's future father came on the weekends to mow the lawn; her mother cleaned our bathroom on Thursdays. I was almost ten when Frau Berger's belly began to swell. From then on I used to watch her through the keyhole every Thursday while she was at work in the bathroom. Until one day she stopped coming. A few weeks later a baby carriage was standing in the shade of the linden tree while Antje's father mowed the lawn. My interest in the former contents of Frau Berger's belly died.

At thirteen I started asking my parents for a dog. Asking turned into begging. I was unlucky in love, not particularly athletic, and much in need of a friend. My parents were strenuously opposed to the idea. They claimed I'd lose interest in the dog before very long and then saddle them with the work. I swore they were being unjust to me.

For my fourteenth birthday I got Todd, a brown cocker spaniel with soft eyes and long ears. We were inseparable. I took him on walks three times a day. No one but me was allowed to feed him. Once I brought him to school, where all the girls swooned over him and I became—for a day—the most popular boy in the class.

Two years later, I was going out with Mareike, and I'd forgotten why I'd needed a dog. Todd was sweet, loyal, devoted, and tiresome. Because I begrudged my parents the triumph of having been right, I clenched my teeth, did my duty, and kept on walking him. Every day our walks got shorter. I'd haul Todd like an object once around the block, and in the end I threw him out of my room, where he'd slept happily at my feet for the first two years of his life. He'd look at me sadly, but without reproach. My bad conscience made me hate him.

His salvation arrived in the shape of little Antje, who came to our door one day and asked if she could take Todd for a walk. From that moment on, Todd was the happiest dog in the world. He loved Antje, and Antje loved him. They'd spend whole afternoons in the town woods. When Antje got a little older, they'd take a bus together and go hiking in the forests of the Neandertal. My mother would give her some pocket money, but the tip had less to do with Antje's expectations than with my family's habit of paying members of the Berger family for their services.

After I moved to Cologne to attend the university, on rainy days Antje would lie with Todd on the floor of my room, listen to my music, read my books, and wait to get older. When I came home for semester break, I'd sit at my desk and try to solve the riddles of some legal homework while Todd and Antje shared a bag of jelly babies on the Flokati rug. If I wanted to go to the bathroom, I'd climb over the two of them. Antje didn't bother me. Her presence had a tranquilizing effect. She was almost sixteen when I inadvertently slept with her one wet afternoon. Since this one-on-one leisure-time activity harmed neither of us, we occasionally repeated it.

Later Antje would say it was me and not Todd she'd been in love with as a child. But a seven-year-old can't approach a seventeen-year-old. Likewise, a twelve-year-old girl has no chance with a twenty-two-year-old student. A girl has to be sixteen before she's capable of making an impression on a man of twenty-six. And so her plan had basically been to wait. During the long hikes in the Neandertal, she said, she had imaginary conversations with me. Even the books in my room smelled like me. She'd crept into my clothes closet for her first exercises in masturbation, she said. I would have thought it impolite not to believe her. I'd learned at court how people shaped the past according to self-created patterns. They'd talk the crudest nonsense with sacred conviction. That was maybe the most important insight I gained from my legal education: he who doesn't tell the truth is still a long way from lying. In my eyes, Antje was such a case.

On the day when I stopped by my parents' house to pick up a few things I'd need on the island, Antje was lying on my bed, doing a crossword puzzle. My mother stood in the doorway and screamed at me. My father backed her up, having left work at the clinic where he was the chief physician for just this purpose. Since he'd paid for my university studies, I owed him my life. That was his position. We agreed that I couldn't expect the smallest financial support when I came back from my reckless adventure, a failure and a disgrace, in a few weeks. I slung my army duffel bag over my shoulder and fled the house.

Antje followed me to the train station, to the train itself, and into my Cologne apartment. She simply refused to leave my side. I was exhausted, and I decided I couldn't forbid her to turn up at the airport at the same time as me on December 31, 1997. It so happened that the pocket money she'd received for taking care of Todd, year in year out, nicely covered the price of a plane ticket.

I'd completed my military obligation with the Army Engineer Divers and trained as a diving instructor with the DLRG, the German Lifesaving Association, during semester breaks from my law studies. When Antje and I arrived on the island, I had more than five hundred dives in my logbook, and from the very first hour I was able to earn money as an instructor. Antje had studied Spanish in school, and in addition she had a real talent for organization. Founding a diving school required a great deal of work out of the water. Antje took on all the logistics, from visits to the authorities and bookkeeping to equipment maintenance, so that

I was able to concentrate on diving right from the beginning. It soon became undeniable that we made a good team.

Todd died a few months after our disappearance from Germany. By then he was almost thirteen years old, but Antje wouldn't accept his age as the reason for his demise. She was convinced she'd killed her best friend in order to be with me. When the diving school started doing so well we could afford to buy the houses in Lahora, she moved heaven and earth to have Todd's breeder send her an identical dog from the same part of the Rhineland. The new Todd actually looked indistinguishable from the old one. He loved Antje, and Antje loved him. I found it weird that she could silence her guilt feelings with such a simple trick.

"I've got a bottle open. One of Nenad's." Nenad was from Slovenia, and for the past twenty years he'd cultivated a vineyard in the La Goria region. "Shall we have a glass and loosen up a little?"

"Good night." I turned to go.

"Jola was here," said Antje.

I stopped. If a client was the subject, that was something else again. Todd lay in front of the couch and slapped the floor with his tail when we sat down. Antje poured a second glass of wine, handed it to me, and held hers up to be clinked. It was her unchanging opinion that I needed to "loosen up." She generally seemed to believe that people were capable of interacting with one another only after an appropriate amount of loosening.

"So what did Theo talk about?" she asked.

"You were going to tell me why Jola was here."

Antje looked at the window, through which there was nothing to see but black night. She leaned forward to pat Todd's head and flicked some fluff off the arm of the couch. For a second I thought she'd invented Jola's visit to stop me from going to bed. Then, however, she began to talk.

Somehow, she said, Jola had grown bored with studying and then had somehow decided to drop over. And since Antje had just finished preparing the tuna salad anyway, somehow or other Jola had stayed to dinner. They'd opened a bottle of Nenad's wine and somehow managed to have a very good conversation.

I asked her not to constantly use the word *somehow*.

First, Antje said, Jola had talked about how much she liked diving and how much playing the role of the Girl on the Ocean Floor meant to her. Overall, Antje said, Jola seemed to be afflicted by an intense Lotte Hass fixation, which probably stemmed from a panic about missing the boat professionally. It was something along the lines of "If I don't get this part, my career's over forever." Antje had found it interesting that a woman like Jola, who appeared so successful and self-confident, would in reality suffer such torments. Despite her 384,000 Google hits, Jola obviously had enormous anxiety issues.

Having registered the information that I wasn't the only one who'd googled Jola's name, I asked, "Well, so what?"

Somehow, Antje went on, Jola seemed to be having doubts about all her hopes and aspirations. She'd begun talking about people's decisions and actions, how they were like pieces of furniture people installed in their lives. That was why someone who did evil could never live happily again, no matter how rich and famous and successful he might be. By the same token, good deeds never arose from love of one's neighbor but always and only from self-love. How to lead your life was therefore not a moral question but an aesthetic one. Of course, there were people who felt more at home with ugliness than with beauty. Because unless you were totally nuts, it wasn't likely you'd do something bad by mistake. In this vein, Antje said, Jola had gone on for a good while, and she'd said a whole lot of remarkable things.

In the first place, I found Jola's line of thought not particularly remarkable, and in the second, I had no idea why I was sitting there listening to the summary of an innocuous conversation. I made these very same observations to Antje.

After a brief hesitation, she explained that there was something about Jola that wasn't right. She'd kept looking around as though some invisible menace was lurking in the room, and more than once she'd seemed on the verge of tears.

Now came the part where Antje invoked feminine intuition so as not to be at the mercy of concrete facts. My lack of interest escalated into anger. When I started to get up, she grabbed my arm.

"Don't you understand?" she asked. "Jola's afraid."

"Of what?"

Antje put on her psychiatrist's demeanor and explained that Jola's real subject had been Theo the whole time. That when she'd talked about people who furnished their lives with evil deeds, Jola had meant no one but Theo.

I wanted to know if Jola had said Theo's name.

No, but somehow it had been clear that the conversation was about Theo.

"Nonsense," I said.

Antje remained stubborn. She said Jola had signaled that she needed help.

I asked whether the word *help* had been spoken.

Likewise no, but at some point Jola had suddenly seized Antje's hand and said, word for word, "You should thank heaven for your Sven."

I hadn't ever been able to put up with the female propensity for psychologizing. With the assistance of a bottle of wine, Antje could construct an entire world out of mere interpretations, a world as dramatic and shimmering as a musical, and then confuse this production with reality. Only women had the ability to be angry with their mates because of bad dreams about them the previous night.

It seemed to me impossible that Jola had dropped over to ask for help, for protection from Theo. When it came to a taste for dangerous practical jokes, she was as bad as he was. I stood up.

"Okay," I said. "Sleep well."

Antje jumped up from the couch too. "Then she said, 'Sven would never do anything to you.' "

I kissed her on the forehead. "It's good that you two get along so well."

"But," said Antje.

One of the pleasant things in life is the fact that everyone is entitled to his own worldview. I took my perceptions to bed with me. I knew tomorrow would be a thoroughly normal day, a day on which I'd go diving with a couple of clients. Beyond that knowledge there was nothing that needed to be taken into account.

JOLA'S DIARY, THIRD DAY

Monday, November 14. Evening.

I'm choking. I can't shake the feeling of being unable to breathe. It's lodged in my throat. As if there's something stuck in there. A cork. A convulsion. Instead of studying, I jump up every three minutes and dash over to the window. I yank it open and suck air into my lungs. I tell myself, That's oxygen! Your body inhales it automatically! You aren't going to die. My heart races so hard it hurts. I try to calm down, to subdue my panic. To breathe slowly, the way Sven taught me to do. If only he were here. If only he would take my hand. Give me his *air to breathe. I need a diving instructor on land. Someone who can teach me how to keep from choking on this crappy life.*

So the old man came out of the shower with a wet towel over his shoulder and that special expression on his face, and already I felt the air go out of me, I got cold, and my inner voice was hollering, Tough it out! You can stand it! It won't kill you! Think about something else and hold still, it'll be over with faster that way!

But the old man just laid a hand on the back of my neck and asked me, friendly as you please, if I really didn't want to go to dinner with them in the little restaurant in Tinajo. I made a frantic grab for the diving books. A thin defensive perimeter. Then Sven arrived and looked shocked when he found out I wanted to stay in. Now I'm staring at the clock on the wall. It's set an hour ahead so that vacationing guests won't miss their programs on German TV.

Studying theory is pointless. Math formulas and page-long descriptions of different pieces of equipment. As if theory could safeguard you in practice. As if the world didn't have ways and means to sneak up on us from behind. And then there's the constant blather about your "buddy." You have to be able to rely on your buddy. You and your buddy must practice underwater communication. Always make sure you're not endangering yourself or your buddy. I'm sick of my "buddy."

I know Theo loves me. Not only because he says so. I see it in his eyes. I feel it in the way he puts his arm around me. Comforts me. Tries to protect me from himself. I know it from the efforts he makes. From the way he honestly tries to be someone else. Often enough, I provoke him, I ask for it. Come on, do it then. Give it to me hard. Stick your dick in my ass. You can't get it up unless you can play the rapist. And so on, until he grabs my neck and forces me to stop talking. To provoke is to maintain control. In some situations, the greatest mercy is the knowledge that at least you've brought them on yourself.

Do people have opposites? If they do, then Sven's the opposite of the old man. Sven watches out for me. How quickly he moved to my side when I swam out over the ledge! He noticed I was losing control well before it became clear to me. His eyes behind the diving goggles. His firm conviction that he could help me. His calm was contagious, and I caught it. He should never have let me go. We would have simply stayed underwater forever.

He sent me a text message a little while ago: "You're in our thoughts." He's always worrying. I've never known anyone who worried so much. I can literally see the wheels turning inside his head. Broody wheels, worry wheels. Sometimes I want to grab his arm and hold on until he stops thinking and tell him, You're a good person.

I try to imagine Sven killing the old man. He grabs him by the throat, pushes him underwater, and holds him down. I'm wearing diving goggles. I sit on the bottom and watch. I see the mortal fear on Theo's face. The sudden understanding that he's gone too far. Drowning's an ugly death. Music by Carter Burwell, as in a Coen brothers film, accompanies the scene. I press STOP.

Everything could be so beautiful. We're on an island, we have money, we're healthy. But everything's ugly. And the more I think and do ugly things, the uglier my life becomes. Like a splendid home furnished with the most tasteless objects. It hurts to have to see that every day. Being inside is unbearable. The open window's not helping anymore. I have to get out of here.

7

By the next morning, the bad weather had finally moved off. Blue sky, bright sun, a friendly little wind. Jola was sitting on the steps of the Casa Raya, wearing cutoff jeans and a top with a narrow halter holding her breasts. Something was missing from this picture, namely Theo. Jola was alone. I knew immediately that he hadn't just gone back in to pick up some forgotten trifle, he hadn't yet left the Casa. I could tell by looking at Jola that Theo wouldn't be diving with us that morning. She looked back at me as if seeing me for the first time.

I stood in front of her and reflected on how we'd been greeting each other the past couple of days. Handshakes? Mutual shoulder pats? Brief waves and simple hellos? Or were we already such good friends that we had to embrace? I didn't like this constant cheek-kissing between near strangers. When it became the fashion at the university to greet people by flinging your arms around their neck, I decided not to go to any more parties. One thing was certain: I couldn't possibly fling my arms around Jola. Not as long as she was wearing that halter top. I realized that on the previous days I'd driven up to the Casa and simply stayed in the driver's seat while Jola and Theo threw their bags into the backseat and got in the front with me. I couldn't understand why I'd climbed out of the van on that particular morning.

"Is something wrong?" Jola asked.

"Where's Theo?"

Her face clouded. She said, "*I'm* paying your fee."

"Is he not in the mood today?"

"The old man's your biggest fan. But he's in bed with a cold."

"Antje will bring him something that'll put him back on his feet by tomorrow."

"But are you ready and willing to go diving with me without Theo?"

I saluted and said in English, "Yes, ma'am."

In the van she sat close to the passenger window, leaving an empty place between us on the front seat. When I turned my head toward her, she smiled strangely, showing the spaces between her incisors. This had the same effect on me as if she'd spread her legs. We didn't speak. I forced myself to keep my eyes on the road.

Everything is will.

Silence on land was something different from silence underwater. It wasn't a normal condition; it was the mute sound track of failure. After fifteen minutes, I couldn't take it anymore.

"So how are you coming along with theory?"

"Fuck theory."

She pronounced the word as if *theo-ry* had something to do with *Theo*. Then we fell silent again.

Finally the van was bouncing along the potholed road that led to the dive site at Mala. I considered it important that Jola's next dive should be in the same spot where she'd had her panic attack the day before. The same principle as getting right back on a horse after a fall. There had been no discussion of this. She hadn't asked where we were going, and I kept having trouble coming up with the first sentence of every single thing I wanted to say.

We stopped and Jola got out. She stretched her back and looked at the ocean, which shone smooth as foil all the way to the horizon. I opened the back of the van and felt gratitude at the sight of all the equipment. Scuba tanks to unload, buoyancy compensators to prepare, weight belts to find. Jola helped me spread out the tarp we were going to change our clothes on. When she crossed her arms to pull her top over her head, I turned back to the van and rummaged under the passenger seat for a mask.

"Where can you pee around here?" Jola said. It wasn't a question, it was a warning. Not a tree or a bush within five kilometers in any direction. Just the gravel road where the van was parked. Beyond that, nothing but rocks and black sand.

Jola went to the other side of the van and squatted down beside the left front wheel. I bent low over the passenger seat, pretending to concentrate on my search, out of fear that she'd be able to see me through the half-open driver's door if I straightened up. A stream struck the hard ground. I could practically feel it splashing on her feet and ankles. The longer the situation went on, the more impossible it became. The splatter seemed to present an increasingly detailed and shameless account of Jola's insides. It wouldn't stop. I stared at the dust at my feet.

Slowly, the hissing became a trickle, and under the passenger door a thin rivulet appeared. It showed no inclination to seep away into the earth. Instead, the little stream was ferrying along a certain amount of dust at its edges, so that it wallowed rather than flowed. It was getting close to my toes. I didn't move my foot. All at once, Jola was standing next to me. Her eyes were not on me but on the ground. On the damp print of my left foot.

"Let's do it," I said. My upbeat tone was a rebellion against her contemptuous smile.

As we made our difficult way down the rocks, she started to stumble. I instinctively reached out my hand to catch her; she took hold of it and didn't let go. I said to myself that when we were carrying heavy equipment and going over dangerous terrain, it was my duty to support her. Her grasp wasn't coy, it was tight and warm, almost like a man's. It felt completely natural to go the rest of the way hand in hand with her.

Before we entered the water, I showed her once again how to protect her mask and diving regulator. I inflated her buoyancy compensator and tested every buckle on her outfit. When her fingers wandered over my suit during the safety check, I closed my eyes. Then I turned around and jumped.

All quiet. Jola lay in the water much more calmly than she'd done on the previous days. It was as though Theo's absence relaxed her. She sank slowly, one hand on her nose for pressure equalization, while her hair floated around her like a living thing. She spread out her arms and legs and hovered in place, gently lifted and lowered by her own breathing. She turned on her back and looked up at the air bubbles rising toward the sun from her mouth like glinting jellyfish. I knelt on the sea bottom and couldn't stop looking at her. We were together down there in the water. Two slow-motion creatures in a slow-motion world. In fourteen years and with hundreds of clients, such a feeling of solidarity, of connection, had never come over me before. Jola approached and landed on her knees directly opposite me. We remained like that for a while, as though we were worshipping each other. A little cuttlefish swam up and looked at us inquiringly. It exchanged its camouflage for a striped courtship display to determine whether we were male or female. Eventually Jola raised her thumb and forefinger to signal, *Okay?* I responded in kind: *Yes, okay.*

I don't remember whose hands reached out first. I do remember taking her by the shoulders and pulling her into my arms, and I remember that she immediately returned my embrace. We couldn't kiss each other, because we had to keep our breathing apparatus in our mouths. We couldn't caress each other, because our skin was covered by a layer of neoprene, and pieces of equipment blocked the way everywhere. The only parts of Jola available to me were her hands and the back of her head. I thrust one hand into the armhole of her buoyancy compensator so that I could at least feel the flattened shape of her breast under the neoprene. Then I turned her around, bent her forward, and rubbed myself against her rubberized behind. I considered whether I dared to undress her. I thought I could grip her weight belt with one hand and carefully remove her buoyancy compensator with the other. Then I'd lay her tank on the seafloor, and she could hold the tank tight in both arms to keep from being carried away by the current. I probably could have managed to peel her diving suit half off. The mere idea of pulling down her zipper and lifting out her breasts while she lay facedown on the bottom of the sea, helpless as a newborn babe, chained by a hose to her air supply—that image alone drove me out of my mind.

Naturally, I did nothing of the kind. We were twenty meters below the surface of the water, it was her fifteenth dive, I was her trainer, and the responsibility was mine. The cuttlefish got bored and swam off. Three butterfly rays hovered close to the ocean floor in the middle distance. Theo would have been ecstatic.

All my adult life I'd considered myself a person with little capacity for love. Occasionally I'd gaze at Antje's face and think that she was really nice-looking. At such times, I felt happy that she was with me. Those brief moments were the peaks of my emotional life. Love, on the other hand, the kind of love that ruined entire families, incited wars, or drove the lovelorn to suicide—I knew a love like that only from the movies. The very idea seemed foreign to me. It was as though I was missing the organ whose function was to engender such a love. And so for a long time I'd believed there was something wrong with me. During my university days, I'd invested a lot of effort in trying to fall in love. That led to sex. But I was too honest to mistake horniness for true romance.

One day after Antje and I had been living together for some years, I heard Don Draper, an ad executive in the television series *Mad Men*, say to a woman, "What you call love was invented by guys like me to sell nylons." From then on, things got better for me. From then on, I stopped feeling deficient. I considered love a mixture of social convention and psychosomatic response. I believed people like Antje felt love because they were assured on all sides that it had to be. Antje had started saying "I love you" to me the first time we slept together. Eventually I learned to reply, "Love you too." I'd simply decided to call a longtime, functioning companionship "love." And I was even relatively sure that Antje and I meant the same thing.

❖

Up until the moment when I embraced the statuesque, neoprene-wrapped Jola on the floor of the Atlantic Ocean. Until she clung to me. Until she thrust one hand between my thighs and grasped me hard, trying to overcome the barrier of the diving suit by brute force. Nothing like Antje's girlish shyness when, once a week, she'd start to stroke the back of my neck. She usually came up behind me when I was sitting on the couch or at the computer and rubbed my neck and tickled my ears with little begging touches until I took hold of her wrists and kissed her purely in self-defense. When we kissed, she'd stick just the tip of her tongue between her teeth and lick my lips instead of properly opening her mouth. She'd giggle and slap her flip-flops on the floor extra loud when she ran ahead of me to the bedroom. She'd always want to lie on her back, because that was the only way she could come.

Thanks to Jola, it suddenly seemed obvious that my lack of belief in love had been the only reason I'd never left Antje. Antje was like the practical, convenient wardrobe we'd bought when we moved into the Residencia, a provisional solution that was still standing in the same place years later because it had proved itself useful and provided no immediate reasons for being discarded. When it came to not providing reasons, Antje was an artist.

◈

By contrast, I wanted Jola so badly I almost lost consciousness. Even in the chilly waters of the Atlantic, I thought I could feel the warmth she was putting out. As if her body was filled with hot liquid. She pulled my head to her and gestured upward with one thumb. I nodded, even though I really didn't want to ascend to the surface. In this underwater world, which wasn't made for mankind, we belonged together.

As a conservative diver, I prescribed a slow ascent. When eight minutes were up, I was helping Jola clamber out of the water. I insisted on our carrying the equipment to the van at once. One behind the other, we climbed up the steep path to the top of the cliff. The offshore wind had freshened a little. Jola's face showed the red imprint of her diving mask. When we reached the van, she pressed me against it, simultaneously trying to pull open the zipper on my back. I pushed her away from me; it was impossible to get out of a diving suit that way. We stood facing each other and peeled the neoprene off our skins. In her haste, Jola wound up hopping on one foot and nearly fell. Then she was naked. She braced both hands on the side of the van and turned her backside to me. I seized her hips. Her breasts swung free, and her wet hair stuck to her back.

It was good. It would have been good. But something was

wrong. It was the way Jola had turned her back to me. Her questioning look, sexy and provocative. *What are you waiting for?* When she did that, she looked like an actress. I rubbed my cock between her thighs. She wasn't particularly wet, but she nevertheless threw her head back immediately and forcefully. She groaned in time with my movements. As if we were playing the leads in some vacation porn movie. I could have penetrated her and gone at it hot and heavy, and we could have finished in a minute. But what would have been the point of that?

Maybe the problem was that out of the water, we were humans. Deep inside me was a dead silence. The intense feelings of a short while ago were hushed. I saw the two of us as though from the outside. The Volkswagen van, the equipment strewn on the ground. A female student and her male diving instructor, on the verge of forgetting his principles. Sex represented a powerful form of involvement. The error of thinking he could enjoy a quickie and emerge from it scot-free had undone many a man before me.

I drew back, patted Jola's ass, and murmured an apology. Then I slipped into my jeans and set about loading the equipment. I'd have to write off the dive site at Mala as currently jinxed. When I settled in behind the steering wheel, Jola was already in the passenger seat. She didn't seem angry. Rather a little absent. She stared straight ahead, as if an important idea had just occurred to her. I briefly put my hand on her knee. Then I needed that hand to shift.

In the course of a man's life, he grows used to the fact that women, with few exceptions, do not wish to go to bed with him. A woman, on the other hand, can take it for granted that theoretically every man wants to go to bed with her. Today I wonder what it must have meant to a woman like Jola to be rejected. Can it really be that fate had required me, at that moment, to bring matters to an end? Unanswerable questions are those best suited to being asked over and over.

JOLA'S DIARY, FOURTH DAY

[pages torn out and pasted back in]

Tuesday, November 15. Afternoon.

Algae produce 80 percent of our oxygen. According to my iPhone. It also says that whole mountains of limestone were formed from marine organisms. Humans use it to make concrete. We build cities out of snail shells and conches. The image appeals to the old man. Maybe he can use it in one of his stories.

A happy mood works just the way a bad one does. You have to take it out on someone. Since there's no one else here, the old man gets to enjoy himself. He lies on the sofa and uses up tissues. I make him some tea, plump his pillows, and acknowledge his suffering as the most tragic in the universe. I read him pearls of wisdom from the Internet. So a good time with one turns into tenderness for the other. Note: a good time, not a guilty conscience.

What I'd most like to do is to tell the old man a completely different story. To give him a detailed account of how Sven, who usually talks the whole time we're in the van—describes the upcoming dive, points out the few sights the island offers, relates anecdotes from his underwater life—suddenly found himself speechless. Instead of talking, he kept turning his head every twenty seconds to look at me. Why don't I tell Theo that? *Because he'd go berserk, that's why. Because he'd beat the daylights out of me, maybe even kill me. Inadvertently. He doesn't deserve to hear a good-time story. And holding my tongue is at least as much fun. So I sit on the bed in the bedroom and laugh to myself every now and then.*

What's so funny? The old man calls out from the sofa.

Did you know cuttlefish change color when they're courting? I call back.

On land I find it difficult to take Sven seriously. Those thick arms, that innocent look. A failed lawyer, escaped to an eternal kindergarten, with 100 percent sun and 0 percent real life. But underwater, he's another person. No, wrong: another being. The innocence becomes self-confidence, the eagerness turns into deepest concentration. So much assurance is never really found in people; only animals have it. I look at him and feel his calmness pervading me, too. I stop struggling. I want only to be close to him.

Today I wasn't afraid at all. The water carried me, it was like slow flying. Sven was waiting for me on the bottom. We knelt before each other like a priest and a priestess. Nature knows only one kind of divine service.

In 1996 the Neoselachii, a group that includes modern sharks and rays, were subdivided according to morphological characteristics into two monophyletic taxa, the Galeomorphii and the Squalea. According to this proposal, sharks are paraphyletic and hence a form taxon, while rays are assigned to a mere subgroup of squalomorphic sharks.

When Theo asks me again what I'm laughing at, I read him that paragraph off my iPhone.

I say, We saw some rays today.

He says, Lucky you, you had a good time.

He could hardly have given me a funnier answer. To tell the truth, we had a very fine time indeed! I have to pull myself together or he'll get suspicious.

The rays glided through the water like slow-motion birds and paid not the slightest attention to us. It was as if we weren't there. Sven's hands on my breasts under the buoyancy compensator. I could feel how hard he was through his diving suit. Our slow ascent was time-release torture. With every meter closer to the surface, our tension grew. Falling for the diving instructor. And so what? Other women who get treated like shit at home fuck the ski teacher or the tennis pro. Lotte Hass married her expedition leader. We practically ran the distance to the car. In spite of all the equipment. If I'd had any idea of refusing him, he would have taken me by force. Never have two people stripped off their diving suits faster. The metal side of Sven's van was hot under my hands. He stood behind me, bending his knees a little in order to penetrate me. There was nothing coarse about it. He was very warm. He thrust into me almost questioningly. Impatience had nearly driven us crazy; now we had all the time in the world. And though all mankind, in order to spare men's feelings, may go on saying that size doesn't matter, I will simply note that Sven has the ability to fill me up. It was sweet to feel my will steadily vanishing. The sound of the surf, the light breeze, the black landscape. Except for us, not a living thing in sight, far and wide. As though life existed only in the sea we'd just climbed out of. Two aquatic animals, coming on shore to mate. When I sleep with the old man, even when it's good, I think about something else. Sven found the rhythm. My knees got weak, and he had to hold me up. He couldn't get enough of my breasts. Whenever I started to think it couldn't become more intense, it moved to another level. I heard myself stammering foolish words. Sven began to cry out my name. When it was over, he literally collapsed on top of me. It was the first time I've ever come standing up.

He dropped to the ground on his back and pulled me onto him. We lay together in the dirt. He twisted my hair into braids and stroked the back of my neck. He said, I love you, Jola. I didn't take it amiss—I knew what he meant. It was a moment of perfect peace.

Theo asks, How come you two went on only one dive?

I say, Oh, you know, without you it's only half as much fun.

He laughs: Little hypocrite.

While we drove up the gravel track from Mala, Sven kept one arm around me. He feels good even when he's dressed. Shortly before we reached the main road, he had me move away and sit at a decent distance. Everybody on the island knows everybody else. Our silence now had another quality. We smiled a lot. When he let me out, he said, See you tomorrow. I said, Give my best to Antje. He said, I will. That meant, Everything, really everything, is all right.

8

It was like déjà vu: Jola was sitting on the same step at the same time, waiting for me. Alone. I backed the van up to the Casa Raya, got out, and said, "Hello." The same mistake. I should have stayed behind the steering wheel. When I was in front of her, she grabbed me by the collar and kissed me on the mouth.

"Morning," she said.

I took a quick look around to check whether Antje or Theo was standing at one of the windows to wave good-bye to us. Thank God we had no neighbors. The geometric pattern of the morning shadows decorated the empty sandlot. "Get in," I said.

I'd decided to try Famara. The flat, sandy bottom there sloped down gradually, so that on most days the surf swirled up floating particles and clouded your vision. In any case, apart from fields of seaweed, shoals of Salema porgies, and a Mediterranean moray eel that was always in the same crevice, there wasn't that much to see. But you entered the dive site directly from the old harbor, which meant that you had to change into and out of your diving outfit right there in the village. It was the best place for us not to be alone with each other.

I talked nonstop during the drive to Famara. My mouth and the speech center in my brain carried out a program I'd given no orders for. For some reason, I expatiated on technical diving, on the enormous expense in equipment and planning required to go down a paltry hundred meters into the sea—a distance you could cover on land in a minute without even noticing it. I explained the tremendous difference between descent and ascent, using the shipwreck expedition I was planning as an example. It would be a matter of a few minutes to dive down to the wreck, and after that I'd have only twenty minutes to inspect it. On the other hand, I'd need more than two hours to go back up, stopping along the way, if I didn't want to endanger my life. The last decompression stop would require me to remain a full hour at a depth of six meters, with light, air, and the dive ship's hull directly above my head. I'd have to hover there, constrained by water pressure and the accumulation of nitrogen in my body.

No-decompression dives were surely the only kind Jola would go on in her life, and therefore in all likelihood she'd never really understand what no-decompression time was. She looked out the window. She was wearing an olive-green miniskirt. It cost me an effort not to think about the shaved pubes under it. Bernie came toward us in his minibus and waved as he passed. I lifted my hand, and Jola imitated me. As if we'd traveled down that stretch of road together a thousand times and greeted Bernie together a thousand times. I knew he'd ask me about her the next chance he got.

We parked on a narrow side street. Two old fishermen interrupted their chess game. A Spanish woman stepped out of her house and poured a bucket of dirty water at our feet. A German shepherd was dozing in the yard under a jacked-up rowboat. In our black diving suits and with our tanks on our backs, we waddled like extraterrestrials through the dead streets. Although it was still early in the morning, the heat was accumulating between the old facades. Jola's face reddened with effort. Before we entered the water, she tried to take my hand. I shook her off. I didn't know what I thought was worse: that things had gone so far the previous day, or that nevertheless I hadn't actually had her. It was probably the combination of both.

Visibility was atrocious and the water as warm as urine. We bobbed around in the murky swill at a maximum depth of nine meters. Not even the Mediterranean moray was at home. It astonished me to think I had entertained, if only for a few supremely lascivious moments, the idea that I'd met the love of my life in Jola Pahlen. I wasn't interested in trouble. For the past fourteen years, my existence had been predicated on the wise decision to stay out of other people's affairs. "Germany" was the name of a system whose entire focus was on what belonged to whom and who was to blame for what. Jola was Germany. She'd come from there, and there she would return. She and Theo had brought a part of the war zone with them to the island. And instead of keeping the greatest possible distance, I'd come *that* close to plunging in with both feet. There was no undoing what had happened. But a man could swerve and still get back on a steady course.

Today I'd add a caveat: provided he knows how to drive. Slamming on the brakes and jerking the steering wheel around is never the right tactic.

"Fantastic dive!" Jola cried, stumbled over her fins, and fell back into the shallow water.

I wondered aloud how many more times I was going to have to explain that you must walk backward when wearing fins. Moreover, I added, it was about time for her to learn how to adjust her buoyancy instead of continuing to lurch and zigzag through the water. It wasn't a matter of lack of talent, no one could be reproached for that. It was a matter of engaging with the fundamental principles of the sport. Or was that too much to ask?

Jola said nothing. I reduced our surface break to a necessary minimum and insisted on executing the day's second dive in the same spot. Because, I said, calm, shallow water was best suited for unsure divers.

We'd set out from Lahora shortly after eight o'clock; it wasn't yet noon when we completed the second dive. While I loaded the van, Jola stood behind me wearing a white terry-cloth robe, which she'd brought for the first time, and a towel around her head. She looked like a model in a catalog of luxury bath accessories. It would have been fabulous to feel her breasts through that thick terry cloth.

"Shall we go somewhere else?"

"I don't have enough cylinders for a third dive."

"Where we were yesterday? Just to go there?"

I turned to her. "To finish what we started?"

She smiled and held out her hand. "Maybe it's only the beginning."

I evaded the hand. The effort not to scream made my voice sound choked when I said, "Maybe you could try not to behave like a tramp for a change?"

She sat down on the curb and started to cry. Softly, without a show. She pressed her face into the collar of her bathrobe.

Fuck the old fishermen. Fuck the woman with the dirty water, who was standing in the doorway of her house again. Hardly any of the indigenous islanders knew me, especially not in Famara. The German shepherd under the rowboat stood up, as if he wanted to see what Jola's problem was. I sat next to her and put an arm around her shoulders.

I said I was sorry.

She asked what I meant.

I said that I'd behaved unprofessionally the previous day and that it would never happen again.

"Sven." She raised her face. Her nostrils were red and seemed to be vibrating slightly. "I'm in love with you."

"Nonsense." I moved a little away from her. "It's the diving. Diving's a liminal experience, and I'm your guide over the threshold. That awakens feelings."

She stretched out her arm and touched my shoulder with one finger.

"Please stop." I held her finger tight. "You have Theo. I have—a girlfriend."

She acknowledged my tiny hesitation with a tiny smile. "Is that so?"

Our conversation needed a new direction. I said, "You're flying back to Germany in ten days."

"I can stay here. I'll take over Antje's job."

I had an instant vision of Jola seated at the computer in our home office, her legs elegantly folded to one side, applying herself to our bookkeeping. I saw her standing at the stove. I saw my hands slip under her dress while she stirred a pot. She turned halfway toward me—and suddenly it was Antje's face, sitting on Jola's neck under Jola's hair and looking at me sadly. I sprang to my feet.

"What exactly are we talking about here?"

"About love, I assume."

"Theo loves you, Jola."

"How do you know that?"

"He told me so."

She looked up at me thoughtfully. "Really?"

The relief I felt encouraged me. "When we went to dinner," I explained. "He said that he couldn't live without you. He said that you're everything to him." I didn't remember his exact words, but that was their general sense.

"And that you can screw me if you want?"

"Of course he didn't say that." I tried to sound indignant.

"That he's got no problem with you wanting me? Because more or less everybody wants me and he's used to it?"

I said nothing. Jola laughed and then stood up as well. "You're really sweet, Sven," she said. She put her hands in the pockets of her bathrobe. The fishermen were openly staring at us. I had to assume they didn't understand German.

"Don't worry about it," Jola went on. "We have time. We can simply wait and see how things develop."

She started to take off her wet bikini under her robe. Apparently the conversation was over. Even though I didn't know what conclusion we'd come to, I felt better. It was as if we'd assured each other that we wanted to remain friends.

A little later, she was sitting in the passenger seat. She'd tied her hair in a ponytail, and she appeared to be in an extremely good mood. "Let's have lunch in Teguise," she said. "After that I'd really like to visit the cactus gardens."

I took my place at the steering wheel. "I'd rather go back to Lahora, if you don't mind."

She laughed as though I'd made a good joke. "Have you by any chance forgotten what I'm paying you for?" The laughing stopped. "Full service. Twenty-four seven. Drive on."

•

It was eight in the evening. Antje was sitting in front of the television and I was at the computer when the doorbell rang. As a general rule, nobody rang our doorbell. You don't arrive by chance at the ends of the earth. If the doorbell did ring, it was one of Antje's Spanish girlfriends, picking her up to go shopping or dropping off a skinned rabbit. A ringing doorbell was no sign stimulus as far as I was concerned. Ordinarily I didn't even raise my head. This time, it was pure instinct that made me say, "Stay there, I'll get it," and go to the door.

Theo was standing outside in the darkness, and he didn't look as though he'd come over to borrow a cup of flour. He was wearing suit pants, no shoes, and a misbuttoned shirt. His eyes and nose were red. He smelled of alcohol. I stepped out of the house and closed the door behind me.

"Congratulations!" He sounded stuffed up. "My heartiest congratulations."

"Theo," I said. "Are you feeling better?"

"Who'd have thought it would happen so fast, huh?" He laughed.

"Who's there?" Antje called from inside.

"It's just Theo!" I called back through the closed door.

"May I step in again?" He pointed at the house. It was hard to tell how well he could be heard inside. His vocal pitch fluctuated between whispering and bawling. "And pay my respects to your little Antje, I mean."

Theo began to stumble. I stepped aside. He bared his teeth. "You're scared shitless of me," he said.

Underwater I found it easy to remain calm in stressful situations. You could even say that the more critical things got, the steadier my nerves became. Unfortunately, this wasn't the case on land. I felt a savage desire to slug Theo. As wobbly on his legs as he was, any child could have taken him. But he was my client.

"*Shitless* is the key word." He pressed one nostril closed and blew out the other. The snot landed right next to the doormat. "Maybe you thought I wouldn't keep my word, was that it? I told you you could have her. I'm only here to get something straight." He pointed an index finger at me. "You're a big dick attached to a coward. That's what you are." As he repeated this assessment, he nodded slowly.

"Look," I said. "How about continuing this conversation tomorrow?"

"You see!" He was getting louder. "Scared shitless, like I said. Scared your Antje will hear me. You're a coward, Sven. I came over here especially to point that out to you."

"Now you have. That's enough."

"That's enough, just like that? If you have the right to fuck my woman, I have the right to give you a piece of my mind."

"I didn't fuck your woman."

"Ah!" It started out as a scream but after a few seconds turned into laughter. "That's so lame, Sven! You're such a chickenshit! At least stick to your guns!"

Suddenly his face was illuminated. His eyes, his shirt, his entire form radiated light. It took me a while to realize that the door behind me had opened.

"Is everything all right?" Antje asked.

I hated the feeling of losing control. Control was the objective of all human striving. Loss of control meant death. I felt my forehead grow cold.

"*Voilà Madame!*" Theo cried out joyously. "Good evening!"

Antje gave me a questioning look. As always, she was trying to establish an immediate understanding between us. My body did me the favor of shrugging my shoulders and contorting my mouth into a helpless grimace.

Theo turned to Antje. "Not much longer," he said. Then he pointed his finger at me again: "You don't dive because you think fish are fantastic. You dive because you feel safe down there."

His tongue seemed to be loosening; he sounded less drunk. I wondered whether he was putting on an act.

"You think you're a first-class individualist. A real man who had the balls to drop out. You weren't going to be stupid and weak like everybody else, you weren't going to play the game anymore. But you're no special case. You didn't even drop out, not really. You weren't up to the challenge. You're the overchallenged prototype of the overchallenged twenty-first century. A whole era of unmet challenges! Do you remember how things looked at the end of the last century? The big chance. The big freedom. Everybody wanted to make something out of it. And then, suddenly, everything was too much. Too much world, too much information, too many possibilities. Everyone's gone into exile, my dear Monstercock. Some escape into bourgeois convention, others choose the countryside or a hobby or nostalgia or even this island. It's an all-encompassing rearguard action, and you're right in the middle of it."

He wiped away some sweat. He'd worn himself out talking. His drunkenness had decreased, and so had his hatred. For a while he stared upward, squinting, at the night sky, as though considering whether concluding his speech would be worth the trouble. "Okay," he declared in the end, "what I want to say is this: your turn's coming. Dream about your personal plans, dream about complete independence. One day your turn will come, just as it comes to everybody else. When it does, you'll think about my words. Good night."

And with that he turned around, walked down the gravel path, and carefully closed the garden gate behind him. We watched him cross the sandlot and disappear into the Casa Raya.

"What was that about?" asked Antje.

"I don't know," I said.

She shrugged. "Probably Vicks NyQuil plus Nenad's red wine."

"That he got from you?"

"How could I know he'd drink it all at one sitting?"

I had to laugh. I was doing fine. I'd done nothing other than stand there, and nevertheless I'd emerged the victor. Or rather, precisely because of that. Everything under control. Antje looked up at me.

"Why did he call you 'Monstercock'?"

I briefly stroked her hair. We went back inside together.

JOLA'S DIARY, FIFTH DAY

Wednesday, November 16. Evening.

I'm just wiping something wet off my mouth and looking to see whether it's blood when my phone rings. It's Hartmut the Great.

Me: Hello, Daddy. Him: the usual stream of words, without commas or periods. I sometimes wonder what would happen if he dialed the wrong number. Would he notice? Nobody can ask questions more beautifully without wanting to know the answers. With Hartmut the Great, it's "How're you doing, good, glad to hear it," a single unbroken sentence. At some point I stopped being willing to listen to him in mute silence the whole time, and since then our relationship has been difficult. A fact that has managed to escape his notice, as far as I can tell.

The old man's in the corner, massaging his knuckles and shivering. I point to the cell phone at my ear and soundlessly form the name Hartmut *with my lips.*

Hartmut talks about all the trouble he's having with his new project, railing against West German Broadcasting, the North Rhine–Westphalia Film Foundation, his slow-assed screenwriter, his young director, who's idiotic enough to take himself for an artist, and, of course, his bitchy leading lady.

Occasionally I go "Mm-hmm" and "Golly." I haven't said anything to Hartmut about Lotte. He could probably get the part for me. Why didn't you say so, baby girl? A little telephone call, a bit of pressure. But after that, Lotte would be dead and not my Lotte anymore. For that matter, I could just blow some director so he'd let me play the sidekick in his new comedy.

Hartmut's still on about the leading lady. What airs she puts on. What she takes herself for. Who does she think she is.

I almost have to laugh. Such relief after the old man's whacked me one. Now he'll think I'm laughing at him, I'm not taking him seriously. Which will make him even more furious. At the same time, I'm afraid. The old man has destroyed my soul. Only destroyed souls laugh when someone hits them. I take care to see that it happens regularly. So he can work it off in small doses. If he should let things build up, he might inadvertently bash my head in one day. I'm most afraid when he doesn't lay a hand on me. If I look at it like that, today's a good day. I'm not even bleeding. The old man always takes care that no one will be able to see anything tomorrow. He can go ballistic, but systematically, please.

Hartmut next attacks the family. Mama's got a new hair color again. The Botox hasn't been a total success. His jokes are the worst: "So I confess to my wife that I cheated on her last night, and she says, 'But Hartmut, that was me you were screwing.'"

How long has it been since his blather could still hurt me? Since I wanted to cry out, Daddy, you're speaking to your daughter! The woman you're talking about is my mother! I believe I started putting up barriers before I could spell barriers. *A good preparation for the old man. I was a young person developing the abilities I'd need when I was thirty. Maybe I should thank Hartmut. Many thanks, Daddy, for making it clear to me early on what shits men are. And for calling at just the right moment.*

Not half an hour ago, while I was sitting up in bed, scribbling away, the old man suddenly appeared in the doorway.

I want to know, right now, what you're writing and why you're giggling like an imbecile.

Fuck off.

Give it here.

Never.

Give it here or I'll break all your bones.

I won't—you will—I won't—you will, just like in kindergarten. The winner's the one who first resorts to violence. Theo ripped a few pages out of my notebook and threw it on the floor. I curled up on the bed while he read them. Interminably. How long can a man take to grasp the information that his girlfriend has fucked somebody else? Finally he crumpled up the pages and let them drop. Very well written in parts, he said. Did I want to be an author now? I didn't answer. I waited for him to grab me. There was a lot of whining instead: I couldn't do that to him. He loves me. Was I trying to kill him? I couldn't leave him. He knows how badly he treats me, he said, how little he deserves me, how often he's cheated on me or at least tried to—in any case, he hasn't forgotten that. But it's different with me, he said, because while he's a bad person anyway, a devil incarnate, I on the other hand am an angel, his angel, innocent and pure. While he spoke, he started drinking. He drank down the rest of yesterday's wine straight from the bottle and pulled the cork out of a new one. His little girl mustn't let herself be soiled by some nonentity, he said, by some diving goon, no matter how completely he stuffs me with his big dick, dirty whore that I am!

And I thought, Hit me and get it over with. Don't wait too long. Fear tied me up. My face was twitching uncontrollably. My inner voice kept screaming, Pull yourself together! Be strong! Be cold! He can't do anything to you! He won't get your soul! But he's had my soul a long time; what I have left is my body, and it lay there defenseless while the old man poured fuel on his own fire. He told me what a piece of shit I was. Didn't I have an ounce of self-respect, he wanted to know, doing it with Zero of the Island, a complete loser who ran away from home so he could play the part of a super-Zampanò here, and why should he have any respect for me, would I actually beg for a little respect, and I screamed, Limpdick! *and finally he whacked me one, and then my phone rang.*

What would Hartmut say if I interrupted him? Sorry, Daddy, I have to hang up, Theo would like to rape me again before he's too drunk. He'd probably say what he's saying now: that he's glad we like the island so much, that he really doesn't have a lot of time to talk, and that he's calling for a specific reason, namely to inform me that Bittmann has set sail in the Dorset *again and will put in at Puerto Calero, Lanzarote, sometime in the next few days. On board, together with Bittmann* himself, *there will probably be the usual riffraff, a little theater, a little film, a little literature. In any case, Bittmann wants to give a small dinner aboard the* Dorset *next week, and it wouldn't do any harm to be in attendance, no harm at all, especially to a woman in my position.*

Hartmut hangs up. I go "Mm-hmm" and "Golly" for a while longer, until the old man's finished his bottle. Then I say, "Okay, Daddy, talk to you soon," and put the telephone away.

The old man's sitting at the table, propping up his head with his hands. That's the position he feels sorry in. Can I forgive him one more time, he wants to know. I'm completely in the right, he says, to cheat on an asshole like him with another man. Because I deserve someone who's nice to me. He reaches out a hand. But I'm in no mood for cuddling. The old man's already so crocked he can hardly open the next bottle. When I see him sitting like that, why can't I gloat? Why does it just seem sad? He looks so old. And so lonely. I know a couple of other lines from his novel by heart: "Men feel hatred when they should feel compassion. With women, it's the reverse."

After today's diving, Sven asked me if I could imagine moving to the island. He was serious. He'd given it some thought. His intentions were thoroughly honorable. He wouldn't listen to rational arguments. As if the world might come to an end next week! I could have laughed, almost. I'm already so screwed up that I start backing away even when people mean me well. Sven cajoled me into agreeing to go back to Mala. He could hardly keep his hands to himself. I asked him to give me time. Let things develop. I sounded like the Dalai Lama, he sounded like young Werther. And yet he's ten years older than I am. Nevertheless, the afternoon turned out lovely. Lunch in Teguise and discreet hand-holding in the cactus gardens. More like a contented married couple than new lovers. The lonely old man faded beyond the horizon.

But there he is now, sitting hunched over the table. It appears that Antje's supplying him with bottles; he's always got one in reserve. As long as he boozes and broods, he leaves me in peace. Maybe Theo and Antje could fall in love, and everybody would live happily ever after. The four of us, next-door neighbors.

9

I couldn't sleep. I kept replaying the scene with Theo in my head. Where did he get off, calling me a coward because I left Germany? The cowards were people like him, people who saw through the game and went on playing it anyway. I'd already heard enough of that kind of talk, complete with set phrases, from clients. They railed against the achievement-oriented society and sent their children to Chinese classes. They rejected the ideologies of economic growth and took to the streets for their next pay raise. They accused executives of greed and searched the Internet for the stock funds that promised the highest yield. They settled down in front of their brand-new flat-screen TVs and watched talk-show discussions about the evils of capitalism. Everybody cursed and swore, everybody played along. It made me want to puke. And in the end, only broken, burned-out types emerged. Guys like Theo. The fact that he was smart enough to recognize the absurdity made things even worse. If he called me a coward, it could mean only that in reality he envied me. The other question was, What had Jola told him? Nothing at all, probably. Theo had probably just been carried away by his imagination. The best thing for me to do was nothing. Ninety percent of all problems resolve themselves if you keep calm.

It was shortly after midnight. I got up and went to the kitchen, where I drank a glass of water and ate some olives and cheese cubes directly from the refrigerator. That wouldn't help me go to sleep. I went into our little office. Emile was sitting on the keyboard, waiting for me. When I reached out my hand, he climbed my fingers like stairs, scurried over my wrist and up my arm, and nestled in the crook. In November, the nights became a little chilly. I had enough body heat to give some of it away. Using one hand so as not to disturb Emile, I turned on the computer, opened *Up and Down*'s home page, and after a brief search found the archived episodes. April 16, 2010: "Deadly Lies." The soft clicking of paws on terra-cotta tiles came from the hall, followed by snuffling in the doorway. Todd entered the room, joyously wagging his tail because he'd found me. I shoved him back into the hall with my foot and closed the door. A snitch was the last thing I needed.

Two guys in a café setting. One, about twenty years old, sported a baseball cap and a three-day beard, which was supposed to make him seem casual and congenial. The other, not much older and properly clean-cut, was dressed in a suit, which immediately identified him as the nice guy's enemy. I had to grin. It was typical: the villain in a television show produced by moneygrubbing jerks was a moneygrubbing jerk. Capitalism denouncing its most faithful servants.

They talked about the nice guy's café. The guy in the suit,

having invested in the nice guy's café, wanted to see some profits now, while the nice guy asked for a little more time to get his business on its feet. The suit started to make some nasty threats, but then a blond bimbo came up to the table and hung her solarium-tanned silicon décolletage over the nice guy's shoulder. I fast-forwarded. The summary had promised an appearance by Bella Schweig. Emile's cold feet moved in the crook of my arm, but then he sat still again.

Bella stood in front of an apartment door, biting her lips. She wore a garishly printed, somewhat-too-youthful dress that nevertheless presented her figure quite appropriately. At last I could take my time and look at her calmly. I could sit there and observe every detail of her face and every movement of her body. She tousled her hair with both hands. She rubbed her eyes and pinched her cheeks. When the camera showed her in close-up again, her makeup was smeared and tears were running down her face. Then she pressed the doorbell. I sat there spellbound. A band of pain tightened my chest. Of course, she was the most beautiful woman I knew, but there was also something behind that beauty, something that went deeper. Something that touched me. The viewer felt a constant urge to call out to her: *You shouldn't do that.*

A good-looking man, older and graying at the temples, opened the door. I liked his plain gray knitted sweater and his dark jeans. Their conversation revealed that he was Bella's ex-boyfriend and didn't want to let her in. But she wept uncontrollably and eventually threw herself into his arms. She'd been in the neighborhood only by chance, she said, and down in the street she'd witnessed a terrible accident. A truck had run over a cyclist. Blood everywhere, she said. Then she fainted.

I thought she did all that very well. And I was glad for her because her partner in that scene looked so much more sensible than the two wankers in the café.

He carried her to a couch and laid her on it with her feet raised. Apparently he was a physician. He touched her forehead with one hand and her belly with the other. The pain in my chest increased. I turned off the computer and sat for a while in the dark. Without my prodding him, Emile left my arm and climbed up on the softly crackling monitor.

When my cell phone rang, I reached the window in one bound and peered through the curtains. The Casa Raya lay in utter darkness. No light shone through the shutters, nothing moved in the garden. I opened my text messages.

"Can't sleep either. Thinking of you. J."

I stood motionless for a long time. My phone screen went black. I heard Todd panting outside the door. There was nothing I could have done next.

10

For a few days afterward, I felt as though I had a fever. The typical combination of weakness, confusion, and nervous euphoria. Actually not an unpleasant feeling. Suddenly the whole world took a step back. It was like watching a movie with me in the lead role. As if life was an entertaining adventure without consequences. My mother used to call that my "don't give a shit" mood. She'd say, "You're not leaving the house, not in that don't give a shit mood. Get in bed and wait until you can think clearly again."

Of course, I didn't really have a fever. Nevertheless, in retrospect it's not easy for me to describe correctly what happened. The days leading up to the dinner on the *Dorset,* where I now believe all decisions were made, flow together in my memory and refuse to arrange themselves in a clear sequence, blending instead into a fuzzy continuum with no beginning and no end. At night I'd wait for Antje to fall asleep so that I could sit at the computer and watch a few episodes of *Up and Down.* I'd set Emile on one arm and pull my cock out of my boxer shorts. I liked to wait until Bella finally appeared, and in general I took my time. I could sit through as many as three episodes. When I was finished, the clock showed it was after one, so sleep was out of the question. I lay on the couch and pondered whether my new passion for *Up and Down* was having a bad effect on my work with Theo and Jola. After careful consideration, I came to the conclusion that what I undertook in my free time had nothing to do with my business relationships. No lawyer would withdraw from a case just because he was having fantasies about his sexy client.

In summary it may be said that only underwater did everything remain unchanged. Theo was back in the company; in spite of his sniffles, he insisted on participating in every dive. I explained the risks to him and forbade nose drops. He took an excruciatingly long time to equalize his pressure, but he managed to get down to the planned depth every time. He'd apparently decided he wasn't going to let Jola and me out of his sight again, not even twenty meters under the surface of the sea. The three of us drifted through the liquid silence, pointing out angel sharks and rays and groupers to one another. We fed sea urchins to octopuses and watched barracudas on the hunt.

Above the water, however, the air between us seemed to vibrate. It was as if we were all three waiting for something to happen. And we had an audience. It started one afternoon when we went shopping. Because I didn't like talking to salesclerks, I maneuvered Theo and Jola past the cheese, fish, and meat counters and made a detour around the produce that customers weren't allowed to weigh for themselves. Then I stood in front of a shelf with olives in glass jars and waited while Theo studied the wine selection two aisles farther on and Jola disappeared into the cosmetics department. She came back with a brightly colored package, put her arm through mine, and held the product up to my eyes.

"What do you think?"

I looked at the photograph on the box—a woman with wheat-blond hair, dressed to kill—and didn't understand.

"Bleach," Jola explained. "Lotte's a blonde. If you want to know how someone thinks, you need to have the same hairstyle."

I tried to free my arm from her grasp.

"You think it'll look good on me?" She snuggled closer.

"I like your hair," I said.

Jola laughed and kissed me on the mouth. When I felt her tongue between my teeth, I forgot myself. It was only a brief moment, during which my eyes closed and my hands grabbed. I thought I was going to fall down. Until I heard my colleague Laura's voice saying, "Are you all shooting a scene for *Up and Down*?"

I could have punched myself in the head. The supermarket was on the way to the beach. Everybody shopped there. Laura looked as though she'd been standing behind us for a good while.

"Or is mouth-to-mouth resuscitation part of the training course?" She seemed to find this question witty.

Jola, whom I'd pushed away from me in fright, leaned against the olives shelf, ostentatiously and provocatively straightening her T-shirt. I raised my hand in a superfluous greeting. "Laura. How are things going?"

"That's what I was about to ask," said Theo. He was standing at the other end of the aisle and staring at Jola. "Why not just kneel down and blow him?"

"Well, okay, see you," said Laura and disappeared.

In some panic, I considered all the people she could tell about this scene. And at the same time, I was searching for the words to apologize to Theo. He came up to me. "Don't worry about it," he said without taking his eyes off Jola. "If you didn't love yourself so damned much, you'd understand you aren't the problem at all."

I withdrew to the magazine aisle. Fifteen minutes later, when they loaded their purchases onto the cashier's conveyor belt, they were joking together. I wondered if I'd been dreaming.

They changed places in the van. Now Jola sat in the middle of the front seat, and Theo leaned against the side window. When she spoke, Jola kept putting her hand on my forearm or my knee. If I told some diving story, she listened gravely and asked questions. If I made a joke, she laughed out loud. In the evenings, she sent so many text messages that I had to switch off the ringer in my phone.

"Thanks for the wonderful day! Your Friend J."

"Missing you. Your Friend J."

"Lotte on a school of fishes: It was as if I were in the presence of a great power that observed me with a thousand eyes. Good, don't you think? So does Your Friend J."

"Shall we go down to the beach? Surf, moonlight, just the two of us? YFJ."

In the mornings it would start up again while I was still lying on the couch. "Looking forward to what comes next. Your Friend J."

I didn't answer. I tried to keep Jola at a distance. Nevertheless, people I knew kept seeing me with her again and again. I wondered whether she could be doing it on purpose. In the Wunder Bar café, she even sat jokingly on my lap right when Bernie came in. I badly wanted to push her off my knees, but that would have looked like an admission of guilt. And so she stayed there while Bernie and I had a brief conversation about the expedition we were planning. The *Aberdeen* was shipshape, Dave knew what was up. If the weather held, there shouldn't be any problem on November 23.

"As easy as a walk in the park," Bernie said in English. He nodded to Theo and went to the counter in search of a piece of chocolate cake. As if he hadn't seen Jola.

Another time she was standing in front of me and rummaging in my jeans pockets for the car key. Before I could grab her hands, Bernie's pal Dave came around the corner. He looked away and didn't say hello. On the promenade in Puerto del Carmen, Jola was hanging on my arm when a group of Spanish women walked toward us. I thought I recognized two of Antje's girlfriends, even though with all the bright dresses and big noses and thick black hair, I couldn't ever be sure about them.

The island was a village. People knew one another. Nothing happened unnoticed. The strange thing was that in actual fact nothing happened, but that wasn't unnoticed either. I began to feel I was always being watched.

While we waited for Theo, who was off somewhere buying cigarettes, I emphatically asked Jola to stop.

"Stop what?" she said, taking my hand.

"That, for example!" I pulled my hand away.

"Maybe I'm just a bit more honest than you." She snatched up my other hand and laid it on her hip. "Tell me that feels bad."

It was always the same: at that very moment, a silver Land Rover Defender drove past us. There was only one silver Defender on the island, and it was driven by Geoffrey, who owned the Lobster's Paradise. Could Jola know that? Could she have seen him before I did? Or was I getting paranoid? The sun turned Jola's eyes into green glass. I liked looking into it. Moreover, I couldn't claim that her hip felt bad. On the contrary. Theo came out of a shop shortly before I let her go.

"Don't let me disturb you, Little Shit," he said.

What was even stranger was how lighthearted Jola seemed at that time. She laughed a lot. Antje, with her simplistic understanding of human nature, would have attributed Jola's behavior to new love. Even though it made no sense, Jola's beaming smiles made me proud. Her face darkened only when she looked at Theo. Theo, who was now calling me nothing but "Little Shit," seemed to find real enjoyment in the situation. He followed our every movement with his eyes, smiled pathologically when Jola touched me, and waited eagerly for what would happen next. I didn't want to form any judgments, but I found Theo's lack of pride repellent. His presence got on my nerves. It was like being permanently exposed to toxic radiation. Besides, I didn't understand what he wanted me to do. Whatever Jola might have told him, he was free to find another diving instructor or leave the island altogether. As long as he continued to require my services, my only option was to do my job, as decently as possible. He could hardly have failed to notice my efforts to keep Jola off me. As best I could, I stayed out of the cross fire. Jola was the one who engaged in blatant behavior. Moreover, it wasn't my fault that we three were together almost around the clock and separated only to sleep. They never wanted to go home after a dive. I chauffeured them up and down the island, trying hard to make the most of its meager sightseeing attractions. We ate duck in Omar Sharif's former villa. We looked into the green water in the sea-level crater known as El Golfo. We trudged around every single piece bequeathed to the island by its artist. On one side I had Jola's overheated chatter, on the other Theo's icy silence. I told myself that only an idiot would have expected to pocket fourteen thousand euros just for a few diving lessons. I was being paid to handle two neurotics who'd anticipated their need of supervision while on vacation. Contrary to Theo's implication, I wasn't so stupid as to consider myself the problem. When Jola took my hand in public, I knew she was doing it for him.

*

During that time I often thought of a talk show that Antje and I had seen years before. A couple sitting on a white sofa had discussed their sadomasochistic inclinations. The two were in their late forties, conventionally dressed, the parents of two grown children. Without subordination, love wasn't possible, the man said. Whoever claimed otherwise demonstrated not modernity of attitude but dishonesty. He declared that equal status or even freedom in interpersonal relations represented an illusion. The difference between someone who lived the S&M lifestyle and a normal citizen didn't arise from the possession or not of an underground torture chamber, but from the fact that the S&M practitioner acknowledged that illusion. The man asserted that the viewers should take the trouble, just once, to think about their own relationships.

Antje and I had sat motionless on our couch. There was something embarrassing about our torpor. It was as if we weren't actually following the program but rather staring frantically straight ahead so we wouldn't have to look at each other.

The viewers could just examine their own sexual fantasies, the woman remarked. She doubted that anyone masturbated while dreaming about gentle foreplay and the missionary position.

About what, then? Asked the moderator, for whom things were not proceeding scandalously enough.

About young things who desired to be put properly through their paces, said the woman. About mothers who did it with their sons. About teachers and their female students, willing prostitutes, Africans with long cocks. Hadn't the moderator ever visited a standard porn site? The name of the game was submission, she said.

The most important thing in life, the man explained, was being able to count on each other. And for that, you needed rules. Then everyone knew what he or she had to do.

And what the other person had to do, the woman added. That gave you a sense of security.

Then what looks from the outside like hell on earth is happiness on the inside? the moderator asked.

If you want to put it that way, yes, the woman replied.

Hell outside, happiness inside: I remembered that image when Jola's hand brushed my belt buckle. I was looking for an explanation. I couldn't get rid of the feeling that Jola and Theo were following the rules of a game I didn't understand. Basically, I don't understand it to this day. It's strange that even in retrospect, no explanation occurs to me. Yet we're supposed to think that explanations are our well-deserved reward for enduring the passage of time. We're entitled to them. We go crazy when we don't get them.

JOLA'S DIARY, EIGHTH DAY

Saturday, November 19. Early morning.

I'm happy. That sounds funny—I wouldn't have thought I'd ever write such a sentence. I don't even recognize myself. A strange woman with bright eyes and a knowing smile. Happiness is always a secret. Happiness always belongs to yourself alone. People write all kinds of drivel about happiness, and it always sounds false somehow. The beautiful part is that neither of us has a clue about happiness. I don't, and Sven doesn't either. That's obvious from his embarrassment. From his tic of pushing me away if I touch him. From the way he's always trying to dodge me. He doesn't want to believe it. Can't believe he deserves it. And then all at once he pulls me against him. Fastens himself to my mouth. In the middle of the supermarket. While his diving instructor colleagues look on, and through their eyes the entire island. We know absolutely nothing about happiness. Sven's Antje and my old man weren't very good guides. We'll have to teach ourselves. Each in his own way. Sven struggles, I press forward. He probably has it harder than I do. More to lose. He's going to have to hurt a sweet person like Antje. And whom must I hurt? Only the old man. That's brutal, that only. *I offered Theo a ticket on the next flight back to Berlin and told him he could stay in the apartment at first. A trial separation. So we can calmly wait and see how everything develops. With me. With Sven. Then we'll figure out what's next. But he doesn't want to go. He says things like, I'm not abandoning the field to Little Shit. I have a right to be cuckolded by you. I'm staying until the bitter end. And: If nothing else, I can always write about it.*

That would be lovely, I throw in. And see how his eyes flash. But he controls himself. Gets a grip. Says, That would *be lovely. Exactly right.*

Of course, I knew he wouldn't go home. Did I ask him just to make him mad? Is it even possible that I want him to stay? Do I need him as an audience? Sometimes I wonder whether my happiness exists only for his sake, only to make him suffer. Whether any Sven would be possible without Theo. Then Sven wouldn't be the end of Theo's story, but only the next chapter in it. A new quality. At this thought, sheer horror seized me.

I cried out, You'll never lay a hand on me again. If I tell Sven about this, he'll break every bone in your body! He'll kill you! It sounded like, Wait until I get my big brother. Was probably meant that way too.

The old man says, You love me. You're not capable of leaving me. A little sun, a little sea, feeling good—you're not the type for that sort of thing, not at all. You need me, Jola. I just have to wait until you realize Little Shit can't make you happy.

I tremble at the thought that he could be right.

At night Sven comes to the window and calls softly. He waits until Antje's asleep before he sneaks out. Which means he still hasn't told her. I'm applying no pressure. The old man has taught me at least one thing: you can't force men to do anything.

We go down near the water. Sven lays a camping mat on some flat rocks. At night the Atlantic roars even louder than it does during the day. The racket drowns out our cries. The darkness is absolute. A kind of darkness unknown in Berlin. Even if the old man were standing a few meters away, he could neither hear nor see us.

Sex and oceans—many corny things have been said about that subject. I'm afraid they all apply. Mostly it happens pretty fast. Then we wrap ourselves up in a blanket and wait half an hour before beginning again. More slowly, with a different sort of force.

Sometimes, in the midst of it all, panic suddenly overcomes me. Something's not right. The whole thing's too improbable. I'm losing control. It's as though Sven could at any moment rip off his face, and someone else's would emerge from under it. My father's. Or the old man's. Then all at once hatred is mixed in with pleasure. I want to draw up my feet and kick Sven in the stomach so that he falls backward into the breakers. When Theo slaps me around, at least I know: this is reality. Unmistakably. Senseless, unfair, brutal reality. No error possible.

Such thoughts soon vanish again. Most likely I'm just not used to being treated well. It scares me.

We go back, not touching each other, and separate in silence. Each to one side of the sandlot, each to a different house. In the morning, when I wake up: a sudden flood of happiness. Like a child on Christmas morning, I know something lovely is in store. I get up and make coffee for me and the old man.

11

We strolled down to the port. The evening was mild. The island enjoys about three hundred mild evenings per year, but this particular evening had something special. The breeze was so soft it made me suspicious again. The contours of people and buildings looked vaguely blurry. On the other hand, all sounds seemed somehow to have sharp outlines. Theo and Jola also noticed something. While we walked along the steep asphalt road, he kept moving closer and closer to her. After we reached the harbor promenade, she allowed him to put his arm around her. She even leaned her head on his shoulder. When I saw that, I felt relief. I let myself drop back a few steps and looked in another direction, as if we weren't together.

The small group of people stood out even from a distance. Gathered at the spot on the quay where the berths for yachts over twenty meters began, they didn't appear to be waiting for a table at one of the restaurants. Rather they were gazing across the harbor basin toward the arrival jetty on the inner side of the mole.

"Can you believe these morons?" Jola said. "They're actually waiting for that Stadler bitch."

Yvette Stadler was a famous German singer and actress, whose name I'd heard for the first time that morning. Antje's Spanish was good enough to extract news from the chatter she listened to on Crónicas Radio, and at breakfast she'd relayed a bulletin: the sailing yacht *Dorset,* chartered by the German protein-bar heir Lars Bittmann, was expected to arrive early this evening at the marina in Puerto Calero. Among the passengers on board was the aforesaid Yvette Stadler. Antje laughed when I asked who that was.

"Just drive over to Puerto Calero and take a look."

"Are you nuts?" I asked. "Why would I do that?"

And there I was. It had been Jola's idea, like everything else we'd done over the past few days. She had on insect sunglasses and a fancy turban, accessories to what she called "going incognito." No matter what disguise she wore, I would have recognized the space between her teeth.

"I'm looking forward to seeing all those dopey faces," Jola said.

"Just imagine, Sven," Theo added. "They've been waiting two hours, and for a B-list celebrity."

It was the first time in two days that Theo hadn't called me "Little Shit." His eyes were gleaming with happy anticipation, which shone under Jola's sunglasses as well. The *Dorset* seemed to mean something to both of them.

"Bittmann always does this," Jola explained. "He gathers together some members of the cultural jet set, sails halfway around the world, and faxes his guest list to the news agencies. The most famous person on the list isn't really on board at the time."

Thinking about German celebrities made me nauseous with indifference. I didn't understand what was so funny about watching a few island tourists waiting in vain for Yvette Stadler. But Theo and Jola were feeling cheerful for the same reason—the first time that had happened in days—and I spotted Dave among the group of onlookers. He was taller by a head than anyone he was standing with. Theo's arm was still around Jola's shoulders. I couldn't have wished for a better statement to make in public; I even imagined we might be at a turning point. I thought maybe Jola had just been using me in recent days to win Theo back. Women pulled things like that, ultimately harmless tricks that led straight back into normality.

"Dave!"

He turned to us, and I could see him register what *he* saw, and in what order: me, then Jola and Theo, and then the fact that they were walking arm in arm while I strolled along next to them, relaxed, hands in my pockets. "Hey," I said to Dave, patting him on the shoulder. We always spoke in English. "What the fuck are you doing here?"

"Just paying my respects to a world-famous beauty."

"Yvette Stadler? Don't tell me you're a fan."

"Christ, no." Dave laughed. "I'm here for the boat!"

"The *Dorset*'s the biggest gaff cutter in the world," Jola explained. "Built in 1926, meticulously restored in 2006. Sails under the British flag."

The look Dave gave her showed his deep amazement. It was as though Jola had just changed from a talking doll to a genuine human person right before his eyes. "So you know about the *Dorset*?" he asked her.

"She's a legend! She held her own against modern boats at the Superyacht Cup in 2007, then took two first places at the Saint-Tropez Regatta the following year!"

Another few seconds and Dave would be proposing marriage to her. "You're saying she can do nine knots?"

That was surely a trick question. No boat wins a regatta with a speed of nine knots. Jola's mouth spread in a wide grin. "You've got to be kidding! Bittmann says she's done seventeen or more, and she was recorded as breaking twenty-two back in the twenties."

It was all over for Dave. Generously and resignedly, Theo removed his arm from Jola's shoulders. Once again, he was lending out his girlfriend.

"You know a thing or two about boats," Dave said.

"My dad's always been into sailing," Jola answered as they took a few steps to one side. "I was co-skipper by the time I was twelve. I knew exactly when to reef the sails or start the engine."

The longing expressed in Dave's body language was something to behold. He bent his six-foot-four frame slightly so he could come as close as possible to Jola's face. While she spoke, he stared at her mouth. Theo followed my eyes. His lips curled in the familiar sneering smile. "Anyone who wants to own a mare like that has to be tolerant when other stallions come sniffing around her," he said.

At first I thought I'd misheard him, and then I didn't know how to reply.

"Look at *me*," he said. He spread out his arms like a Mafia godfather. "I put up with you banging her. So you have to put up with the Englishman gawking at her a little."

"Scotsman," I said.

The upper part of a mast appeared over the top of the mole. The ship the mast belonged to must still have been a good distance away. Before long we could see the topsail, and a little later the gaff. Apparently the mast was some forty meters high. The *Dorset* was big. And fast. No wonder Dave had crossed half the island to welcome her. Even though he now had eyes only for Jola. The others in the waiting group stretched out arms and index fingers and pointed out the tip of the mast to their companions. Some of them carried binoculars.

Theo's hand gripped my arm. Another favorable statement. Everyone could see how well we got along. I briefly wondered when I'd started using the word *statement* in connection with appearing in public.

"One advantage," Theo said, "is that I've always got a guy standing next to me who's going through the same shit I go through." He patted my shoulder encouragingly.

"Thanks all the same," I said. "But let me make this clear one more time: I'm not 'banging' Jola."

"Perfectly clear." He was staring squinty-eyed at the harbor entrance. "You screw her with great tenderness."

The *Dorset* was rapidly approaching. The skipper had probably received instructions to head into port under full sail. It made an undeniably impressive sight.

"Not that either," I said. "Seriously. We're not having an affair or anything like that."

Theo spun around as though something had bitten him. All the former friendliness in his demeanor was gone. He said, "Do you know what honor is?"

I shook my head and got angry, both in the same moment. Of course I knew what honor was. I just didn't understand where the question was leading. Moreover, our public statement looked like it was about to degenerate horribly.

"I thought not." Theo laughed. "I've already explained it to you. Not so long ago. Bang her. Enjoy it. But don't lie to me."

"Can you lower your voice a little?"

"Can you act like a grown-up?"

"Look, Theo." I moved closer to him and spoke softly. "I don't know what Jola has told you—"

"Get out of here!" He said it loud. A few people near us looked our way. Dave and Jola also turned their heads. "You know it. I know it. The whole island knows it. You two don't even bother to hide it. So do me a favor and stop with this shit."

"But we haven't—"

"Theo!" Jola yelled.

Either she knew him well enough to read his mind, or the past few days had damaged my reflexes. While I was still wondering why Jola was yelling, Theo already had me by the shoulders. I was too flummoxed to defend myself. I saw people jumping out of the way in slow motion. Then I was tipping backward off the quay wall. One crystal-clear thought flashed into my consciousness: *Don't fall on the landing stage.* I pushed off before I lost the ground under my feet, did a half turn in midair, and dove into the water. I knew at once I wasn't hurt. I swam a few strokes close to the bottom. It was surprisingly warm in the harbor basin.

Little fish nibbled at the keels of the anchored boats. I kept telling myself, *Surface. Breathe. Laugh.* My breath was running out. I surfaced, inhaled, saw twenty anxious faces looking down at me from the quay wall, and laughed.

Only the *Dorset*'s final maneuvers put an end to the laughter and talk about my plunge into the harbor. While the yacht's sails sank down together, I stood in my own private puddle. We could hear the skipper's orders. The tourists became deadly serious. Suddenly every one of them was looking through binoculars. The diesel engine started up, and the *Dorset* sailed majestically into the harbor at Puerto Calero.

I thought of this line: *My heart burns for love.* That was exactly how I felt. The *Dorset* showed what true beauty signified: not symmetry, but the combination of power and elegance. Pure power came across as crude; mere elegance was vanity. Only the merger of the two had the force to touch you at the deepest part of yourself, which was exactly where I found myself touched. Jola was standing very straight on the edge of the quay, held by Dave's and Theo's arms in turn. The yacht looked as though it was putting into port for her sake. Proud and strong and yet so susceptible to storms. I stood in the background and played the good-natured diving instructor whose clients' idea of a joke was to toss him into the drink. I felt love and pain and sadness and wasn't sure whether they weren't all the same.

◈

Two hours later, behind the wheel of my van, I laughed all the louder, despite the terrible mood that had come over me. My clothes, in the meantime, had dried. All possible jokes—about being launched or getting baptized or cooling off—had already been cracked on the quay. But Jola was still in top form. Her crumpled turban lay among the equipment, her sunglasses hung from the rearview mirror. Her bare feet, which she braced against the windshield, left behind an impression that could still be seen weeks later when the glass fogged up from inside. She and Theo were recapitulating the *Dorset*'s arrival. Their focus wasn't the beauty of the vessel, it was the fact that Yvette, as predicted, had not been among the guests. Jola mimicked Bittmann, the way he'd spread his arms out as he stood on the gangway and said, first in German, "My apologies, folks, Yvette has canceled," and then in English, just in case the entire crowd wasn't made up of German sightseers: "Sorry, guys, Yvette couldn't come." Next Jola parodied the yacht's five passengers. In Jola's version, they had gone down the gangway at the exact moment when the disappointed crowd dispersed, and then they'd had to stand around like stranded orphans, hoping that someone would recognize them. I'd simply seen five people leaving a ship. They'd looked perfectly normal to me, but in Jola's and Theo's eyes each of them was apparently a laughingstock. Jola bent over with laughter and practically put her face in my lap. On other such occasions, I'd shoved her away from me. I'd begged her not to crowd me. In my best killjoy voice, I'd pointed out that I had an automobile to steer. But now I tried to get ahold of her hair. I wanted her to keep lying on my lap. And it irritated me that she was already leaning toward Theo's side again. I would have liked to say something. But I knew neither the literary critic nor the woman who directed plays nor the photographer. All that remained to me was my own joyless laughter, designed to show that I belonged.

Back in Lahora, I parked the car and stood for a moment at the gate to watch Jola and Theo cross the sandlot and disappear into the Casa Raya. They had turned down my suggestion that we go to Giselle's for some fish soup. Jola wanted to cook. I went into the house, found Antje sitting on the terrace with a book, hauled her into the bedroom, and threw her on the bed. Unlike what happened in movies, I had no trouble whatsoever calling her by the right name.

JOLA'S DIARY, EIGHTH DAY

Still Saturday, November 19. Evening.

Little girls wait for the white knight who's going to lift them up onto his horse and ride away with them. Grown women, on the other hand, negotiate contracts. Our latest deal: the old man will leave me alone if I jerk him off on demand while telling him about Sven. About Sven's giant cock, which fills my mouth and throat so completely I nearly choke. About Sven's big balls, which lie in my hands. About how Sven grabs me and fucks me so hard I think I'll fall apart.

But humiliation is a complicated business. The old man sits there on the sofa, his semi-stiff member between my fingers. He clutches the cushion with one hand and my hair with the other while he listens to dirty stories about me and our diving instructor. The question of who's humiliating whom in this scene must be neither posed nor answered. He's a forty-two-year-old writer with just one published novel to his name. His pants are tangled around his ankles, his face red with effort. A tormented, self-tormenting creature.

I told him so. Whereupon our deal was canceled again. He pulled up his pants and ran into the bathroom. The victim had abandoned her own integrity for a sweet moment of triumph. I love to gaze into Theo's eyes and see something shatter in there. I love to see the infinitely wronged look that comes over them because the traitor who thrust in the dagger was, of all people, me. Such a wonderful feeling. For a few seconds I know—no, I clearly see*—how much he loves me. When can you actually* see *love? It's a rare and precious experience. I'll think about that if he comes back and*

12

After Antje fell asleep, I got out of bed. I'd overexerted myself, I'd had no dinner, and we'd done it twice in succession. Antje had put herself at my disposal for the second go-round as though for an athletic endeavor in which she functioned as both playing field and spectator. My knees were trembling. For several minutes I stood before the opened refrigerator, contemplating Antje's left-over, cellophane-wrapped tapas. Todd's reproachful look identified me as the kind of villain who won't even give the needy what he himself doesn't want.

After a couple of pointless turns around the living room, it became obvious that the magnetic attraction the computer was exercising on me could no longer be attributed to anything else. As before, I shut Todd out of the office, and while the machine booted up I looked around for Emile, who didn't want to show himself that evening. By now I'd seen enough episodes of *Up and Down* to be able to follow the plot, to find characters appealing or unappealing, and to predict with some certainty when Bella would turn up next. I'd really been enjoying Bella's appearances since she'd gone back to her old boyfriend the doctor. There was a lot of kissing, sighing, and groping, even though it was thoroughly obvious that the doctor wasn't about to end the affair he was having with a nurse. For her part, Bella was only using him so she could get her hands on the drugs that would help her avenge herself on a director who hadn't cast her in a role she'd very much wanted. Bella had just caught the doctor in flagrante delicto with the nurse and was making quite a scene when I heard music. Loud music. I stood up and drew the curtain aside. Out in the hall, Todd started to bark.

I was gazing right into the Casa Raya. When the living room was lit up at night, it looked like a stage. I saw—I wasn't exactly sure what I saw. I saw two people who seemed to be dancing exuberantly. They embraced, staggered backward, circled each other, crashed together. Every now and then one of the figures would disappear, as if he or she had fallen or briefly run out of the room. Immediately afterward they'd be stumbling around again, locked in another embrace, falling on the floor together, getting back on their feet.

The desire to be with them made me press my face to the windowpane. I saw a kind of energy over there that never manifested itself in my life. Which was, therefore—it came to me in a flash—not rightly a life. Both my hands were flat against the glass, and I was staring with wide-open eyes. I would have sacrificed everything to be a part of that scene. Beyond control. Beyond strategy. Beyond escape. Even when I realized that what I was watching was no dance. At first I was repelled, but then the need to run over there became even more urgent. But I stayed where I was. I clenched my fists on the glass. I wasn't interested in stopping whatever was going on in the Casa Raya; I wanted to join in, that was all. To plunge in. To scream over the music and be someone else, someone other than Sven, the nice diving instructor. I didn't know which was more frightening, what I saw or my reaction to it. Across the way, one of the figures raised an object high overhead. A relatively large object. A living-room chair. The nice diving instructor would have long since intervened. Whatever was going on over there, he would have stopped it.

Instead it was Todd who showed some initiative. His little body darted down the gravel walk in front of the Residencia. Yelping hysterically, he raced across the sandlot, ran up the steps to the Casa Raya, and flung himself against the door. The music stopped, the lights went out. The logic machine in my head, working lethargically, concluded that someone must have let the dog out of the house. I spun around. Antje was standing in the office doorway. I shot a quick glance at the computer monitor. The screensaver was hiding Bella's face.

Antje, who'd followed my eyes, said, "Oh, Sven, not to worry. I know what you do in here anyhow. You never clear your browsing history."

I didn't know what a browsing history was. I stared at her. Her blond hair was disheveled, an effect I'd helped produce.

"What's going on?" she asked.

I wasn't able to come up with an answer to that one either. I couldn't take my eyes off her dressing gown, which was printed with strawberries. *Why strawberries?* I wondered.

"Your friends are slowly starting to get on my nerves, do you know that?"

I finally managed to unclench my teeth. "They're not my friends," I said. "They're our clients."

"Right you are, Sven, sure," Antje said and went back to bed.

Disgust suddenly overcame me. Over in the Casa, all was still. I lay down on the sofa to wait for morning.

JOLA'S DIARY, NINTH DAY

Sunday, November 20. Very early morning.

Bella Schweig's a slut. But always a victim. Never a perpetrator. Who wants to be a perpetrator? Nobody. Except maybe at the moment of perpetrating the deed. But the deed is brief. And forever after, all sympathy belongs to the victim. The victim impulse is part of human nature. The smallest child will whack another kid and cry, "He started it!" Four-year-old girls master the innocent-as-a-lamb eyeblink by practicing it in the mirror. People form couples and share houses and join clubs and parties and societies so that there will always be someone else to blame everything on. The art of playing the victim is easy when you're performing with a suitable costar. Someone stupid enough to accept the buck when it's passed. Someone who'll lash out without thinking and then beg for forgiveness. Such a willing perpetrator yields huge innocence dividends! Innocence with interest, an innocence retirement plan. If you have your own perpetrator, you never have to worry about the victim role again.

Who'd want to break off such a profitable relationship? Nobody in her right mind. The perpetrator smiles a little, zing, and the judicious victim's back in a win-win situation. So do I go for self-esteem, self-protection, a modicum of self-defense? Not a chance. I'll stay where I am, comfortably ensconced in my own woe, domiciled in doom. Let's not forget, there was my difficult childhood, a father who was never there unless a party was being thrown, and a mother locked in combat with the passage of time. Such conditions apparently suffice for a lifetime of self-sacrifice on the offspring's part. What difference does a bloody nose make, as long as you know it's for a good cause? Even when the bleeding won't stop.

Tomorrow the old man will tell Sven he broke the chair by sitting on it too hard. He'll laugh and demonstrate how he threw himself down on the thing and wham, it fell apart under him. Ha-ha, the good island food, ha-ha, the good island wine! He'll generously offer to pay for the chair—with my money, by the way—and we won't be stingy. Maybe he'll use too many words to describe a basically insignificant event, but he's a writer, after all, and as such used to embellishing his lies.

Sven will believe him. Sven's had no experience with lies. The way he gawked when we were down at the port! The loneliness without end that spoke out of his eyes. A ship will come in, but it won't be his. Meanwhile he's the one asking for more time. Let's not rush things. Let's make no waves. He still hasn't told Antje. But I know what to think about that. It's not for lack of love. Men are simply cowards. That's why they make such good perpetrators. No, stop: Sven's no perpetrator. Sven's a victim himself. All you have to do is listen to him to know that. He didn't leave Germany as a winner, he left as a loser. And now he likes to drone on about the war zone.

"Are you going back to Theo?" That's what his eyes said down at the port. My silent reply: "Have I left him, then?"

Sven didn't stand under the window and call me last night. All the same, after the old man went to sleep, I walked down to the edge of the rocks overlooking the sea. Down to our spot. But the pounding of the waves scares me. It's as if the bit of rock I'm sitting on could be ripped away at any time.

I don't dare to think about how I behaved in the van earlier. How I sat between lover and life partner and sucked up to both of them. I made jokes about Bittmann's guests to please the old man. Because he'd acted friendly for a few minutes. Because he'd tried to fight for me by throwing Sven in the water. The perpetrator acts, zing, and the victim's back. If I could look at it from the outside, I'd have to puke. I'd turn the music loud out of sheer nausea so no one could hear my screams and punish me for being not only a disgusting whore but also a disgusting ass-kisser.

The truth requires only a few words: I'm at the end of my rope. Taking a lovely trip together, maybe even turning myself into Lotte, trying for happiness with someone new—rubbish, all of it. I'll always go back to the old man, again and again, until he destroys me. I need help. Sven has to make a decision. This isn't your standard case, where the man can take his sweet time deciding which woman he prefers and in the meantime amuse himself with both. What we have here is an exception. If Sven really wants me, he has to do something.

13

"Hold on, Sven, I have a confession to make," said Theo, standing inside the door on the driver's side of the van. I was behind the wheel, having just dropped him off, and about to drive over to the Residencia. I'd put the van in gear, reached out to close the door, and there he was. It was about seven thirty in the evening and had been dark for a good hour already. Theo leaned across me and switched off the engine.

Jola hadn't come diving with us that morning. Her monthly visitor, Theo had explained. After our second dive, he'd talked me into doing a third and then a fourth, speaking so urgently I wondered whether he wanted to go home at all. It was already dusk when we climbed out of the water for the last time. Now my main thought was dinner. Antje had called to tell me she was cooking paella.

"I'm really sorry. It was stupid, but I don't want you to think we're wrecking your whole guesthouse. It was an accident, truly, I have no idea how it could have happened. Maybe too much good island food. In any case, I'll obviously pay for the damage, no matter what it costs."

"What did you break?" I asked.

"Oh, I haven't told you yet?" He laughed.

My expression didn't change. I'd been thinking about the situation all day long, but I hadn't made any sort of progress. I'd persuaded myself I wasn't even sure whether there *was* a "situation." The answer to the question of what was going on, if indeed something was going on, kept slipping through my fingers. I felt ashamed and didn't want to know what I was ashamed of. In a way I'd even been glad to see that Jola wasn't going to come diving with us. My head felt like an overheated engine. Maybe I was just exhausted. What I needed was a tranquil dinner with Antje, preferably with candlelight and soft music. A miniature paradise.

"Absolutely vast," Theo said. His head was tilted back, and he was looking up. "You can't see this in Germany. There's the Milky Way, directly above our heads. The starry sky you've got here is a work of art."

He looked at me admiringly, as though the firmament were a result of my efforts. "All right, then," I said. "Good night, Theo."

"I hope it wasn't an heirloom," he said. "The chair, I mean."

Obviously Theo wanted to be asked what had happened. I bit my lip. And then I put the question anyway: "What happened?"

"Don't have a clue, man." Theo was looking up again. "Maybe I dropped down on it too hard. The thing just came apart. Mind-boggling, all these stars."

"Were you . . . dancing?"

Theo removed his gaze from the universe and contemplated me pensively for a while. "Let's say the evening got a little wild."

"Is it possible that the chair . . . went flying?"

"I threw it across the room in anger. It hurt pretty bad at first. Maybe you noticed the bruise on my thigh."

I could have said with some certainty that there was no bruise on Theo's thigh.

"But not to worry, nothing else got broken." Theo laughed. "Then we heard the dog barking and turned off the music. I hope our rumpus didn't wake up you and Antje."

"No," I said.

"So don't look like that." Theo nudged my shoulder. I immediately raised a hand to fend him off. I didn't want him touching me.

"I'm not allowed to have fun with her anymore? Look, she's not your property, got it?"

"She's my client, Theo. That's all."

"That's the correct attitude." He nodded gravely. "She's paying you to see to her every need while she's on vacation."

"She's paying me for diving lessons."

"Okay." He folded his arms. "Let's clarify things, once and for all. We're alone, nobody's listening. We'll talk man-to-man. Understood?"

I nodded. I felt an enormous need for a thorough clarification.

"I've allowed you to give her a little pleasure," said Theo. "But my relationship with Jola is none of your business."

Exactly my take on the matter. I relaxed a bit.

"So I'm asking this for the last time: stop denying the obvious. It's bad form."

"But I've . . . ," I began, but then I fell silent at once. It wasn't worth the trouble. He wasn't about to believe any assertion of mine.

"Good boy. Just keep your trap shut." Theo lit a cigarette. "The whole thing may seem weird to you. Believe me, I don't find it so great either. But Jola refuses to go back home, and I refuse to leave her here alone. So we're going to stay through the remaining six days, and after that you'll never see us again. Maybe you and she will exchange a couple of e-mails, but before long the correspondence will die out and the thing will be forgotten. You'll get on with your life and I with mine."

I felt sudden relief. Even though Theo was proceeding from false premises, he was speaking to me from his soul. It was almost as if I were listening to my own thoughts. Rational and clear. Free from the strenuous and, all things considered, totally superfluous confusion of the past few days.

"We can get along extremely well in the time we have left," he continued. "Provided we behave like adults."

He drew so deeply and appreciatively on his cigarette that I had a sudden urge to smoke one myself. Apparently reading my mind, he held out the pack to me and gave me a light. I inhaled and coughed, enjoying the slight dizziness.

"Games aren't in your line anyway, not if I'm any judge." He stretched out his hand and said in English, "Fair play?"

I was still trying to figure out what I was promising while we shook hands. The gist appeared to be that I was to stop contradicting him on the subject of my alleged affair with Jola. Which didn't mean I was admitting anything at all. In legal matters, a fundamental principle states that silence does not constitute a declaration of intent. Remaining silent means neither yes nor no. It means nothing at all. It's a legal nullity. He who remains silent doesn't lie. I pressed Theo's hand. He slapped me heartily on the shoulder.

"I knew it," he said. "You're all right, Sven."

He seemed to think our conversation had been of the utmost importance. We threw our cigarette butts away. "The great thing is, now we can talk," Theo said. He looked up at the stars again. "Like me, do you sometimes get the impression that Jola's not completely right in the head?"

The question took me by surprise. "I don't know," I stammered. "Actually, no. Maybe I haven't known her long enough."

He laughed as though I'd made a joke.

I said, "It's a principle of mine never to judge other people."

"No judgments, huh?" Theo nodded thoughtfully. "What a luxury that must be. Then I suppose you can't say whether you think she's pretty?"

I had to consider that one. Without a doubt, Jola was beautiful. To say so didn't seem like a judgment but rather the statement of a fact that any normal person would observe and acknowledge. Of course, the very observation of a fact might contain judgmental elements; that couldn't be ruled out, but I had no desire to discuss it. I had even less desire to talk shop with Theo about his girlfriend's qualities as if we'd chartered a yacht together.

"I want to go home and get something to eat," I said.

"Never mind," said Theo. "This is new to you. You're not used to it. And I appreciate your discretion. Wait a minute, I've got something to give you before you go."

He reached into his hip pocket and pulled out some sheets of paper, folded at least four times into a little packet. He must have carried those pages around all day long.

"You wanted to read something of mine," he said. "Hope you enjoy it."

The packet he placed in my hand immediately started to unfold. The pages were typed. I pressed them back together.

"Say hello to Antje for me. Tell her we're nearly out of wine. Fabulous sky, fabulous stars you have here."

He'd reached the steps of the Casa Raya when he turned around again. "I apologize for throwing you in the water yesterday. And don't forget to tell me how much I owe you for the chair."

The door closed with a crash behind him. Only when the lights went on inside the Casa did I realize that it had been totally dark inside. As if Jola weren't home. Except that when you were at the ends of the earth, you needed a car to go anywhere, unless you went to the water, so where was she? In her bed asleep, perhaps. Or maybe sitting in darkness at the dining-room table and staring into space. I tried to think about paella, but I didn't feel hungry anymore.

•

That night I dreamed about Jola. She was dancing in front of a desk where two men were sitting. One of them was Theo, and I didn't recognize the other. There was no music to be heard, so Jola's bare feet struck the floor all the more loudly as she danced. She was trying out for a new role. She wore diving goggles and the red bikini. While the men watched her, they were jerking off under the table. Jola ended her dance before the men had reached their goal. A wrenching pain in my lumbar region made me aware that the second man at the table must be none other than myself.

"Lovely, Frau von der Pahlen," Theo said to Jola as she stood before us, breathing hard. "And now please spell *Montesquieu.*"

Jola stuttered, Theo laughed. I wanted to go into action. I wanted to jump up and shout that I was no judge, that I would deliver no verdict, that I had nothing to do with the whole affair. But my mouth was so dry I couldn't utter a sound, nor could I move my legs.

"Not even a guess?" said Theo.

Jola started crying. Now she was dressed like Bella Schweig, and she was telling her ex-boyfriend about the accident out on the street.

"Better try somewhere else." Theo scribbled something on a little card and handed it to Jola. "Death is a business that's always hiring."

My hands flew forward and seized Theo by the throat. Before I could tighten my grip, Jola came closer. She wasn't actually in the room, she was on a large video screen. She smiled and spoke to the camera. "Don't turn us off. We'll turn you off," she said.

I screamed and sat bolt upright in the bed. Antje rolled over and looked at me in the semidarkness.

"Serves you right," she said, turned on her other side, and went back to sleep.

The next morning I woke up in the living room. I needed a little while to get my bearings, but I slowly realized that I was on the couch. Antje was asleep in the bedroom, and the house was absolutely quiet. Apparently that "Serves you right" had been part of my dream. The pages of Theo's story lay scattered on the floor next to me. Although I couldn't remember reading them before falling asleep, I knew for sure they were somehow connected to my dream.

I swung my legs over the edge of the couch and sat up. For the first time in four nights, I'd had several hours of uninterrupted sleep. I felt sick. It occurred to me that I didn't know why and for what I was alive. Then I got to my feet and went into the kitchen to make coffee.

14

At first I believed it was a coincidence and then that it was my imagination, but on my tenth day with Theo and Jola, it became a fact: people were crossing the street to avoid me. It happened three times in a row on the main tourist drag in Puerto del Carmen, where we'd gone for ice cream between dives. First there was a group of local Spanish women, possibly part of Antje's circle of friends. Then a married couple who might have been the owners of one of the holiday houses that Antje managed. And then two older men I couldn't connect either to Antje or to myself. They all came toward us, looked at me, and crossed over to the other side of the street. Jola and Theo didn't seem to notice anything.

My paranoia was probably a result of Bernie's telephone call. My telephone had rung that morning at breakfast. It was Monday; the great diving expedition on the *Aberdeen* was to take place in two days. A few questions still needed to be cleared up, but it turned out that Bernie was calling for another reason. He asked me how things were going in a tone usually reserved for addressing pregnant women and cancer patients. "How are things *going*?" Because I didn't understand what he was getting at, I said nothing. Antje looked at me attentively, holding a slice of bread and honey in front of her mouth. I stood up and went out onto the terrace.

And then Bernie really started in on me. What did I think I was doing. What was going to happen now. Didn't I care about my job. Didn't I have any shame. What did Antje have to say about all this.

It took me a while to understand that his subject was me and Jola. Actually, I liked Bernie. He was a person with a strong foundation, a basic agreement with himself that prohibited him from being friendly without good cause. This made dealing with him uncomplicated. In my opinion, most problems arose not because people wanted to harm one another but because they didn't know what to talk about. They'd cast about for a topic, and outside of the weather and malicious gossip, there was simply nothing that could keep a conversation between two people going. With Bernie, it was different. He was taciturn and gruff and therefore incorruptible.

But on this particular morning, he talked and talked and refused to give it a rest. He got on my nerves. Speaking in English, naturally, he called me a "prick" and a "dumbarse" and came at me with the divers' "Do It Right" doctrine. And all of it at machine-gun speed, even though he knew I didn't understand English very well on the telephone.

I said, "Fuck off, Bernie," and hung up. However, I couldn't get his call out of my mind. I didn't know what Bernie or Dave or anybody else had heard. He hadn't sounded worried, he'd sounded irate. I needed Bernie, Dave, and the *Aberdeen* on Wednesday. Planning for the expedition had been going on for months, and I'd invested a pile of money in new equipment. What I most felt like doing was going out and taking the first person I saw by the collar and yelling in his face and asking him who he thought he was, sticking his nose in other people's affairs like that, and demanding that he and his island friends stop spreading lies about me. Wars started that way, through the appetite for rumor. Through readiness to believe, always, the worst about other people. I was more than pleased when we got back into our diving suits. The neoprene formed a thick skin that kept the world out. I looked forward happily to another half hour when I wouldn't have to share the air I breathed with humankind.

A measure of my perplexity was that we dove again off Playa Chica, the beach at Puerto del Carmen. By that time, Jola and Theo knew all the island's dive spots. Barracudas, groupers, and angel sharks were no longer a sensation. One of my personal goals was to surprise my clients again and again. But few of them stayed longer than ten days, and hardly anybody undertook more than two dives per day. There was a limit even to the number of sightseeing points in the Atlantic Ocean. I had slowly run out of ideas. Under the ledge east of Playa Chica, there was a cave spacious enough to be safe. It was the last thing I had to show them. After that, we'd have to fill the remaining days with boat diving.

I swam close to the seabed, turning around every few seconds to check on my two companions, making sure they didn't get tangled up in an anchor cable or caught in somebody's lost fishing line. Although Bernie and I launched cleanup campaigns from time to time, Playa Chica remained the dirtiest spot on the island. To our left, Laura and a group of beginners were churning up sludge. Above us, children were jumping off the quay, feet first, prepared to kick an ascending diver in the head. Snorkeling tourists hauled their bellies through the water and looked down on us, never dreaming how badly their backs would be sunburned that evening. The drumming of motorboat engines was constantly in our ears. We couldn't leave the cove behind fast enough. We headed for the rim of the ledge, from where we would venture into deeper waters.

We didn't get that far. We were barely twelve meters down when I spotted it where it lay, buried in sand. It was over a meter long, surely a male. Electric rays always reminded me of the snowmen my mother baked out of cookie dough for Christmas. Two circular discs, one large and one small, joined together in a single flat object. Also known as torpedo fish, electric rays could generate life-threatening electric shocks.

Laura liked to tell the story about the time she was letting the current carry her backward so that she could keep an eye on her dive group. As she drifted, she disturbed a torpedo with her fins. The creature shot up from the ocean floor, did a full somersault in front of Laura's nose, and struck her on the elbow. Two hundred volts, underwater. Not necessarily enough to kill you as long as you remained conscious. Laura compared the feeling to being punched hard in the solar plexus. Supposedly, she could still remember what went through her head at the time. She thought she absolutely mustn't pass out, because the beginning divers wouldn't be capable of saving her. She thought if the panicked fish zapped one of her clients, she could toss her diving instructor's license into the trash can. And she thought it was a good sign that she was still able to have such thoughts. She made it to the surface with her group. I took over Laura's clients for two weeks, until she felt able to get back in the water.

I raised my hand and signaled to Jola and Theo that they should kneel on the bottom. Then I pointed to the torpedo fish and drew the fingers of my other hand in a slashing movement across my throat. Both Jola and Theo nodded. They'd understood what my gesture meant: *deadly.*

I had them come a little closer. One meter was the approved distance. Electric rays were basically nonaggressive. If they felt they were being attacked, they'd defend themselves within a predictable radius. There was a trick I'd tried a few times since Laura's experience, and it had always worked. I took off one fin, held it with both hands, and beat the water a few strokes, right above the torpedo. The compression wave blew the sand off the fish's back. Now you could see its snowman shape and its marbling. An extremely pale specimen. I wagged my fin a few more times, touching the ray's tail, trying to provoke a reaction. I wanted it to perform a somersault. Jola and Theo were seeing an electric ray for the first time. It could provide their overdue sensation, something they could record in their logbooks. When we were back on dry land, I'd explain to them about the strength of the electric current the torpedo could produce and tell them Laura's story; maybe I'd even claim it for myself.

But nothing happened. The ray's body oscillated slackly with the movement of the water. The thing looked like a big cleaning rag. I made a few more efforts, waving my fin as though I were fanning a campfire. Either the fish was in a really deep sleep, or he simply wasn't going to let himself be disturbed. Finally I gave up and set about putting the fin back on my foot.

What came next is best described in the simplest words: Jola shoved Theo. She picked the right moment. Theo had leaned forward to take a few snapshots of the apathetic torpedo with the underwater camera. He was holding both arms out in front of his body and had shifted his center of gravity well forward. There was scarcely half a meter's distance between the camera and the skin on the ray's back. In this position, Theo was knocked completely off balance by Jola's push. Even though the water resistance slowed his movement, he tipped forward too fast to react properly. Instead of twisting himself to one side, he let go of the camera and stretched out his arms to break his fall on the seafloor. But that was where the torpedo was lying. Theo made some desperate rowing motions in an effort to maintain his distance and avoid touching the fish. I was too far away to reach him with my hands, and so I kicked out at his thigh, hoping to change the direction of his fall. It could have worked. But at that very moment, everything became too much for the torpedo. A tremor went through its still-flaccid body, which stiffened itself into concentrated strength.

No one knows how things look from an electric ray's viewpoint. Instead of giving Theo a heavy jolt of electric current, the fish decided to flee. With a few powerful lashes of its tail, it propelled itself away from us. Ten meters on, it already felt safe enough from further disturbance to sink back down to the bottom and shovel sand onto its back with the perimeter of its disc-shaped body. On the spot where the torpedo had just been lying, Theo was crouched on all fours. His heavy breathing caused a column of air bubbles to climb up above him. I didn't even try to hold him back when he arbitrarily broke off the dive and began his controlled ascent.

I had no idea what I was going to do or say once we reached dry land. Instead of structured thoughts, images shot through my head. Of me sitting on a bench up on the quay with Jola and pulling a sea urchin's spine out of her foot. Of her struggling with Theo in darkness, wind, and rain atop a steep cliff in Famara. All that seemed so astonishingly far back in time that I wondered how long it had actually been since they arrived. However, when I tried to comprehend the immediate here and now, in which the three of us were swimming landward on our backs, I was compelled to the realization that this image too seemed like a memory. As if the present were nothing more than an especially distinct flashback to the past. Even the best plan—a severe tongue-lashing or the irrevocable decision to tell Jola and Theo to go to hell, once and for all—would have done nothing to help me along. Because no one could have prepared himself for what came after we'd clambered up the slippery steps to the quay. No one could have foreseen it. Bent under our heavy tanks and wearing our dripping rubber suits, we'd slipped through the holiday makers on the promenade and finally reached the van. Jola's entire body was shivering. Not with shame, not with excitement, not even with cold; she was trembling with anger. She set down her scuba tank, threw her fins on the ground, ripped off her diving mask, and immediately went on the attack.

"Are you crazy, doing *this*"—she drew her hand across her throat—"when the fish was alive?"

"That," I said, also making the slashing gesture, "was a deadly fish!"

She stared at me aghast. "So when you stirred up the sand around it, were you doing that so we could see it better, or what?"

"I wanted to wake it up so it would do a somersault for you."

"That close to us?"

"It wasn't my first electric ray, Jola."

"All the same, it was as pallid and limp as a corpse. I thought it was dead!" She repeated my gesture yet again. "Theo could have been killed!"

"Because you shoved him!" I shouted.

"No!" She stood right in front of me, her arms folded, her breasts molded as though in plastic under the tight neoprene. It briefly occurred to me that maybe she wasn't angry at all, that she simply enjoyed putting on such a performance.

"Because you gave a signal that wasn't agreed on in advance," she said. "Haven't you ever heard that you're supposed to use only prearranged hand signals? For safety reasons? That's one of the 'Do It Right' principles you value so much, isn't it?"

Her tone of voice was slowly getting on my nerves. I said, "It's a gesture everybody understands."

"No it isn't, as we see."

"But *you* shoved Theo!"

"Don't try to turn the tables on me. You're the one who bears the responsibility. You communicated badly, so you alone are to blame. If something had happened to Theo, you'd have had to answer for it."

She turned around and went over to Theo, who was leaning

against the van, smoking a cigarette. He looked like a detached observer, waiting with quiet curiosity to see how the scene would develop. The bit of sidewalk we were standing on felt like a stage to me too. Not a good feeling.

"Sorry, Theo," Jola said. She stroked his cheek as though he were a little boy who'd cut his knee. "It was supposed to be just a stupid joke. Theo and the dead fish. Ha-ha."

"Forget about it," Theo said, drawing on his cigarette and not taking his eyes off Jola.

"It was Sven's mistake. Complain to him."

She threw a last, annihilating glance at me over her shoulder and then stalked around the van and out of my sight. There was no other possible way to exit the stage.

That was probably the exact moment when I should have understood the game Jola was playing. She'd dropped enough hints. Along with Lotte Hass's biography, Jola had been reading countless nonfiction books about diving and the underwater world. And she, of all people, was supposed not to have known what an electric ray looked like and what my warning sign had meant? And when I tried to goad the torpedo into reacting, she'd thought—what? That I was playing around with a dead fish? I should have made it my business to recognize what was consistent in Jola's behavior. Lawyers are supposed to have a sixth sense for patterns. But I wasn't a lawyer, after all; I was a diving instructor. Instead of wishing the two of them a nice vacation and taking to my heels, I came to the conclusion that Jola wasn't completely wrong. If Theo had collided with the ray and suffered a fatal accident, I might have been accused of involuntary manslaughter.

Maybe even of murder. The motive would have been clear if half the island had taken the witness stand and testified to my alleged affair with Jola.

We separated for the rest of the day. Theo and Jola wanted to stay in town a little longer, go to dinner later, and take a taxi back to Lahora. I was grateful for the evening off. I steered my Volkswagen van through the volcanic landscape, alone and enjoying it.

It's easy to judge your past self. How stupid you were, how little you grasped. Patterns, though not necessarily explanations, show themselves only in hindsight. So with all our efforts to do everything right, we can still be sure to arrive notoriously too late.

JOLA'S DIARY, TENTH DAY

Monday, November 21. Afternoon.

I don't have much time. He could come back at any moment. I'm in the Wunder Bar *café, surrounded by German tourists. There's a piece of cheesecake and a cup of filter coffee on the table. It's 3:32 in the afternoon. Scarcely an hour ago, Theo tried to kill me again. Sounds like the beginning of a crime novel. But it isn't. Maybe I should compose an appeal for help while I'm sitting here: Dear Sir or Madam, if you find these notes, please inform the police at once! Inquire as to the whereabouts of a certain Jolante von der Pahlen. Has she disappeared? Has something happened to her? Please tell the police it was no accident! They should question the writer Theodor Hast, and they shouldn't forget he's a true master in the art of twisting the truth. That's his profession.*

It was so brazen, the way he attacked poor Sven! He said he'd misinterpreted Sven's hand signal and assumed the fish was dead. The dead fish and the actress—ha-ha. I wonder if he concocted that story before he decided to push me onto an electric ray? Or is he ingenious enough to come up with such explanations spontaneously? In any case, he actually threatened to file a complaint with the police, while the truth was that Sven would have been perfectly justified in showing us the door. But the race is to the cheeky. In the end, Sven really thought he was to blame for everything.

Now the old man's looking for an ATM. He wants to withdraw a hefty sum from my account so he can take me out to dinner this evening. Such a failed murder attempt calls for a celebration. He probably didn't even want to kill me. One doesn't break a pretty toy on purpose; one merely wants to find out how much it can take. One wants to see it perform a two-hundred-volt dance at the bottom of the sea. To watch it roll up its eyes, twitch epileptically, swallow water, lose consciousness. What fun.

Did he think Sven wouldn't see him push me? Or was he determined that he should? Maybe it's not really about me. Maybe it's some kind of suicide attempt. Maybe Theo beats me right in front of the living-room window and shoves me onto a lethal fish before Sven's eyes as a way of provoking Sven. Until he has no other choice but to avenge me and hang the old man on a rock the next time we dive. Theo's clever enough to know that staging an accident would be easy for an experienced diver like Sven. No marks. No witnesses. If that's so, I'm less than a toy. Less than an instrument. Only a kind of lure. The piece of cheesecake in the mousetrap.

Maybe I'm going crazy. I don't feel anything anymore. Then again, my brain's working incessantly. I remember wanting to talk to Sven. He'd rescue me, I thought. But then he suddenly seemed surreal to me. A flat, cardboard figure. As though I'd invented him. How can you be rescued by your own invention? Please let me in on that secret when you're finished giving your statement to the police, dear sir or madam. And don't forget to speak with the coast guard. They must search the Atlantic Ocean for the remains of the actress or the writer. Maybe even for the remains of both. Down forty meters deep.

15

Before I reached the sandlot, I could already see that Antje wasn't home. In all our years in Lahora, I'd never been able to teach her to shut the gate only when the VW van was parked on the property. Whenever I came home, I always had to climb out and open the gate. There were days when that inconvenience galled me to my soul; on this day, however, seeing the gate standing open caused me only frustration. It meant that Antje wasn't there. I'd been looking forward to spending the evening with her, to eating and chatting, to discussing the day just past and the new day tomorrow. To putting our heads together under the light of the dining-room lamp. It almost seemed as though I was observing that scene through a lighted window, while I myself stood outside on a cold, wintry German street.

Without Todd's yapping, the house positively boomed with silence. There was nothing extraordinary about Antje's driving to town in the afternoon to do some shopping, meet girlfriends, or tend to a holiday apartment. It was only that she usually called me up before she left and asked what I was doing at the moment and whether she should come to the dive site and bring fresh scuba tanks or hot soup. When there was nothing on schedule for the evening, we'd sometimes arrange to meet for coffee and cheesecake at the Wunder Bar café. Or to take Todd for a walk on the promenade. Suddenly it became clear to me how much had changed since Jola and Theo arrived on the island.

I put the wasp-waisted espresso pot on the stove and filled a big glass with lemonade. "Making things nice for yourself" described a method women resorted to; nevertheless, male though I was, I was determined to give it a try. I picked up the scattered pages of Theo's short story from the floor near the living-room couch and put them in the proper order. I carried the coffee, the lemonade, and a bucket of ice cubes out to the terrace and pushed a deck chair into the shade.

Two hours later, I called Antje's number. All I got was her voice mail. Just in case she was in a dead zone, I called her three more times at intervals of a few minutes.

It had cost me an effort to read Theo's story all the way through. In the end I'd felt downright loathing for the typed pages themselves. It was as though the content of the words had bled onto the paper. As though they might dirty my fingers.

The sun had sunk behind the flat roofs of the neighboring houses. Antje knew a lot about literature. I wanted to ask her how much real life entered into storytelling. Would she think an author who described something abominable in great detail must necessarily have had practical experience in his subject? I didn't understand why Theo had given me that story. The feeling it had produced in me was that I never wanted to see him again. Several times, while I was reading the thing, I'd been on the point of calling up Bernie and asking him whether he'd agree to take over my clients. One of my basic principles was to accept money from my clients only at the end of their course, which meant that I hadn't yet seen a cent from Jola and Theo. If I terminated the contract now, I could most probably kiss all fourteen thousand euros goodbye. Antje and I needed that money badly. That was why I wanted to talk with her. I wanted to ask her whether it wouldn't be better to cut all ties with a guy who was capable of writing such stuff. I figured she'd look at me as though I'd made a joke. She'd say something like *You want to ditch the best contract you've ever had in your life because your client wrote a story about two people who aren't nice to each other? Hasn't anyone ever informed you that literature is never about nice things, not even on islands? You're acting like a child who's seen a scary movie and now he's afraid of the dark!* Maybe the wretched feeling I had would go away if I could hear her talk like that.

Her voice mail again. Antje never turned off her cell phone. That little gadget was always freshly charged and ready to work. For her, the ability to be reached constituted a kind of proof of existence. Just as some physicists thought that if no one looked at the moon it wasn't there, Antje believed that anyone who couldn't be called up disappeared. Voice mail, one more time. I resolved not to try her number again. Fortunately, I wasn't the sort of person who always jumped to the direst possible conclusions. You just had to bear the normal probability distribution in mind. Getting in an automobile accident was much less probable than losing a cell phone or not hearing it ring. Even in Antje's case. It struck me that I couldn't think of anyone I could ask about her. I didn't even know the names of most of her girlfriends, much less their phone numbers. Quite apart from the fact that holding a telephone conversation in Spanish was a physical impossibility for me. Bernie didn't really have anything to do with Antje, and if I called him and inquired about her, he'd answer by immediately asking me what the devil was going on with us. I had no contact with her parents in Germany. And in any case, it was only eight in the evening.

A strange restlessness drove me to pace through the house. I might also have been a little queasy. And probably hungry as well, but I couldn't make up my mind to eat anything. As though attached by barbs, Theo's story hung on my thoughts. There was even something baleful about the sunset in the beginning of the story, when he had his two characters go out for an early evening walk: The sky was an arrangement of bloody pieces of cloud, as if some enormous being had exploded overhead. The gathering darkness was a cloak, the gulls' cries a jeering sound track. Even a literary lowbrow like me could tell that the woman wasn't identical with Jola. Her name was different too. On the other hand, she seemed to share many of Jola's characteristics. First and foremost, a dark beauty. And a certain unpredictability. It slowly became clear to me why I didn't care for literature. Like jurisprudence, it was about the art of judging. The author acted as the highest judge, decided the facts of the case, called in witnesses, and in the end handed down the verdict. Punishment or acquittal. Unlike in the legal process, there was not even a possibility of appeal.

I roamed around the living room like a man looking for something. Everywhere in the house, there were objects I would have sworn I'd never seen before had they been pointed out to me in some neutral place. It was time for me to get a grip on myself.

I went into the kitchen and whisked three eggs and some Maggi seasoning sauce, tore off a big chunk of bread for dipping, and carried everything into the office. By way of distracting myself, I wanted to watch one or two episodes of Jola's series. If it succeeded in making me sleepy, I'd be able to take advantage of Antje's absence by spending a night in the bed for a change.

For the sake of completeness, I'd started watching the series in chronological order from Bella Schweig's first appearance. I sat at the computer, opened the *Up and Down* archive, and clicked through to Episode 589. Just as I hit the START button, I saw him. He was lying on his back just a few centimeters away from the mousepad, his four delicate legs with their high-tech suction cups thrusting stiffly upward. It was as though he'd been positioned to send a message: *Look here, this thing's dead.* I jumped up and probably cried out. Emile. The chill of his little body burned itself into my hand. I prodded him with my index finger again and again, tried to warm him, turned him right side up, and set him on my arm in the usual spot. He fell back onto the table, reduced to a piece of rubbery matter. I thought there was a vaguely chemical scent, perhaps insect spray, in the room.

In the middle of my reflections on which would be more absurd, throwing a friend down the toilet or burying a reptile, the doorbell rang. Without Todd's hysterical barking, the rooms seemed so unfurnished that I myself thought I wasn't home. Antje had her own key and would have made more noise upon arriving. The doorbell rang again. Three short, three long, three short. It was someone who knew the Morse alphabet. Even without that hint, I would have guessed who was outside.

When I opened the door, she fell into my arms. I caught a fleeting glimpse of her mascara-smeared face. She hadn't had makeup on that afternoon. Her shoulders were twitching. She clung to me hard. Sobs shook her body all over. I held her in my arms and buried my nose in her hair. We hadn't even said hello. While I inhaled the smell of her, I felt myself becoming indifferent to everything else. To the torpedo fish, to Antje, to Theo's story, to the gecko. I thought, *I mustn't think about anything anymore, I mustn't want anything more.* She told me through tears what had happened, but I barely understood what she said.

She and Theo had taken a walk on the promenade at sunset. Suddenly Jola had spotted a swimmer struggling with the current far from the shore. Her first impulse was to jump into the water, but Theo had held her back. They ran around pointlessly for a long while before finding a lifeguard. Meanwhile a crowd had gathered on the promenade, a coast guard boat was on the way, and a helicopter was arriving from one of the other islands. They were all too late to recover the swimmer alive. I thought fleetingly about Bella Schweig, who turns up weeping at her ex-boyfriend's place with a story about a cyclist run down in traffic.

While I stroked Jola's hair, I told her that tourists often died on the island. They drowned or fell from bicycles or paraglided into a cliff or got drunk and drove off the road. There was a whole rescue industry dedicated to helping people who fell victim to their leisure activities. There were helicopters, boats, hospitals . . .

I'd probably long since stopped talking, assuming that I'd said anything at all. In any case, I found myself on the living-room couch again, with Jola on my lap. Her hair formed a black curtain, behind which we kissed. A great peace came over me. As if I'd finally arrived. The tension of the past several days fell away. There was no more conflict, no doubts, no confusion. My hands felt completely at home on Jola's body. Nothing about her seemed unfamiliar to me. The room revolved around us, and so did the house, the island, the whole world. The universe had found its center, from which it expanded and into which it would one day collapse.

Until Antje was standing in the room. I'd heard neither her car nor her key in the door. Todd growled at Jola. I wasn't able to react. I simply sat there blinking. As though Antje's entrance had turned on a dazzling light, had subjected us to pitiless illumination. A diving instructor with his half-naked client on his lap, caught in flagrante by his domestic partner.

"Okay," Antje said. "We can handle it this way too."

In duty bound, Jola jumped from my knees, took a few steps away, and rearranged her clothes with downcast eyes. I'd lost all further interest in the scene before it got properly started. As soon as I stopped touching and smelling Jola, she looked like Bella Schweig again. The way she was staring at the floor, her hair hiding her face, her hands smoothing her T-shirt over and over. Maybe the actors' curse was that they couldn't stop playing themselves.

Antje stood three meters away, unquestionably identical with herself. She was quivering. I felt impatient. *Where were you so long, I have urgent matters to discuss with you, I wanted to ask you a few things. Can we please call a halt to this nonsense and have dinner. A glass of wine, the warm lamplight on the table.* In the actual situation, there was nothing to say. Once again, I'd let myself be caught off guard by a chimera. Jola was a mistress of her trade. I would have gladly gone back to the usual order of the day, even though I knew, of course, that such a thing couldn't happen without further ado. Because it was becoming absolutely necessary for someone to speak, I asked the only question that interested me: "Why did you kill Emile?"

That worked as though I'd thrown a switch and activated a brand-new, hitherto-unknown Antje. She didn't even raise her voice. In fact, she spoke rather softly, but with a sharp edge in her tone more penetrating than any volume. "Actually," she said, "I was willing to let the whole thing rest. All this"—she made a sweeping movement with her arm that took in me, the house, and herself—"is more important to me than your childish affair. But I won't allow myself to be humiliated. Bringing your lover here now is just outrageous."

"Jola's not my lover."

The edge turned into hate. "Maybe," Antje said, "I've made it too easy for you the past few years. I've let you withdraw further and further into your own world and lose all sense of reality. In the end, it's probably all my fault."

Her speech was seriously getting on my nerves. That wasn't the Antje I knew. She didn't sound like the girl who'd lain on the floor of my room at home, eating jelly babies with the first Todd. She sounded like a public prosecutor. Moreover, I now knew that she had Emile on her conscience. It was typical of female perpetrators to avoid answering the main question and to react instead with recriminations. I had no desire whatsoever to thrash the matter out. I didn't want dinner anymore either. I just wanted to get in bed, pull the covers over my face, and sleep for twenty hours. After that, everything would be normal. Normality was the least a person could demand of life. But Antje wasn't finished yet. She looked at me pensively, hesitating as though she had to make a decision. Then it came.

"Let's put everything on the table," Antje said. "I've got a lover too. His name's Ricardo. We've known each other for a year."

I stared at her, dumbfounded.

"It's a draw," she said, smiling painfully. "Maybe the only chance for a new beginning." She swept her hair off her face and took a deep breath. "I love you, Sven. Unlike you, I have no problem saying so. The thing with Ricardo is purely sexual. You're a pretty sporadic lover. And sex is very important to a young woman like me."

When she came closer and put out a hand, I stepped to one side.

"Don't worry," she said. "I've always taken care to protect you. Nobody knows about this. We're in Spain, after all. Only Valentina and Luisa are in on it, because I sometimes need help with logistics."

I didn't know any Ricardo. I was convinced she was lying, and precisely *that* was what hurt. Her wish to wound me wounded me. It was so important to her, she'd stooped to an absurd story that insulted us both. "I think you should go now," I said.

She began to weep silently, nodding as she did so. While she was in the bedroom, stuffing some things into a travel bag, I realized that Jola wasn't there anymore. She must have dissolved into thin air at some point during Antje's lecture. In any case, I couldn't remember when she'd left.

Antje came back in. She stood still in the middle of the living room, uncertain about what form to give her farewell. I would have liked to stand up, take her in my arms, and say a few nice words. But I remained on the couch, empty-headed and heavy-legged, unable to move. At some point, Antje turned around and left. I heard Todd's paws clicking on the tiles in the hall. I heard the front door close and Antje's Citroën start up. Then the sound of the engine faded into the distance. The ensuing silence was different from what I'd imagined it would be. Less restful.

JOLA'S DIARY, ELEVENTH DAY

Tuesday, November 22. Morning.

Life can be so strange. A naked nightmare one moment and wonderful the next. As Daddy used to say: Child, never forget you're a girl. When you feel like shit, it's because of hormones. Or Mama: The question isn't how you feel, but how you look. Or Theo: You only feel lousy so I'll feel guilty.

Sven said, I'll kill the son of a bitch. Before that, he said, Everything's going to be all right. Both times, he looked as though he meant it.

Sven as a murderer—unimaginable. Even though by now I can actually imagine just about anything. All I have to do is walk on the promenade and someone starts dying. A little spot out on the sea. It's weird, the things that cross your mind at times like that. When I wanted to get in the water, I was thinking only about what a good swimmer I am, and that I could do it. And that such a heroic deed would get news coverage in Germany as well as here. And that in the end they'd have no choice but to give me the role of Lotte Hass. I could see it already: I'm sitting in my apartment, candles lit, music playing, and on a shelf the Silver Bear from the Berlin Film Festival. The cell phone's switched off, because I can afford the luxury of being unreachable. I'm sipping wine and reading one of the scripts from the pile on my desk.

But the old man held me back. While we searched for a lifeguard, he was probably thinking about how he could use the scene in a story. Two desperate tourists run up and down the beach, and out in the sea a swimmer struggles for his life. Stark and brutal. Nothing kitschy. When someone's dying, that's always art.

One hour later we were on the promenade, standing a little apart from the other rubbernecks. We watched the swimmer's body on a stretcher as it was raised up to a helicopter. There wasn't much to see. It was completely covered by a tarpaulin. We couldn't even tell if it was a man or a woman. Seeing that packaged corpse didn't bother me. I don't cry at funerals, either. Grandma, Grandpa, Uncle Lukas, Aunt Miriam—the Pahlen family is numerous and given to drink. I never cried on any of those occasions, they didn't matter. What's the fuss about, when we all know we're going to die? In the presence of death, everybody acts as though it doesn't exist. It's the opposite with love.

But when the helicopter lifted away, the tourists relaxed their necks, and the old man pressed me against him, I suddenly knew what I must do. Apparently I had to come here in order to realize it. I had to meet Sven. I had to see someone drown. You only live once. That's something Daddy always says, but he just means you shouldn't have any consideration for anybody else when it comes to making money. I watched the helicopter fly away and decided to live my life without Theo, starting now. Because I can't do it alone, Sven will help me. Only four more days. Things have to be clarified before our time here is up. I must force Sven to come to a decision. I must tell him what the old man does to me. Then we'll see how serious Sven is.

Theo wanted another drink, so he went to a pub and I took a taxi. Antje's car wasn't parked in front of the house. That was a sign. I immediately rang the doorbell at the Residencia. Sven opened the door and pulled me into his arms. I pushed him away. I wanted to speak as soon as I could, before I changed my mind.

Some creased typewritten pages were lying on the coffee table. I recognized the font at once: Theo's old travel typewriter. He's got it with him in case some inspiration comes to him while we're on our trip. The thing is hellishly loud. He must have used it when I was diving without him. The sly dog. And him constantly moaning about his ongoing writer's block. There can't be any doubt that the story's about me. The old man likes writing about women. He calls them Lola, Nora, or Josa, lights up the dark torture chambers of their souls, and describes with gusto the ways they destroy their male victims. He probably wrote the piece especially for Sven. The title could be "So You'll Know What You're Letting Yourself In For." But the text appeared to have missed its intended effect. Sven was still talking to me. Or rather, listening. The words just came pouring out. Tears ran down my face. The pressure must have been enormous. It was the first time I'd ever told anyone. As I spoke, I had a lot of trouble with word choice. Should I say dick or penis, pussy or vagina, asshole or anus? In any case, what I told him sounded harrowing. It frightened even me. It was as though I was living through what I was talking about, really living through it for the first time, right then. As though it became steadfast reality only when Sven heard it.

Sven said, Everything's going to be all right. And then, later: I'll kill the son of a bitch. I wonder whether one might be the result of the other. Of course, he won't kill Theo. Both of us know that. I was sitting on Sven's lap. He held me tight, rocked me, kissed me, shielded me, put me back together. And then Antje came in. Sven didn't even try to defend himself. He'd probably decided a long time ago. He needed only a final push, just like me.

I left while Antje was talking. Not because I found it disagreeable, but out of respect. Later I heard the dog, and then Antje's car drove off. Still I remained seated at the table in the Casa Raya, staring into the darkness. I felt it would be better to let Sven spend the night alone, even though everything in me cried out to him. The old man came home and fell into bed at once. I spent the rest of the night out by the sea.

Now I'm looking at the rose-colored sky and wondering if the future isn't just a mug's game. In half an hour Sven will drive his VW van onto the sandlot and toss out his cheery "Good morning," as though every morning's a good morning, especially this one. The old man didn't come looking for me—maybe he's done us all the favor of dying in his sleep. The sea is calmer than usual, as if its mind is elsewhere. The obvious indifference of the elements soothes me somehow. Do what you want, the sky and the rocks and the ocean say. We really don't care. How many of you do you think have sat gaping at us and thought yourselves special? Doesn't bother us. You all scuttle around and make a huge fuss and then you go away, one after another. Nothing remains from your little catastrophes; whole islands go missing now and then in ours. That at least is something, although not much, because after all, who cares about an island?

The smartest thing to do in the face of so much indifference is simply to be glad. To be happy. Sven and I are a couple now. What that means exactly will reveal itself soon enough.

16

Tuesday, November 22, 2011. A near-perfect day. Light north-northeast wind, no more than twelve kilometers an hour. Expected high temperature: twenty-four degrees Celsius, seventy-five degrees Fahrenheit.

A typical November morning, in other words. I stood on the terrace in my boxer shorts, cup of coffee in hand, and thought about damp cold and the smell of rotting cabbage. About the ground fog that hung over the fields until noon, the wetness that crawled under your jacket and numbed the skin on your thighs as you walked. I thought about the days when the sun went down before there was ever any proper daylight. No wind, no sea, no sky. Just mute silence, and behind it the hum of the Autobahn. The silhouettes of apple trees with all their leaves gone and a couple of wrinkled brown fruits still hanging on. The silhouettes of my parents, hand in hand, my mother (helped by shoes and hairdo) taller than my father. And about knee-high, something that was always in motion and never cold: Todd the First, practically overcome by the sheer joy of a family walking party. "Cold, but lovely," my mother would say. Antje was also somewhere in that fog, still no higher than a fence post, her hair gleaming blond. There was the memory of the summer, the certain knowledge of the fall, the prospect of a wet winter, and the abstract hope for a spring that still lay much too far in the future. There was the year and the season. Had anyone told me fourteen years ago I'd be on the island in November and I'd miss, of all things, the bad weather in the Rhine Valley, I would have told him he was out of his mind.

I stood there drinking my coffee in the warm breeze that morning and longed for temperatures a few degrees below freezing. For fumes rising from my cup. For the possibility of putting on a sweater. I'd slept wonderfully in the big bed, a deep, dreamless sleep that stripped my soul and promised a new beginning. When I woke up, the silence in the house—no radio, no clattering dishes, no dog's paws—had reminded me of winter.

Twice a year, Antje flew to Germany alone to spend a week with her family. I thought of those days as holidays, even if I had to work and the annoying task of washing the dive suits every evening fell to me. Not that I was usually tormented by her presence, but her absence opened up rooms. I stretched out. I did a lot of thinking, without being able to say later what it was I'd been thinking about. By the end of the week, having stretched myself out and thought myself out, I'd look forward to the moment when the place would come back to life.

Lights went on in the Casa Raya. I saw Theo stagger into the living room and over to the little kitchen, where he paused, as though he couldn't remember what all those appliances were for. Then he filled the espresso pot with water and set it on the stove. He stood in front of the open refrigerator and drank something from a bottle. I couldn't tell whether it was juice or wine. Though as a matter of fact, bottled juice wasn't available on the island. Theo scratched his head with his right hand and stuck his left down the back of his pajama pants. He ate a few spoonfuls of something in the fridge, maybe olives or caviar. He emptied the bottle and dropped it on the floor. He poured out his coffee, took a sip of milk from the open carton on the counter, and immediately spat into the sink. Hadn't Antje told them they should buy only long-life milk on the island? Anything else went bad almost at once, even in the refrigerator. Theo took his black coffee into the bedroom.

When I envisioned the future, I imagined a contradictory picture. I firmly believed that Antje would come back. She'd never spent more than a week away from home. I couldn't manage the diving school for longer than that without her. She was surely staying in some girlfriend's house, and I figured she'd keep up the Ricardo act for a few days in order to punish me. Then, one evening, suddenly she'd be there again. At the same time, I saw myself waking up in the morning and gazing at Jola, asleep beside me in the double bed. I saw Antje lying in the bathtub and Jola standing before the mirror. While Antje made breakfast, Jola set the table. I saw Jola sorting invoices while Antje sent e-mails to clients. Snow was falling outside the windows.

I went back inside, shaking my head. I hadn't taken care of the gecko yet. I tore off part of a paper towel, picked up Emile's cold little body, carried him into the bathroom, and threw him in the toilet. He wouldn't flush down. I covered him with toilet paper, flushed, waited, flushed again. Until he finally disappeared.

⁂

They were both standing in front of the house. I hadn't reckoned on more than one of them. On this morning, as on every morning, they waited at the foot of the Casa Raya's front steps while I backed the van across the sandlot. Jola wore a red dress with a swaying skirt that I hadn't seen before. Theo looked like he wasn't awake yet. I got out of the van, walked up to Jola, put my hands on her waist, and kissed her on the mouth. I didn't know why I did that. I hadn't planned it. Nor did it feel good.

"Whoops!" said Jola.

Theo looked past us, gave a slight nod, and smiled.

Some fuse in my head must have blown overnight. In the van, I gazed at Jola from the side and stroked her cheek with my forefinger. I put a hand on her knee. She seemed happy, but also a little mixed up. She wasn't wearing a brassiere. At the dive site, when she turned her back on Theo and me to take off her dress and get into her suit, I had to keep my hands still. I felt like a boy forbidden to test out his new toy, even though it had so many functions he'd yet to discover. Theo was suddenly full of questions about technical diving. Only then did I remember that tomorrow was the day I'd been waiting months for. My fortieth birthday, one hundred meters underwater. No matter what the wrecked ship's original name had been, I was going to rename it after myself. A few more preparations remained to be made; there were tanks to fill, various pieces of equipment to check, calculations in the dive plan to be gone over one last time. The impending expedition seemed far away to me, like something I'd already lived through and concluded. That perception had to change. I needed my full concentration. I answered Theo's questions without properly listening to myself. While I was explaining that helium, even under high pressure, had very little narcotic effect, and that this was the reason why divers at hundred-meter depths breathed a helium-oxygen mixture, I looked at Jola, who was standing a little away from us. She returned my gaze with her head slightly tilted to one side, like someone contemplating a piece of furniture, uncertain about which room to put it in.

I thought about how urgently I needed to make a few decisions, and this immediately put me in a bad mood. Then I reflected that such decisions were best left to fate, and my mood improved. I said that the thermodynamic law of ideal gases didn't take the interaction between gas atoms into account, and that therefore it was advisable to fall back on the van der Waals model when using helium. I thought that I had as valid a right as anyone to follow the laws of logic. Which meant that if Theo, Antje, Antje's girlfriends, Bernie—if the whole island—assumed that I was having an affair with Jola, then it was only logical that I should actually have the said affair. The thought appealed to me. A man who didn't want to lose his reason had to make sure that idea and reality were coextensive. As a general rule, one adapted ideas to reality. Sometimes the opposite method was the simpler one. An affair with Jola would ease the sting of Antje's unjust accusations, give my conviction a retroactive basis, and put me back at the negotiating table. I'd had enough of feeling that I couldn't explain anything because no one would believe me no matter what I said. I composed a text message to Antje in my head: "Just slept with Jola, so you can stop thinking I'm a liar." Let her try to get over that.

Jola watched me as I thought. She appeared to know what was in my mind. I smiled. She smiled. I laughed. She shook her head. As though she couldn't rightly believe what she read in my thoughts. *Come to your senses,* her look seemed to say. All the same, she'd been coming on to me for days. It bordered on the miraculous that a woman of her caliber was prepared to go to such obstinate lengths to get a man.

I'd apparently broken off my helium lecture at some point in the middle; nevertheless, the Boltzmann constant and Charles's law of volumes were still hanging in the air somehow. Theo looked unsatisfied.

"Okay," I said. "Let's go for a dive."

•

Three hours later, when the dive was over and we were back in the van, Jola asked me, "Do you own a dinner jacket?" I said I didn't. "Then a clean pair of jeans and a white shirt will have to do," she said. "But with long sleeves!"

She hadn't asked me whether I wanted to go out with them.

"Dinner on the *Dorset,*" Theo explained. "Aperitifs at seven."

I gave some brief consideration to what Antje might be planning for dinner, but then I recalled that Antje wasn't home. My aversion to parties was irrelevant in this case. Theo and Jola were scheduled to depart on Saturday. The time remaining until then must be utilized, deliberately and thoroughly. Relishing the thought, I swung the van through the open gate and onto my property.

"Would you like to come in?" I asked in Jola's direction, addressing her as casually as possible. Theo burst out laughing and left the van. Jola extended an index finger, poked me on the nose, and got out too. Her sports bag dangled jauntily from her shoulder as she walked over to the Casa Raya and disappeared inside.

With his back to me, Theo was standing on some indefinite spot between the gate entrance and the sandlot, approximately where the sidewalk would be in a German village. As he turned around, I could see a cigarette between his lips. He was crying. It was a weird sight: the forty-two-year-old man with the old face, the burning cigarette, the tears. Like a still shot from a movie that Antje would have liked.

"When we were children," Theo said, "we wouldn't have imagined we'd come to this one day."

His flamboyant talk of the past few days was still in my ears. *I'll put up with you banging her,* he'd said. *Just stop denying it.* As my mother would have observed, there's no pleasing some people. Right there and then, I found Theo repulsive. He wasn't only smoking and weeping, he was also smiling, all at the same time.

"Just imagine," said Theo. "Seeing that drowned swimmer didn't bother her a bit. It was almost as if she was enjoying it."

He wiped his face with his cigarette hand. With the other, he made a regretful gesture, as though sympathizing with me about something. You had to hand it to him—he certainly had a knack for producing shock effects. Without turning around again, he crossed the sandlot and entered the Casa Raya.

❂

Jola wore a silver-white dress that gave off a pale, liquid shimmer and reacted to her slightest movement. Her dark hair was braided and wound around her head like a wreath. She was breathtakingly beautiful.

She had made sure we'd arrive fifteen minutes late. As we went up the gangway, she took my arm. The conversation on board fell silent. Theo walked behind us. I felt ashamed to be wearing jeans.

It was a moment I'll never forget. Bittmann, tuxedoed and filthy rich, stared at us wide-eyed, as if he were standing on a raft while I steered a luxury yacht in his direction. Because of Jola, my jeans suddenly presented no problem; on the contrary, they seemed like a clever gambit.

A young girl wearing a man's suit and a 1920s hairdo served the aperitifs: Aperol spritzes. My question as to what those might be made everybody laugh. A guy who was a singer in an East German band ordered a beer. On my left a young black man wearing gym shoes and a hoodie was grinning nonstop. I asked him how he liked the island. He understood neither German nor English nor Spanish. I couldn't speak French.

We stood in a circle on the quarterdeck. The *Dorset* radiated light to all points of the compass. People in Morocco could probably see that something was going on here. A couple of children whom Bittmann had permitted to take a tour of the ship ran up and down the deck. Their parents were on the quay, so curious they didn't know what to do. We gazed at the starry sky, or rather at what there was to see of it behind the haze of the *Dorset*'s lights, and said, "Fantastic" and "Spectacular" alternately. Jola greeted a tall man in his sixties named Jankowski, whom Bittmann introduced as Germany's most important literary critic. Next to Theo stood a lady wearing a multicolored shawl; according to Bittmann, she was the star director of the Schauspiel Köln theater. The other guests included a famous photographer with unwashed hair and the noted East German singer with his beer. The young black man was an artist from Burkina Faso who glued together collages of plastic bags; an exhibition of his work had opened in a gallery in Hamburg a few weeks before.

"Jola Pahlen and Theodor Hast need no introduction," Bittmann said. "And this is . . ."

"My personal trainer," said Jola, raising her glass to me.

I found that mortifying and therefore laughed with everyone else.

"Lovely to have you here," Bittmann thundered, and all the glasses met in the center of the circle. "To art and culture!"

"To art and culture!" the guests shouted to the stars, and I began to have an uneasy feeling that my dinner companions, no matter how well or little they were acquainted and whether or not they liked one another, all belonged to a kind of club, a club whose membership didn't include me. It had been an eternity since I'd last stepped into a museum. I didn't read books, didn't listen to music, rarely watched a movie, never went to the theater, and couldn't even stand the works bequeathed to the island by its local artist. Such things, I felt, required me to make myself small and to tilt my head as far back as possible.

"Art is always where you aren't," Antje had said to me one day. She meant this observation as a reproach, but I considered it a compliment. Maybe it was an either-or proposition: you could love nature, or you could love art. Nature needs no admirers. It works, in every respect, by itself. I took another glass of Aperol from the flapper's tray.

"I wouldn't have recognized you," Jankowski said to Theo. "The photograph on your book must be a little old now."

"As old as the book," said Jola with a bewitching smile.

"When will we see something new from you?" Jankowski asked.

"I'm working on a big project," said Theo. "It's a social novel that—"

"Great," said Jankowski.

"He writes short stories," I remarked.

"Touché!" Jola cried out and pressed my hand. Jankowski laughed.

"Short stories," he said, winking at me. "What do you know."

I saw Theo's jaw muscles working, felt unclear about what exactly I'd just done, and emptied my glass. Bittmann shooed the children off the yacht and invited us to move to the dining salon on the lower deck.

With an elegant naturalness that surprised even me, I stepped back and let Jola go first down the stairs. Antje was one of those women who got irritated when someone held a door open for them. Jola inclined her head like a queen, gathered up her dress, and descended the steep steps. The action of her thigh muscles showed through the clinging material she wore. An athlete's legs. I looked from above at her artfully braided hairdo. The impulse simply to turn around and run home grew almost overwhelming. The other guests crowded down the narrow steps behind me. *Everything is will,* I thought. Without knowing what I meant by that. One after the other, we plunged into the *Dorset*'s belly.

Down there, the past was waiting for us. The restorers had returned the interior of the *Dorset* to its original 1926 splendor. Cherrywood paneling on the walls. Cream-colored leather upholstery on chairs and armchairs. Every door handle, every little wall lamp, every drawer pull was polished brass. The large skylight in the ceiling overhead reflected the candles on the dining table. Over the sideboard, an oil painting of the "Big Five": the five biggest racing cutters of the 1920s sailing in a regatta, the *Dorset* in the midst of them. *Shamrock, Westward, Britannia*—I couldn't think of the fifth schooner's name. Jola would certainly have known it at once.

The flapper had duplicated herself. The two of them were now passing out glasses of Moët & Chandon, an activity that required them to snake among the guests. The presence of nine people standing in the salon showed how small it actually was. We formed a miniature group of banqueters in a miniature banquet room. The noise level rose. Glasses clinked. The champagne was excellent. The girls distributed refills. When she laughed, Jola clutched my forearm, which I was holding bent at an angle, like a waiter. The warmth in the room seemed to emanate from her body. At last, Bittmann suggested we take our places at the table. The seating arrangement was up to us. We sat down. Jola was on my right, the black Frenchman still on my left. Theo sat at the other end of the table, far from Jola, who now belonged to me. That was exactly what I thought: *She belongs to me.* I let myself lean back, laid my arm across the top of Jola's chair, and laughed at a joke I hadn't understood at all.

Scallop and swordfish carpaccio with lime-tomato marinade.

The photographer scarfed down the appetizer in something under two minutes. Then he wiped the marinade from his mouth and declared that the European economic crisis would widen the gap between rich and poor. Bittmann pointed out that the Riesling we were drinking came from a good friend's vineyard on the Mosel River, where a coalition of the righteous was staunchly protesting against the building of a bridge. The star director chimed in, observing that the people were in the process of being repoliticized. Jankowski asked the singer, who was washing down his scallops with beer, why there were so many Nazis in the former DDR. The young black man and Jola chatted in French, leaning across me from both sides in order to hear each other better. The star director talked about her latest play, in which actors who'd spent weeks conversing with hookers, junkies, and homeless people played hookers, junkies, and homeless people. She spoke rapidly, making frequent use of the word *authenticity.* When I asked who'd written the play and what it was about, Jankowski went into a paroxysm of laughter. He struck the table with the flat of his hand and cried out, "Sven, you're priceless!" Jankowski had liked me from the start. The director's answer was drowned in the general uproar. Theo looked at me from the other end of the table in a way I couldn't interpret. The evening was getting better and better. In Jola's mouth, French sounded like a song with no beginning and no end.

Black ribbon pasta with lobster sauce.

The photographer, his shirt sprinkled with droplets of sauce, asserted that the financial crisis had signaled the definitive end of capitalism. The singer informed us that his band had been supporting projects to combat right-wing extremism ever since the reunification. Jankowski, nodding distractedly, listened while Bittmann praised the real economy.

"Oh, Lars," cried the director, who'd been a little marginalized. "It's so wonderful, the way you always bring it off!" She wasn't referring to rising sales figures, but rather to something about dialogue and the connection between culture and politics. Shouting loudly, Theo asserted that the finance economy was the metaphysics of poker players. The twin servers circled the table tirelessly, Riesling bottles in hand. The little curls on their temples hadn't budged an inch.

King prawns in sesame tempura, served on a cucumber bed with papaya tartare.

I wasn't properly listening anymore. I thought about Germany, where these people lived when they weren't sailing off the coast of Africa. I knew how they felt. They were confronted daily with the task of accommodating their own personal crises to the bank crisis, the financial crisis, the climate crisis, the energy crisis, the education crisis, the euro crisis, the pension crisis, and the Middle East crisis. For fifteen minutes in the evening, every evening, they watched people on television elucidate for them the imminent decline of the West and the inability of politicians to prevent it. Meanwhile the viewers clung to the totally private and slightly embarrassing hope that, in the end, everything would nevertheless remain as it was. Just keep on going. Their lives were wholly dedicated to keeping on going. To crossing hours and days and things to do off the list, one after another. Although the future appeared to them like the place where the coming catastrophe would be accomplished, they fought their way doggedly through the trenches of the present. They were soldiers who'd lost their faith in victory and cared exclusively about their own survival. They didn't desert because they didn't know where to go. In a world without differences, there was no such thing as exile.

I looked around. The temperature was rising steadily; alcohol and candles were heating up the little salon. I felt my cheeks glowing. My shirt stuck to my back. I recognized the anxiety behind the papaya tartare. All the faces were laughing in the way I recognized from Jola: with their mouths open too wide. They all talked like Jola: emphatically, with broad gestures that put glasses and candlesticks in danger. A wave of sympathy washed over me, flipped me around, ebbed away, and left behind a sandy feeling of love for the people at the table.

"It's too bad you can't fondle wine," Theo cried. He'd been watching me the whole time I was looking over the others. Our eyes met again and again. He seemed amazingly relaxed. He clearly assumed he'd be taking Jola back to Germany with him on Saturday. I had the distinct feeling I must not allow that to happen. *Bide your time,* I told myself, and raised my glass to Theo. He lifted his glass as well and sent me a little nod. Jola gave back her plate practically untouched, which nobody commented on.

Cream of celery soup with chard-wrapped salmon roulades.

The evening metamorphosed into a tableau of light, heat, and noise. In my memory, the conversations around the table are covered up by loud music, something classical, somebody's ninth whatever, but at the same time, I'm not completely sure there was any music at all. I didn't turn down the twins' offers to refill my glass. And Jola's nearness intoxicated me. She kept groping me, laying her hand on my shoulder, on my arm, on my thigh. She leaned against me, and I could smell her hair. She whispered into my ear, and I could feel her breath. There was a dark red film of wine on her chapped lips. Smeared mascara ringed her eyes. She dug her fingers into my shirt while she laughed. *Too bad you can't drink a woman,* I thought. During those minutes, I believed I'd never before loved anybody so much. In fact, my sympathy with the others at the table had its source in the profusion of my love for Jola. The East German singer and his faith in beer, the lady director's strident isolation, Jankowski's tragic perception of his own past, the young African, locked inside himself, Theo's pretended serenity, the social-climbing Bittmann and his protein bars—all that provided an overflow basin for my feelings. My affection poured itself over them, fused them into a wedding party that had journeyed from far-off Germany in order to celebrate my marriage to Jola. The mere presence of these people made us a couple, for which service I owed them my thanks. They all moved me to tears. Jola and I, individually and together, moved me to tears. I put an arm around her and felt her soft yielding as I pulled her against me. Ever since the king prawns, I'd been hiding a semi-erection under the table, a reaction to the scent of Jola's perfume. I knew what lay ahead of me. I saw Jola in my bed, in my kitchen, in front of my computer, in my living room; I saw Jola as an island resident, wearing shorts and flip-flops; I saw her talking to clients and helping run the diving school. Along the way, I'd train her to be a diving instructor in her own right, and she, Jola, would recover from Germany day by day, month by month; she, Jola, would laugh more softly and gesticulate less and become more and more beautiful. In my fantasy she didn't give up her career, she only downsized it, and occasionally I accompanied her to Germany, where we lived in an apartment overlooking the rooftops of Berlin and went out to events in the evenings. She wore the shimmering dress and I was at her side, the same as now. Film premieres, television awards. Jola in the spotlight, and I the silent observer. People looked at me askance. Photographers took pictures of us. I smiled, unspeaking; now and then Jola pressed my hand. On the return flight, we imitated the people we'd met and laughed so much that the other passengers complained. Jola was wearing enormous sunglasses so as not to be recognized, and after we landed she said softly, "Welcome home." One morning she'd bring me coffee in bed, gaze at me for a long time, and tell me she was expecting a child. Even that was something I could imagine.

Terrine of various fish in octopus mantle over sautéed sugar snap peas.

I started out of my reverie. Something had changed: the light, the ambient noise, the guests' looks. I was apparently in a state of extreme sensitivity, in which I could detect the tiniest vibrations. When Bittmann began to speak of Yvette, I knew something was wrong. Or better, I knew something was going to go wrong in a second.

Yvette was such a dear, according to Bittmann. He'd known her a long time. A fabulous beauty, he said. And of course, a superb actress. Yet despite her accomplishments, she'd remained the same. Still the nice girl next door.

Maybe the movement I felt beside me was Jola, suddenly sitting up a little too straight. In any case, the noise level around Bittmann's voice seemed to drop down so far that I could hear every word he said. The music, if in fact any was playing, fell silent. Everybody listened.

Yvette had sailed on the *Dorset* before, Bittmann said, and she would have very much liked to come along this time too. A good addition she would have been, because by now she was an expert sailor.

"But seasick," the lady director cried out.

"But seasick," Bittmann confirmed.

"Could you all please stop repeating the word *seasick*?" Jankowski asked.

"But you refused my pills," the photographer cried.

"Ingwer! Please!" cried Jankowski.

They laughed together about something that had happened on the boat a few days before. It was Theo who took it upon himself to bring the conversation back to its topic. He asked, "So why couldn't Yvette be here this time?"

It was clear that all the guests aboard the *Dorset* knew the answer already. Theo too looked as though he'd been informed. Bittmann had probably told him earlier what Yvette Stadler's present occupation was. Theo just wanted to make sure that the matter would be gone over in public one more time. When he asked his question, he was looking at Jola, not Bittmann. His face shone with pleasant anticipation. He looked like a man scarcely able to suppress his laughter. I felt Jola tense up beside me. As though her body were preparing for a life-threatening assault.

"Yvette's on the shores of the Red Sea as we speak," said

Bittmann. "Beautiful spot. A few years ago, on our legendary tour, we ran into a heavy storm. We were all drenched to the skin, and when we finally reached the new marina in Hurghada, Boris and Til, wearing nothing but underpants, jumped into the water and—"

"But what's Yvette doing down there by the Red Sea?" Theo asked impatiently. He was grinning. He'd obviously lost all desire to control himself. I had the impression that Jola was starting to tremble.

"She's preparing for a new role," Bittmann said. Now he too was looking at Jola. "Surely you've heard about it? From your father?"

Jola didn't react. She extended a hand toward her wineglass, reconsidered halfway there, and put the hand in her lap.

"What role is that?" asked Theo.

"Well, they're making a film about the life of this woman deep-sea diver." Bittmann was speaking to Jola again. He assumed that such news would be of professional interest to her. "I can't come up with her name at the moment."

"Lotte Hass," Theo said.

"Yes, maybe so."

Bittmann still had noticed nothing. Everyone except him and the African had lowered their spoon to their terrine bowl. They gazed at Jola, who had turned as pallid as a corpse.

"In any case, we must keep this among ourselves until the official press conference. I know about it only because it was Yvette's reason for declining my invitation. Otherwise she would've come aboard in Casablanca."

Theo turned toward Jola. "Wasn't that role the reason why we came down here, love?" he asked. "The reason why you're taking this diving course?"

"But casting . . ." Jola cleared her throat. "But casting doesn't start until the week after next."

Her voice toppled over at the end. I admired her. She fought against domination like a bull in an arena. Theo thrust in the next lance. "Wasn't your heart set on playing the Girl on the Ocean Floor?"

"What I told you was insider information," Bittmann said. "They made an internal decision that Yvette absolutely had to get the part."

"Didn't you say"—Theo started laughing again—"didn't you say this was your last chance?"

"Jola . . ." Bittmann looked stricken. "Don't tell me you intended to try for the role yourself."

"Because otherwise you'd never be able to get out of that soap-opera shit?" Theo slapped the table with delight. "You'd never be taken seriously as an actress? You'd just be an aging TV whore nobody would remember in a few years?"

Jola had lost. She'd lost against Theo, against the people around the table, and especially against herself. A gasp escaped her throat. She sprang to her feet and ran out of the salon and up the steep stairs. I wanted to go after her and was already half out of my chair when my eyes fell on Theo. He broke off laughing to raise his eyebrows and shake his head. That meant *Let her go.* I sank back down. He kept looking at me while his chest began to quiver with laughter again. *Now what was that?* His eyes seemed to ask. *You couldn't give your new girlfriend any help at all? Fucking beginner.*

Amid the general silence, the African turned his head from one side to the other and asked in English, "What is?"

After a longish pause, Bittmann said, "I feel very sorry about that."

"She'll get over it," Jankowski opined.

"I don't think so," said Theo.

"Dessert?" Bittmann asked.

Vanilla panna cotta with pistachios and red wine jelly.

When the dessert plate lay in front of me, I couldn't hold out any longer. I murmured an apology and left the table. Before I reached the main deck, my cell phone rang. I thought it must be Jola and answered at once. It was Bernie. He spoke in English, and pretty rapidly at that. A stream of mostly incomprehensible language rushed past my right ear. Every now and then, single words I could understand briefly emerged from the torrent: "Fuck"; "Dave"; "*Aberdeen*." I heard the word *crazy* twice.

"Bernie," I said. "What's the matter?"

"You can have the fucking boat. But don't ever ask me again."

"Pardon?"

"Aren't you listening, man? You can take the *Aberdeen* out tomorrow morning. But forget about us! Dave—is—not—coming—and—neither—am—I, understand? It's the last thing I'll ever do for you. You've lost your fucking mind."

"But, Bernie, why won't—"

The conversation was interrupted, because Bernie had hung up. I tried to call him back, but he didn't answer. I went up the last steps to the deck, stood next to the mast, and stared into space. In front of this space was a section of the ship's rail. Jola was leaning against it, looking at me. She too had a telephone in her hand, and she held out the illuminated screen so I could see it. For a moment I imagined Bernie had also called her to cancel the expedition.

"Text message from my father," Jola said. "Bittmann's right. Stadler got the part."

So much for that, I thought. Weeks of preparation, all for nothing. I had no chance of finding people to replace Dave and Bernie on such short notice. And December would bring the winter currents, which would make it impossible to reach the wreck. At a stroke, my whole project was dead. Deferred until some future date that, try though I might, I couldn't imagine would ever come. I didn't even know what the following days would bring. The following week. I felt my life disintegrating into its component parts. For months I'd envisioned celebrating my fortieth birthday, my personal farewell to the first half of my existence, at a depth of one hundred meters. Having to abandon that plan undermined everything else. I didn't have the slightest idea why Bernie had canceled at the last minute like that. All I knew was I couldn't rely on anything anymore.

Jola put her cell phone away. Side by side, we leaned on the rail and looked out at the massive breakwater formed by the lower edge of the night sky. A cold wind snatched at us from all sides. I wanted to put my jacket around Jola's shoulders and discovered I wasn't wearing one; at some point in the course of the evening, I must have taken the coat off and hung it on the back of my chair. Everything struck me as unreal. The *Dorset* wasn't a normal ship; she was a seafaring piece of Germany. And that was the way I felt: German. Overburdened, disoriented, disgusted by the world.

"Is something wrong?" Jola asked.

I told her about Bernie's call, and she laughed sardonically.

"So we've both had the ground under our feet yanked away. Me a little more than you, maybe. But I'm not so sure about that."

There weren't many people who could recognize another's misery alongside their own. For a while we were silent, gazing out to sea. Then the five minutes began, the five minutes I've gone over in my mind again and again during the past several weeks. Never before have I regretted such a short span of time for so long. Jola seized my arm, looked me in the face, and said, "We'll do it tomorrow."

I didn't grasp what she meant at first, though I felt the effect of her smile. It crossed my mind that I'd come up on the deck to comfort her. To help her gather up the shards of her life and build a new life out of them. I took her in my arms. From that moment on, my body made all the decisions itself. Instead of patting her consolingly, I pressed her against me and kissed her throat. She shoved me away so that she could keep looking at me. "You're diving down to your wreck," she said. "Theo and I will sail the *Aberdeen*."

My arms took hold of her again. Now my body was asserting its claim. My fingers slid over the sheer fabric of her nearly nonexistent dress. Her scent was a spinning whirlpool, drawing me downward. I wondered fleetingly whether I'd ever mentioned to her that Dave's cutter was called the *Aberdeen*.

"Such a load of shit." Jola turned but didn't pull away. "With the old man as master of ceremonies. The devil." She gave a cooing laugh. "A devil. That's what he is. Nothing more and nothing less."

I'd lost the thread and no longer knew what she was talking about. Which didn't bother me. While those seconds were passing, there were a great many things I had no interest in. Things that no longer existed for me. The night. The boat. The wind. Past and future. As though they'd all been obliterated. I had Jola's dress hiked up around her hips, and she, half shoving, half carrying me, maneuvered us onto the foredeck, where two large chests stood.

"What time does it start?"

I paused. She'd stiffened her back. Obviously, she was waiting for an answer to her question. I said, "What?"

"The expedition."

"Fuck the expedition," I said.

"No!" Jola shook her head so hard that a strand of her artfully braided hair came loose. "The expedition is still on! Lotte Hass is all over for me, nothing can be done about that. But your diving expedition, that's really going to happen. Now more than ever. Do you understand?" She was getting louder. "I'm . . . we're not giving up!"

Very slowly, it was becoming clear to me that she was serious. "I don't have a crew for tomorrow," I said.

"Theo and I will be your crew."

I lowered my hands. "That won't work, Jola. You need experience for such a thing."

"I was steering ships before I could walk. Do you really think a cockleshell like that's going to be a problem for me?"

"The wreck's several kilometers offshore. In that kind of expedition, I'm putting my life in the hands of my crew."

"And you'd rather trust the asshole who just left you high and dry? Rather than me?"

Jola twisted her fingers into my hair. Despite the wind, her hands were surprisingly warm. Her face came nearer. Eyes, nose, lips, all in close-up. Like a flash, I had the feeling I'd gone through that scene once already.

"The crew has to watch the surface of the water every second," I said. "They have to read the wind. Interpret the current."

Her skirt still up around her waist, Jola sat down on the lid of one of the chests. She leaned back a little; her knees shot out and clamped my hips right and left. Her panties had a silvery sheen. I slipped two fingers under them and watched myself lift up the fabric.

"Child's play," Jola said.

She was dry. I thought nothing of it at the time. I pulled the silvery material completely to one side, went down on one knee, and separated the folds of skin with my tongue. She laid her hands on my ears. Now it would happen. It had to happen. It was why Antje had left me. It was why the whole island looked at me funny. It was something that fate had long since made a supposition, so attributing it retroactively to fate seemed imperative. Everyone has a right to logic. Jola's hands pressed against my head as though she intended to crush my skull.

"Will you take us with you, Sven?"

I stood up and kissed her. I wanted her to taste herself.

"Sven! The expedition!"

She wasn't wearing a bra. My lips effortlessly found her nipples under the fabric of her dress. I braced her tailbone with one hand and with the other unbuttoned and unzipped my jeans.

"We'll get it done tomorrow, the three of us together?"

"Yes," I said.

"Seriously, Sven!"

"Yes, dammit."

"Do you promise? Do you swear?"

"Yes."

There was nothing behind her for me to lean her against. I would have to hold her good and tight to keep from knocking her off the chest. By the time I'd concluded that train of thought, she was already standing two meters away. Her dress hung smoothly, right down to her ankles. She looked perfect. Except for the loosened strand of hair and the two wet spots on her breast.

"Come here," I said fatuously.

She observed my cock, which was poking out of my open pants. "We should get some rest," she said.

"Please."

"Look at your watch."

I was so confused, I obeyed her. Ten after twelve.

"Happy birthday, Sven."

She stepped close to me again and kissed me. I briefly felt her fingers on my stomach.

"Believe me; tomorrow's going to be a great day. First your diving adventure, and then the rest."

The heels of her shoes resounded sharply on the gangway planks. When she was on land, she turned around. "We leave at eight, as usual?"

"At six," I said. "We need the tide."

"Good night."

"Wait," I called out. "Let me give you a ride home."

She kissed her hand to me and walked quickly along the quay. A taxi was waiting a few meters farther on. There's no possibility that it was parked at that spot by chance. Somebody must have called it. I stood watching the red taillights for a good while, until the cab reached the end of the rows of shops, turned left, and accelerated up the mountain. The inside of my head contained not even the echo of a thought. I put my clothes in order and went belowdecks to collect my jacket and Theo.

JOLA'S DIARY, TWELFTH DAY

Wednesday, November 23. One A.M.

Small injuries are painful. Banging your toes against the annoying angle between the bathroom and the bedroom, a defect overlooked by some drunken architect when the premises were inspected. Whacking your shin against the coffee table in exactly the same spot where there's a dent in the bone from your last collision. Tearing off half a fingernail on the upholstery of your car seat. That sort of thing hurts abominably. Your whole body reverberates like an orchestra without a conductor. Bright spots dance before your eyes. And then comes the hate. You want to blow up your car. Smash the coffee table to smithereens. Set your house on fire, annoying angle and all. You're prepared to kill. For revenge.

It's completely different when you're shot. Your body presents no resistance to the first bullet. Then come the second and the third. Bam, bam, bam. The metal bits burrow effortlessly into your flesh until they lodge somewhere. There's no pain. You look down at yourself, mildly surprised. The bloodstain spreads; your stomach feels warm. Not unpleasant at all. Dying can be easy. Maybe you make a last effort to register the expression on your murderer's face. Overjoyed by his accuracy, he squeezes off another shot and then another, even though they're not really necessary. He looks around to make sure everyone has seen that you're dying. For a moment, you think he's going to take a bow. He's chosen his audience carefully. The kind of people who are delighted to be on hand when somebody croaks. To hide their enjoyment of your agony, they stare embarrassed into their fish terrine. They fold their hands piously so as not to applaud. With whatever strength you have left, you turn and run. Just to deny them the pleasure of witnessing your definitive collapse. The murderer laughs. You can hear his voice in your head. Well, how do you like this, it says. And you thought you had me by the balls. I win in the end. Take note of that. You little slut.

So then I was standing on the deck of a sailing yacht in the middle of the night and waiting for the pains to start. But I waited in vain. No hate, no anger, no longing for revenge. Even Lotte, who's kept me alive for so long, suddenly lost all importance. I only felt the wind cooling my fever and wondered what was going to happen now. Was I supposed to board an airplane on Saturday, bury myself in my Berlin apartment, and rot away, nice and slow? A gradual process of decay, carefully overseen by the old man? The thought was absurd. Yet at the same time, I had no idea how I could begin a new life. I wasn't at the end anymore; I'd moved beyond it.

When I heard steps on the stairs, I thought it was Theo, coming to apologize. Or in other words, to examine at close range the damage he'd caused. But it was Sven. My first impulse was to send him away. The last thing I needed was somebody making clumsy attempts to comfort me. But Sven was already blathering before he reached the deck. He came up to me, stared at my forehead, and talked. Laid his hands on my shoulders, shook me, and talked. At some point I realized he wasn't trying to comfort me. Not even a little bit. It wasn't about me at all; it was about his diving expedition. The fabulous shipwreck exploration. His private birthday celebration one hundred meters underwater. It couldn't happen, he said, because Bernie and Dave, for some reason he didn't understand, had pulled out. The worst-case scenario. He asked whether I'd be able to assist him. He wanted us to be his substitute crew, me and the old man. Of all people!

Out of sheer amazement, I gave him sensible answers. I said I thought it wasn't a good idea. Neither Theo nor I had the necessary experience, I said; it would be better to postpone the expedition.

But a postponement was out of the question. The winter, the currents, the wind. All that planning. And his birthday. He'd been working weeks and months to prepare for this one day. He'd invested untold amounts of money. And I'd been steering ships since before I could walk, right? I told him what he knew better than anyone, namely that the wreck lay several kilometers off the coast, and that he'd be putting his life in the hands of his crew. But he didn't give up. He said he trusted me more than he did the two Scottish assholes who had just double-crossed him. Was I going to leave him in the lurch too? And then once more, from the beginning: the planning, the currents, his birthday. Tomorrow morning or never. I had to help him. Absolutely had to. He begged me: Please, please, please. Like a little boy. Shining eyes, red cheeks.

While he talked like a waterfall, I wondered whether he understood what had just taken place at the table. Or whether it simply didn't interest him. Could a man actually be so egocentric that he'd consider a canceled dive more important than the total emotional destruction of the woman he supposedly loves? I didn't say anything else, I just listened. Such steadfast pigheadedness astounded me. It was like some elemental force.

Until what he was doing dawned on me. And it was so clever, so sensitive, so thoughtful and right, it almost brought tears to my eyes. He didn't want the expedition for himself. He wanted it for me. He'd realized at once it wouldn't be any use to talk about Lotte or Theo. Or about the fact that my shitty life lay in shitty ruins. He wanted to redirect my attention and give me a chance to concentrate on real things: water, wind, boat. Things he understands, things he knows will be good for me. He wanted me to fight, to be the person he needs, the one who must help him. Sven himself canceled Bernie. He sent him a text message and let him know he needed only the Aberdeen, *without any crew. Because he wants to sail with me. It's his way of reminding me of something I can do very well, though I do it far too seldom: I know how to keep a boat on course.*

All at once I smelled the sea and felt the Dorset's *slight movements. I was alive again. All the pain was still there, but so was joy. I lived* toward *Sven, as though love were a direction. I took him in my arms. The stream of his words dried up immediately. I said I'd come with him. It would be a fantastic expedition, I said.*

He said, I need Theo too. I said, Then Theo's coming with us. He said, Theo's important. We can't do it without Theo. I said, Don't worry, he'll come. Then Sven wanted to know if I could promise that. I promised. He made me repeat the promise. Both of us, Theo and I. Tomorrow morning at six, in front of the Casa Raya. Ready for action. Sven stressed every single word. Like we were plotting a bank robbery. I kissed him. He stroked my hair. I wasn't interested in thinking about the future anymore. Not even about Saturday. Only about now and tomorrow morning. Then Sven said it was late. He told me to take a cab and go to bed. He'd bring Theo home. We all needed at least a few hours' sleep.

The sleeping part's hard. I've got so much to think about, so much I'd like to write about. But Sven's right. We need sleep. I think I can hear his van driving up. The light has to be off when Theo comes in. I'll stop now.

17

"Sweet," Jola said, and jumped aboard.

The *Aberdeen* is a converted fishing cutter, nine meters long, with a small cabin, two single berths, and all-wood construction. Nineteen sixties diesel engine, seventy-five horsepower, six knots. Although it was still dark, Jola inspected the helm stand while I unloaded the steel cylinders from the van. The VW's headlights illuminated the quay. We were the only people in sight. The Marina Rubicón was still asleep. Unlike Puerto Calero, this harbor contained no luxury yachts; instead there were little vacation vessels, family boats, small, trim cutters—a floating campground in the last minutes of nighttime peace. A narrow streak of dawn appeared behind the promontory.

"Only radar and radio?"

I handed her the bag with the portable devices: depth sounder, GPS, chartplotter. She gave a satisfied nod and started to set things up. I lugged aboard my dive suit, stage tanks, and chests with other accessories. Theo sat on a bench a little apart and dedicated himself to transpiring alcohol.

"Almost exactly four kilometers southwest of here? So about twenty-nine north, fourteen west?"

Jola was good. Very good. The wreck lay at latitude 28°50'33.8" north, longitude 13°51'8" west. I gave her the exact coordinates and felt myself relax. Jola was wearing jeans and a checkered shirt and moving about with great assurance, as if she sailed the *Aberdeen* on the Atlantic Ocean every day. I believed I could rely on her ability. Theo, staring off in another direction, lit his third cigarette.

I find that day difficult to describe. My memories aren't like a coherent, linear film; they're individual images, still shots, like a puzzle with half the pieces missing. At the same time, every single detail is probably important right now. *Herr Fiedler, do you really think we're interested in the horsepower of an old fishing cutter? Don't you think we'd rather hear about the impression Frau von der Pahlen made on you on the morning of November 23, 2011? The allegations you've brought us are very grave, Herr Fiedler! Give us a chance to believe you! Was Frau von der Pahlen different from usual? Did she act despondent? Aggressive? Hysterical? Come, come, Herr Fiedler, you can surely offer us a few descriptive words. This cannot be so difficult!*

But it is. Jola was always "different," every day; with her, there was no "usual." If I honestly ask myself whether anything struck me on that particular morning, whether I could have known or at least sensed what would happen in the next several hours, I must answer with a clear "No." It's possible I wasn't paying sufficient attention. I might have been concentrating too hard on the upcoming dive. On going over my equipment, which I checked at least five more times. As far as I noticed, Jola acted neither despondent nor aggressive. Maybe a little too chirpy. Which, after the events on the *Dorset*, wouldn't have surprised me—had it crossed my mind to give any thought to such matters. Above all, she struck me as being in a very good mood. She seemed to be looking forward to our adventure. It was obvious that the *Aberdeen* gave her great pleasure; it was as if she was finally in her true element. And I liked the way she looked in jeans and a work shirt. Even more, actually, than the way she'd looked in her evening dress.

*

As soon as she was finished installing the navigation devices, Jola jumped onto land, pulled Theo off the bench, and sang, "Sailing, sailing, over the bounding main," in his face. He lurched into motion, grumbling, a burned-down cigarette clamped between his pale lips. The previous night, I'd needed a full hour to tear him away from his audience. He couldn't retell the tale of Jola's defeat often enough. How she'd spent the past weeks preparing for the role of Lotte Hass. How she'd read books, taken a diving course, even pinned a photograph of the lady in question to the wall over her bed. How she'd made her future, her happiness, and her very self dependent on being allowed to play Lotte. And now: Yvette Stadler. Theo didn't seem to notice how embarrassing his behavior was. Or didn't care. He told us again and again that it was the end of Jola. The end of arrogance and pride. From now on, he said, she'd be nothing but grateful if someone should volunteer to attend her slow decline. Her daily aging into insignificance. He, Theo, was prepared to perform that service. He could imagine no finer occupation than observing and documenting Frau von der Pahlen's disintegration. Preferably over the course of decades. The slower and more excruciating, the better. In the end, Theo said, he would turn this story into the novel of the century. A thousand-page metaphor for an undignified age. Only Thomas Mann's *Buddenbrooks* would be comparable to it in scope and importance. This evening was the end of Jola and the beginning of a tragic masterpiece. . . . Theo kept talking like a maniac. At some point, I grabbed him under the arms and pulled him off his chair. I didn't so much support as carry him up the steep stairs. Corpses and drunks are heavy when they're not floating in water.

Now Jola cried out, "Come on, old man! You of all people should try to enjoy our little excursion. You don't have much time left."

I figured this was a joking reference to his alcohol and tobacco consumption, but Theo seemed to take Jola's words literally. "What does that mean?" he asked. "Time for what?"

They were facing each other, standing near the quay's edge. *Swaying a little on the brink of the abyss,* I thought. *Their favorite position.*

"For taking boat trips," said Jola. "After all, you're flying home on Saturday."

"And you aren't?"

For the next few seconds, we stared at Jola as if she were an oracle about to deliver the final pronouncement on our fates. I suddenly imagined, with crystal clarity, what it would be like if she should disappear into the sky above the airport on Saturday afternoon. She'd be at my side—and a moment later she'd be gone, vanished, as if she'd never existed.

Jola raised her nose to the wind and gave her verdict: "North, eleven knots. Ideal conditions. Like sailing on a duck pond."

She saw the looks on our faces and laughed. Then she jumped back on deck, verified that my gear was loaded on board, and started the diesel engine. A few minutes later, we reached the end of the breakwater and chugged out into the open sea. A little to the east, the first ferry to the neighboring island was getting under way. Theo sat on the bow, waiting for the invigorating effects of the north wind. Jola stood at the helm. She didn't look as though she needed any additional tips from me. I left it up to her to hold the course and started my diving preparations. The trip out wouldn't take more than an hour, and for starters, the urinary sheath required several minutes. Sitting on deck with my back against the wheelhouse, I rolled down my swimming trunks and slowly massaged myself until I reached the proper degree of stiffness. I dedicated the utmost care to fitting the sheath and applying the adhesive tape. If the sheath slipped off, I'd have no choice in the coming hours but to pee in my wet suit. On the other hand, I'd been in the Red Sea with an experienced diver who suffered a contusion of the ureter because he'd taped too tightly. Eighty meters down, he was seized by the most fearsome pains. A quick ascent to the surface was not an option, not at that depth. Never. Not at eighty meters, and most certainly not at a hundred. As my army diving instructor used to say, when you're deep underwater, you've got a glass ceiling above your head. You solve your problems down there or not at all. I knew enough stories about people who'd died while on dives. In most cases, it wasn't even possible to track down what had gone wrong. I preferred to go over every detail twenty times and come back up alive.

I put on my undersuit and wet suit. Fastened the hose to the urinary sheath. Checked fins, mask, gloves, hood, weight belt, dive light, backup dive lights, battery packs, knife, camera, surface marker buoys, reels, plastic bags, dive computer. Sat on the boat rail and breathed into my back. Now I could feel the aftereffects of the previous night's drinking. A slight dizziness, a throbbing at the temples. Under normal circumstances, residual alcohol would have been a reason to call off the expedition. But this wasn't a normal situation. It was—I don't know what it was. A desperate attempt at self-assertion. I forced myself to concentrate. The last minutes before a dive were the most important of the entire expedition. I turned my gaze inward, went over all the points of my gas plan one more time, visualized every single movement. My intensity seemed to rub off on Jola and Theo. They maintained a resolute silence. The farther the *Aberdeen* got from land, the more the onboard tension increased. Even Theo looked as though he was slowly coming to full consciousness. When he wasn't squinting at the Atlantic, he was eyeing me thoughtfully. I didn't try to sustain his gaze. I was glad to have a day when he wasn't my responsibility. I could keep my mind on more important matters than the question of what was up with him.

The diesel engine's decibel level and stroke rate diminished, the steady noise of the bow wave became softer and then fell silent. I joined Jola on the narrow helm stand and looked at the GPS. She'd hit the coordinates exactly and had moreover maneuvered the boat into the best anchoring position. The depth sounder showed an elevation in the ocean bed. The wreck lay a little east of us, around 107 meters down. Its outline was clearly recognizable on the sonar screen. I placed my hand between Jola's shoulder blades so that she'd know how proud I was of her. She pushed past me and prepared to cast the anchor. No one had spoken a word since we left the harbor. At that point, I no longer doubted that the expedition would go off without a hitch. All Theo had to do during the three hours of the dive was to watch the water surface and look out for my buoys. If he should prove unreliable, Jola would share the task with him. She'd keep one eye on the instruments and the other on the Atlantic. Bernie and Dave were good, but when it came to boats, Jola was obviously better than the two of them together.

I spent the next ten minutes fastening seventy kilos of equipment to my body with snap hooks. The six cylinders with the different gas mixtures seemed particularly heavy. I was sweating feverishly in my hermetically sealed dive suit. The biggest challenge consisted in standing up, fully outfitted, in the rocking boat, making my way to the stern, and putting on my fins. When I was finished, Jola gave me the "okay" sign, and I responded in kind. I'd just as soon have gone over the side amid general silence, but Theo had constructed a question out of his various preoccupations, and he just had to ask it. He took hold of my wrist to prevent me from dropping into the water before he could speak.

"Suppose we disappeared with the boat. Would you die?"

"Almost certainly," I said.

Theo let my arm go and nodded approvingly, as if giving me points for mortal danger. I let myself tip over backward. Before I hit the water, I thought I heard Jola's voice call out, "Happy birthday, Sven!"

My fortieth. When I was a kid in school, there used to be stickers that read ATTENTION: TODAY IS THE BEGINNING OF THE REST OF YOUR LIFE. For the first and only time, that inane dictum seemed appropriate. It just needed an additional line to indicate whether it was a promise or a threat.

As soon as I was in the water, the familiar calm came over me. The weight of the dive tanks had disappeared. Under me there was neither firm ground nor empty air but instead a liquid three-dimensionality that I could traverse in any direction I wanted. No swells, visibility excellent. I grabbed the anchor cable and began a brisk descent. Soon the current caught me, and I hung on perpendicularly, like a banner in the wind. Sixty meters down, the first brief stop to change over to bottom gas. Soon afterward, the wrecked ship came into sight, a gigantic shadow in the everlasting semidarkness of the ocean floor.

I'd figured this dive would be an extraordinary experience. All the same, my own reaction surprised me. With every meter, the closer I sank to the wreck, the more my hands started to shake. I felt as though all the hairs on my body were standing up. The ghost ship below me was as long as a football field and broken into two pieces. The bow had separated from the rest of the ship and lay a little distance away from it. The ship's waist appeared to be well preserved, except for a loading crane that had snapped off and fallen diagonally across the bridge. The stern loading crane still stood upright, as did, in fact, the entire steamer. The *Fiedler*, as I'd baptized her, looked as though a mighty hand had placed her there to wait for a secret future assignment. If—as I guessed—

she'd sunk sometime during the Second World War, no human eye had looked on her for about seventy years. On the deck down there, people had once lived and worked, sung and quarreled, had harbored thoughts and feelings, and in the end had most probably gone to the bottom together with their ship. I was hovering above an inscrutable past that was principally, in the way of pasts, a graveyard. No one but the fish had taken care of those dead bodies. Maybe they were still to this day unaccounted for. Maybe there were grown grandchildren somewhere who believed Grandpa had absconded to America in the middle of the war and left Grandma alone with two little ones.

The most impressive feature of the *Fiedler* was, beyond a doubt, her enormous funnel, which towered at some distance from me. I decided to leave the anchor cable, swim over there, and negotiate the rest of my descent alongside the chimney. Because of the sunken ship's imposing size and the strong current, I had to make sure I'd be able to find the cable again. The anchor would surely creep some distance over the seafloor; on the other hand, visibility was better than I'd expected that far down. I let go of the cable, battled against the current with strong fin strokes, and got my camera ready. The effort was worth it. I was looking down into a black maw big enough to swallow a cow. A dense school of sardines, as pliant as cloth, as agile as a single creature with a single will, wound around the funnel. When I got close, they formed dents and bubbles, but then they immediately went back to circling the chimney. One level down was a large battery of barracudas, too satiated to hunt. I pressed the shutter-release button. Those photographs would be the envy of the entire island.

I quickly completed the final stage of my descent. From this point on, time would speed by. I couldn't spend more than twenty minutes at that depth, and twenty minutes was the blink of an eye, particularly considering the size of the object I proposed to investigate. I took a plastic bag from my pocket, inflated it with gas, and released it. It fluttered upward like a frantic jellyfish doing battle with a family of different-size air bubbles. The marker made a beeline for the surface, where Jola would see it and interpret its meaning: *I'm down, everything okay.*

Then I started to swim. Against the current, but at a leisurely pace, because haste underwater only used up gas, strength, and nerves. I swam along the ship's steel walls, which were as high as a house and covered with a closed layer of mussels, sponges, and soft coral, here and there decorated with sea urchins and starfish. It was a living, breathing, and ever-hungry vestment that hardly offered a glimpse of the metal underneath. The barracudas watched me and found me boring. While I had to keep working my legs hard, they hung almost motionless in the current.

I saw the quarterdeck, the main deck, and the bridge. The lifeboats were all properly in place; everything had obviously happened very fast. I noted the signal bridge, the Morse lamp, and the radio mast, which was overgrown to the tiniest branch with mussels and anthozoans. I inadvertently broke off a little stony coral from the bulwark and felt ashamed. I took meticulous care not to get tangled in any of the long-lost fishing nets that clung to the wreck here and there like giant spiderwebs. A hole in the ship's side allowed me to peer into the engine room. I reached the detached bow, which lay separate from the rest like a wrenched-off body part. The break was a colossal, gaping wound. I guessed the ship was a British collier, maybe a merchant vessel built in the Roaring

Twenties and later put into service by the Allies. I'd have to come back here many times to look for the ship's bell or the shipbuilder's plaque, for identification plates in the engine room, for dishes or utensils embossed with the shipping company's emblem, for the manufacturers' marks on the engine telegraphs and the binnacle, before the secret of the *Fiedler* would be unlocked.

It was time to return to the anchor cable. I was slowly reaching the point of sensory overload anyway. There were too many impressions. I wasn't processing them anymore, only registering them. Ground tackle, king posts, fan cowls, deckhouse. Thousands of dolphinfish, amusing themselves by pursuing me. Once again, the ship's screw captured my attention. It was a four-blade bronze propeller with a diameter of about five meters. The rudder, which had been swiveled hard to the left, could have told an entire story. And I was curious to hear it. I wanted to sit on the seafloor and grow gills so that I could breathe freely. I wanted to cast off my equipment and move into the captain's cabin. The barracudas would surely have had nothing against that; there was room enough for all. The wreck was as big as an apartment complex. I could have made myself at home in there. After all, I knew how life worked underwater. It occurred to me that during the previous several minutes, for the first time in days, I hadn't thought about either Jola or Antje or Theo. That was the pass I'd come to. Jola and Theo had brought Germany to the island—and with it a war that wasn't mine, that had nothing to do with me. Nonetheless, they'd turned me into a combatant. Up there on the land, there was no longer any refuge I could escape to. The whole island was a battlefield. I couldn't stay out of it anymore. My living space had been destroyed, like the habitat of a creature on the way to extinction. Down here was the only place I could still be. Everything felt right here. The planet *Fiedler*, discovered by myself. A realm nobody could follow me into. All I'd have to do was take off my equipment, breathe through gills, and . . .

I reached the anchor cable. Twenty-two minutes; deepest point, 109 meters. Not good, but acceptable. Apparently I'd forgotten the time for a few moments while contemplating the ship's screw. I was breathing too fast—I had to get a grip on that. From this point on, the old rule from the Bible held good: don't turn around, don't look back. I couldn't be interested in the wreck anymore. Now my entire focus must be on my measuring instruments, with whose help I had to bring the factors of depth, time, and gas mixture into perfect proportion.

I made my way up the anchor cable hand over hand, a little faster at the start because the cable sagged in the current, and then more slowly so as not to surpass the proper ascent speed. My first stop came at seventy-five meters, where I changed gases and then waited a further two minutes without taking my eyes off the dive computer. Constantly monitoring the parameters required my complete concentration. At three minutes per meter, up to a depth of forty-five meters; there a five-minute pause, including another gas change. Then continuing upward with increasingly longer decompression stops to twenty-one meters, where I had to wait twenty minutes and noticed for the first time the increase in the current. My arms and hands were already aching from clinging so tightly to the anchor cable. As soon as I noticed those aches, I started thinking I couldn't hold on one second longer. Using one hand, I fished the mooring rope out of my pocket and attached myself to the cable. The next hour and a half was taken up with the coordination of ascent and stops, and I had no opportunity for reflection. For the first time, I looked up. The *Aberdeen*'s oval hull lay obliquely above me. It was a reassuring sight. Some part of me must have secretly reckoned with the possibility that my support ship might disappear. It was hard to imagine that Jola was actually up there. My desire to see her and report on my meeting with the *Fiedler* was like a pang in my belly. At the same time, I already felt disappointment at never really being able to describe to her what I'd experienced, because there were no suitable words for it. The eternally dusky undersea world, the sleeping ghost ship, the pitiless dimensions of past, ocean, and death—that was all trapped inside my head. No one but me had seen those sights. I'd have to work hard with Jola to help her develop the abilities necessary for diving down there with me someday. Maybe she could do it in a year or two. Then we'd share the same memory forever. The *Fiedler* would marry us.

Now I was being pulled upward as powerfully as down. Below me was darkness, above me light. The boundary between all conceivable opposites ran straight through me. I hung between bright and dark, above and below, yesterday and tomorrow, life and death. My instruments told me what direction I should move in, and when: higher, immediately. I unhooked the mooring rope and worked my way up the next fifteen meters, making various stops of four to thirteen minutes.

The glass ceiling lay six meters below the surface. I had to remain at that depth for an hour, alternately breathing pure oxygen and bottom gas, while the *Aberdeen*'s hull was directly above my head, so close it seemed I could touch it by stretching out a hand. Below me was the vitreous blue water mass of the Atlantic, in whose uppermost layer I found myself. There was nothing for eye or hand to fasten on except the anchor cable, which was quickly lost to sight in the deep. Now everything was pulling me upward and nothing down. I wanted out. Out where I could talk, breathe, get dry. So as not to lose my nerve, I strenuously avoided looking up.

Barely ten minutes had passed when I heard a loud splash. Something heavy must have fallen into the water. I raised my head and looked up toward the surface. A person was floating next to the boat.

Now they're ruining everything, I thought. *The careful plan, our agreement, my trust. The spirit of the expedition. Because they got bored. Or too hot. Because they decided to abandon their posts and go for a little swim while I'm finishing down here.* Disappointment took my breath away for a moment. Until that moment, everything had gone well—had gone perfectly, in fact. I couldn't believe I'd been so wrong about Jola. *She begged me to go along on this expedition.* She'd wanted to be my partner, a person on whom I could rely 100 percent. Or had she? My reason was exhausted, and I could see I was arriving at strange conclusions. All I knew for sure was that the little swimming party up there represented an attack on everything I held dear.

Then I realized that there weren't two bodies swimming in the water, only one. And that one wasn't swimming, it was sinking.

I can see him in memory, gently drifting down toward me. In reality, he must have dropped like a stone. Nevertheless, I had endless time to reflect, or so it seems to me today. *Jola,* I thought. *Something's happened to her.* To be more precise, what I thought was: *Now it's happened.* As though it had always been a given that something would, to her.

Against the light, the body showed like a dark spot that grew larger as it came nearer. Its contours billowed in the agitated water. *This person has to return to the surface at once,* I thought. I'd already let go of the anchor cable and would have simply swum up if the rope hadn't held me back. My reason seized the opportunity to yell my instinct down: *You're staying where you are!*

If I surfaced now, the nitrogen inside me could expand fatally. Or make me very sick: vomiting, breathing difficulty, paralysis of arms and legs. I might pass out with blood running from my ears. Moreover, I didn't know what had happened on the *Aberdeen.* Jola wasn't making any swimming movements. Had she hit her head and fallen overboard? But then why wasn't Theo making any attempt to rescue her? Was he asleep in a fog of alcohol fumes? I thought it was something else. I thought Jola and Theo must have had another quarrel. He'd knocked her down and thrown her into the water. Or she'd been injured in the struggle and fallen over the rail. In any case, it was clear, as the seconds went by, that Theo was purposely letting her drown. If I broke the surface with the unconscious Jola, I ran the risk of his attacking us both in the heat of the moment. Or he might simply start the boat and chug away. Even if he didn't become aggressive, I still couldn't assume he'd do whatever it would take to get me to the nearest decompression chamber. And not even considering the question of whether I'd survive long enough for that. *You solve your problems down here or not at all.*

The interval between the moment when the body hit the water and the moment when I unhooked my mooring rope couldn't have been more than a few seconds. I swam away from the cable on a course to intercept the sinking body, but I made sure not to ascend as I did so. Our paths intersected at a depth of six meters, a short distance off the port side of the *Aberdeen*'s bow. I thrust out both hands, grabbed cloth, and got pulled down a little way. I struck out hard with my fins until at last I could free one hand and use it to inflate my buoyancy compensator and thus make up for the additional weight. Swimming on my back, I towed my unconscious companion to the anchor cable. My unconscious *male* companion. With one arm around his chest, I used my other hand and the mooring rope to attach myself as tightly as possible to the cable again. Technical diving, my instructor always said, is the art of doing everything with one hand. Without looking.

Time changed tempo and direction. Up until then, events had gone past as though in slow motion, but now they rushed at me with the speed of light. In retrospect, I see a vortex, at whose center I'm struggling to save a life. Before me is a face with closed eyes and half-open mouth. An underwater face. A face that seems to belong to a corpse. Theo's face. Not Jola's.

From 1992 to 1995, I spent a large part of my semester breaks as a rescue diver. I knew how drowning worked. In the first phase, the victim made uncoordinated movements, gasped frantically for air, and therefore swallowed water. In phase two, a reflex closed off his larynx. That was what gave Theo a chance. As far as I'd seen, he'd been already unconscious when he fell into the water and had therefore skipped phase one. It was possible that this was a case of dry drowning, and that no water had reached his lungs. Even on land, freeing the breathing passages from water was a difficult undertaking. I'd never yet heard of anyone who rescued a drowning man while remaining submerged. But maybe Theo had entered the suffocation phase, which would be followed by spasms and apnea, but not before two or three minutes had elapsed. If that was the case, I could reactivate his breathing reflex by giving him oxygen, and I wouldn't have to resort to resuscitation measures.

That wasn't something I thought. It was something I knew. There was no time for thinking. I'd long since switched to trimix, and in one hand I was holding the diving regulator with pure oxygen, ready to put it in Theo's mouth. The greatest danger for both of us was the possibility that he'd come to and panic. It's by no means unusual that drowning people kill their would-be rescuers. But I couldn't think about self-defense, not as long as Theo and I were hanging on an anchor cable six meters underwater. It wasn't possible to put any distance between me and the drowning man. The only reason he wasn't still sinking was that I was still holding on to him. If he started thrashing around, he could easily rip out my own air tube. He could cling to me in a panic, damage my equipment, immobilize me. Drowning men possess superhuman strength. They're more dangerous than any hammerhead shark.

And that was the moment when it happened. A tiny moment that showed me who I'd become in the last fourteen years.

I hesitated.

I asked myself for whom or what I was about to put my life on the line. For a man who terrorized the woman I wanted. Who would never give her up, because he considered her his property. Who had no real occupation and was of use to no one. Who missed no chance to point out that he was weary of life. I had only to release my grip. I could let Theo go and look away while he vanished silently into the lower depths. No one would ever connect me with his death.

It was only for a brief moment, but I hesitated.

Then I shoved the diving regulator between Theo's teeth. I took pains to close his lips around the mouthpiece in such a way that the least possible amount of water could get in. I held his nose and pressed the purge button. A rush of air bubbles shot up. The pressure pumped air into Theo's lungs. He suddenly opened his eyes very wide. He couldn't see much in the brine. He could only sense my embrace and the cold water and the likelihood that his life was about to end. He dug his fingernails into my forearm and whirled around like a fish. As best I could, I protected my air hose from the imminent attack.

But Theo didn't attack. In spite of the stinging seawater, he stared into my face at extremely close range. His head was shrouded in a whirl of bubbles. His lungs were pumping so hard that there was barely any distinction between his inhalations and his exhalations. The sight of him acted like a sign stimulus. We were diving instructor and diving student. My student was hooked up to my emergency air supply and hyperventilating. He was staring at me because he loved me, the way helpless nurslings love their mothers. I squeezed Theo's forearm several times to get his attention. His eyelids fluttered. Some part of his brain made an effort to concentrate, and I nodded encouragingly, as if to say, *Good. Like that.* He watched as I slowly moved one hand away from my mouth: *Exhale. Wait.* I brought the hand back to my lips. *Inhale. Slowly.* I pointed to him and repeated the gesture: *Exhale. Inhale.* It took a little while, but eventually he joined in. His breathing slowed. We found a common rhythm. His body abruptly relaxed. He became so limp that I had to hold him more tightly. We'd done it. He allowed me to turn him around. I could hold him better from behind. From the way his back shook, I could tell he was weeping. On impulse, I gave him a hasty pat-down. The reason why he was being pulled down so inexorably into the deep was stuck in his jeans pockets: lead. Lead weights, that is, from my reserve supply. I removed the weights, and they headed for the bottom at high speed. I helped Theo take off his shoes and his jeans. The clothing also sank into the dark depths below us, but at a more leisurely rate.

After that, holding on to Theo was child's play. I detached my substitute mask from its strap, drew it over Theo's face, and adjusted it until it sat right. Theo tilted his head back and blew air out of his nose to expel water from the mask. Now he could see me as clearly as I could see him. He raised a hand, made the "okay" sign, and smiled. His lips were blue from cold. As I answered his sign, I felt like crying too. He might have been an asshole, but his fortitude was preternatural. He didn't even try to ask me, in pantomime, why we weren't going up to the surface. He'd apparently been listening to me closely during the past few days.

We spent the following thirty minutes switching back and forth between the different gases, checking our air supply again and again, and performing together some gymnastic exercises that were supposed to keep Theo from hypothermia. We did knee bends, rolled our wrists and shoulders, swam one behind the other in little circles around the anchor cable. We were connected by the air supply as though by an umbilical cord.

When my required decompression time was over and I could complete my ascent without danger, I signaled to Theo that we were going up. I took hold of him from behind again and carried him laterally a little way, until we were no longer directly under the *Aberdeen*. When we reached a safe distance from the boat, we slowly rose to the surface. The air tasted warm and sweet. Theo began to pant. It's quite possible that he'd only just grasped where he was and what had happened. By all rules of logic, he should have been dead. Maybe he imagined himself in a next world that looked confusingly similar to this one.

Jola stood in the stern, waving and seething. "Fucking hell! Why didn't you send up the deco buoys? Can you imagine how worried I've been?"

I wondered if she'd gone crazy, but there was no time to answer that question or any other. I gave instructions, brought Theo over to the *Aberdeen*'s stern, and closed his fingers around the side rails of the boarding ladder. He didn't have enough strength to pull himself up. I explained to Jola how she should grab hold of him and shoved up from underneath until Theo plopped on the deck like a wet sack. He'd used up his last ounce of strength and lay there like a corpse. I hurriedly removed the things I'd put on him while he was underwater—dive mask, hood, gloves. I ordered Jola to pull off his soaked shirt, and then I sent her to get some towels, a thermal blanket, and the emergency oxygen kit. She obeyed. Theo not only lay there like a corpse, he also looked like one. His skin was waxy yellow. His closed eyes were sunk deep in their sockets. His lips, hands, and feet were appallingly blue. A thin stream of blood ran out of the hair near his left ear. I felt a laceration and a great deal of swelling. While we were underwater, I hadn't noticed the wound. I was just thinking that he shouldn't be moved for any reason when a coughing spell caused him to rear up. I rolled him into a stable position on his side, and salt water came gushing from his mouth. Jola brought the kit. I pressed the breathing apparatus to Theo's lips and said to her, "Drive the boat."

"He wanted to kill himself," she said. As if I'd asked a question that required such an answer. My mouth contorted in disgust. Suicides may stuff lead weights in their pockets, but they don't whack themselves across the head with the big water-pump pliers usually kept in the engine room belowdecks.

"Drive!" I shouted at her. "Drive as fast as you can!"

She dithered a moment and then turned around and ran to the helm stand. The engine sprang to life. A speed of six knots had never been slower. I wrapped Theo in the blanket, gave him oxygen, massaged his limbs. When I was sure I could leave him briefly alone, I crowded next to Jola at the helm stand and made a radio call. Then, when my cell phone finally found a network, I called the hospital. They promised to send a helicopter.

The rest of the return trip seemed endless. While I knelt beside Theo, who gave no more signs of life, my mind kept returning helplessly to how normal he'd seemed underwater. Downright calm and relaxed. As if everything was fine.

I first noticed the coast guard when their Zodiac inflatable boat hove to alongside us. We were still two kilometers from land. Jola turned off the engine. All at once, the *Aberdeen* was full of people. The situation proved too much for me. I frantically warded off the rescue personnel's hands. I may even have tried to keep them away from Theo. "*No tocar! No se debe mover!*" *Don't touch him, don't move him.* My own voice sounded shrill in my ears. Someone pushed me aside. They laid Theo on a stretcher and lifted him over the rail. Jola clambered over behind him. A guy from the rescue service grabbed my arm and tried to get me to leave the boat too. I struck out at him. The *Aberdeen.* I couldn't just leave her out there. The Spaniards exchanged a few quick words, pointing to me and shaking their heads. "We be back here!" one of them called out in English. The outboard motor roared and the Zodiac sped away, leaving a wake of white foam behind it.

And suddenly I was alone. I savored the stillness. No people, no birds. A little wind and the lapping of the waves. The fading sound of the outboard motor as the Zodiac, now far off, hurtled landward. I made no move to get the *Aberdeen* under way again. I simply stood there. Still in my dive suit. I hadn't even dried my hair. I couldn't tell whether I was sweating or freezing. The here and now took my breath away, like a pressure of one thousand bars. As though I were lying on the deepest spot in the Atlantic Ocean. A helicopter rose up above Playa Blanca. It was the last I saw of Jola and Theo.

18

She'd hidden it in such a way that it would pretty much have to be found. Not placed it so obviously that it seemed to have been planted. Nor, however, was it concealed so well that any island police inspector, no matter how dim-witted, could overlook it.

I have hardly any memories of the day after the Wednesday diving expedition. It's as though that whole Thursday has been expunged. Maybe I slept completely through it. Or spent it staring unseeing out the window, stupefied by the emptiness that surrounded me. On Friday morning I ran out of the house before breakfast, armed with vacuum cleaner and mop pail, as if my life depended on doing the usual post-guest cleaning in the Casa Raya. Normally that would have been Antje's job. She would have done it on Saturday afternoon, right after Theo and Jola's departure, so that the house would be ready for the Sunday arrival of our next clients. I, meanwhile, would have taken the day off. But Antje wasn't there anymore, and I had three free days. I didn't even dare to think about Sunday. It seemed to me completely implausible that I'd spend part of it waiting in the airport terminal, holding a sign with the names MARTIN & NANCY. That mental image belonged to a universe that no longer existed.

When I stepped into the Casa Raya, I felt as though someone had punched me in the pit of the stomach. They were still there. They'd left the house only briefly to take a stroll by the sea. At least, that was the statement their stuff made. Everything was hanging around as though still warm from contact with them. There were clothes on the floor. Toothbrushes in the bathroom. An open book on the dining-room table. Only the dried coffee dregs in the cups revealed that some time had passed.

I walked around for a while without knowing where to begin. The unmade bed. The remains of a hasty breakfast. Jola's bikinis hanging over the shower-curtain rod. Tidying up and cleaning had never been my strong points. Most of all, however, I couldn't bring myself to touch anything. The objects all looked to me like props in an amusement park's haunted house.

Then my paralysis metamorphosed into a frenzy of activity. Swift as the wind, I gathered up all the clothes that were lying around and threw them into the washing machine. I cleaned out the closets and meticulously distributed their contents between the two wheeled suitcases. I carefully removed Lotte's photograph from the wall. In the bathroom I packed the toilet kits, never taking longer than a second to decide what belonged to Jola and what to Theo. All at once, things sorted themselves. I washed the dishes, pulled the sheets off the beds, took fresh linens from the bathroom closet, and set about making the beds with the clean sheets. When I lifted up the big double mattress, there it was. On the slats underneath. A black notebook.

I knew immediately what I was looking at. The dates. The handwriting. A few pages torn out and then glued back in. I started reading at random:

What would Lotte have done? When I tried to get up, he put his hands around my throat. I told him to let me go. He tried to shove himself into my mouth. I clenched my teeth. He pressed on my windpipe. My lips opened and I gasped for air.

I dropped the notebook as though it had burned my fingers. Then I picked it up again and laid it on the table. When I'd finished vacuuming and dusting the whole house, cleaning the bathroom, and remaking the beds, when the two suitcases were standing packed and ready at the door, the black notebook was still lying there. The local police inspector would have jumped for joy. The discovery I'd made had been intended for him. If there was one person in the world who wasn't supposed to get his hands on that notebook, that person was me.

Apparently Jola had figured on never going back to the Casa Raya. Even more certainly, she'd assumed that *I* would never set foot in it again. Had Theo drowned as planned, she would presumably have waited until I was back on board the *Aberdeen* and knocked me out with the water-pump pliers too. She'd have taken off my dive suit, maybe arranged a few signs of struggle, and then informed the police by radio. *Help! My partner's been killed! The murderer's here, right next to me! Twenty-nine north, fourteen west. Please come quick!* They would have arrested me while we were still at sea and taken me to the police station for questioning. Jola would have come along as a witness. The suspect: totally distraught. The witness: well prepared. Her statement carefully thought-out and more convincing than mine. Two rivals who have learned to hate each other's guts in the past ten days come to blows on a boat. Between them is a woman who's been abused by one of them and is trying to start a new life with the other. A woman too weak to prevent the catastrophe. Jola wouldn't have accused me; instead she'd have sought, through her tears, to defend me. Confusion and anxiety in perfect balance. And, if possible, in fluent Spanish. *It's all my fault, Señor Comisario. Herr Fiedler was only trying to protect me. He was at his wit's end, just as I was. I should never have told him about any of that. What would you do if you knew the woman you loved was being beaten by another man?* Por favor, *if you will, imagine that. What would you do?*

I would have remained in custody. The stupid police inspector would have privately expressed his respect for me, man-to-man. Then he would have set to work checking Jola's statement. He would have asked half the island about our affair. The guests on the *Dorset* would have been questioned concerning the previous evening's bitter altercation. Divers would have been sent to look for Theo one hundred meters down and might even, in spite of the current, have found his body. With a bad head wound and scuba divers' lead weights in his pockets. The police would have searched my house and, it goes without saying, the Casa Raya. And in the end, they would have discovered the rather ostentatiously hidden diary. Germany would have filed a request for extradition. My trial would have been held there.

In the course of the past few weeks, like a man obsessed, I've gone over Jola's plan again and again. Its complexity. Its refinement. The sheer cold-bloodedness with which she'd developed and then implemented her calculations, one by one, carried along by her conviction that life works like a crime novel: no weak points allowed. Of course, one might believe that only a sick mind would be capable of such painstaking malice. But Jola isn't crazy. It follows, therefore, by an *argumentum e contrario,* that what she did was normal. Maybe not strictly so, statistically speaking, but still within the ordinary human spectrum. Even though she did it extraordinarily well.

I called up Bernie. Countless times. At first he hung up, and then he refused to take my calls. When he was finally ready to talk to me, I asked him why he'd backed out of the expedition the night before it was supposed to take place. He told me that as far as he was concerned, I was the one who'd backed out. He said he got a text message from me informing him that I still needed the boat but not the crew, and that I wanted to go on my expedition with Jola and Theo instead. Right away, Bernie said, that had seemed to him like an idea conceived by a madman.

A text from my phone, just as described in Jola's diary. I found the message in my "Sent" box. She'd mimicked my bad English so well that I wondered for a moment whether I'd written the text myself. On the *Dorset,* Jola had sat next to me the whole time. Practically on my lap. Of course she'd had access to my telephone. I couldn't help admiring her ingenuity. It's said that hostages identify with their captors as a way of coping with their own situation. Maybe believing that Jola's brilliant is the only way for me to bear the unbearable.

I've tried to feel sorry for her. If only a small part of what she says about Theo's excesses is true, she's lived through hell on earth. A defense lawyer would say that a woman who's been brutally and systematically abused over a long period of time finds herself in a permanent state of psychological emergency. He'd arouse the compassion of judge and jury and plead for their recognition of extenuating circumstances. But Jola doesn't need any extenuating circumstances. She's not the accused. I don't feel like pitying her. Nor can I manage to hate her, even though she was prepared to put me behind bars for the rest of my life. Loving her for that would certainly be absurd. Maybe fascination is what you've got left when you don't know how you should feel.

Did she arrive on the island with her plan already formed? Or did she come up with it only after she got here? If so, when? Was it some kind of game at first, and then at a certain point it turned serious? Did Theo's behavior on the *Dorset* finally tip the balance? Or was it my refusal to have sex with her by the beach in Mala that got everything rolling? Looking for answers, I've read her diary so many times I know some passages by heart.

*

On Saturday morning, I lined up the van, went over to the Casa, and picked up the two suitcases. I left in good time for the return flight to Berlin that Jola and Theo had booked. Their tickets and identification documents were in my shirt pocket. It was as though I was driving ghosts to the airport. When I passed the spray-painted EVERYTHING IS WILL, I turned my head to the right. The passenger seats were actually empty.

I thought about the past Wednesday, the day of the murder

attempt, about how I'd driven the same stretch of road on the way to the hospital. I'd brought the *Aberdeen* back to her anchorage as quickly as I could and forced myself to off-load at least the most expensive pieces of my equipment. After tearing across the island like a mental case, I was made to wait at the hospital reception desk. Half an eternity had to pass before the hospital was able to confirm that one Theodor Hast had been admitted more than two hours previously. When asked whether I was a relative of the patient, I stupidly answered, "No." Nobody could tell me anything about his condition. No physician was available for me to talk to. Whether one Jolante von der Pahlen was present in the hospital could not be determined. In any case, no patient with that name had been admitted. When I tried Jola's number, I got a dial tone. She was refusing my calls. Before long, her cell phone was turned off. There was no reception on Theo's phone either.

People wearing robes and slippers meandered through the lobby, eyeing me curiously. Every thirty minutes, I went back to the reception desk and repeated my questions about Theo's condition. Always with the same result: no further details were available, and I couldn't be allowed upstairs. I could only wait for Frau von der Pahlen to come down to the lobby, perhaps to get a drink from the coffee machine, as many patients' relatives did. Then, I was told, I could talk to her.

Darkness fell. The woman at the reception desk was relieved by a doorman, who produced a thermos bottle and switched on a little television set. I got some coffee from the coffee machine. The lobby was empty. It was very quiet. I gazed at the tall glass walls and through them at palm trees and cactuses and behind those the twinkling lights of the island's capital city, and I felt a strange peacefulness. Above me, people were sleeping, some of whom didn't know whether they'd survive the night. I stretched out on the bench. My leaden weariness almost felt good.

When I awoke, a young nurse was sitting in the doorman's place. The TV was off, the thermos bottle had vanished. Dawn was breaking outside. When I requested information about Theo, the girl immediately reached for the telephone, asked questions, and listened to the answers, which poured out of the receiver in a stream of high-speed Spanish. After she hung up, she explained to me in English that Theodor Hast had already been transferred to the central hospital on the neighboring island; the transfer had taken place the previous evening. As far as she understood, Theo would undergo a few final tests and then take a direct flight back to Germany from the airport on the other island, probably in the course of that very afternoon.

I thanked her and drove home. I figured Theo's condition must be at least stable. Getting his head cracked open, half drowning, and then spending an hour in cold water—that was enough for circulatory collapse and severe hypothermia. In that condition, you could die if you didn't get help. But Theo had been helped, he'd turned the corner, and he'd be back on his feet soon. In Germany. Only when I was driving their luggage to the airport did I completely grasp the fact that I'd never see Theo and Jola again, that they'd literally vanished into thin air.

The woman working the check-in counter hesitated a long time and kept asking me to repeat what had happened. A diving accident. Air ambulance back to Germany. She compared the names on the tickets with those on the identity documents several times. Finally she nodded. She promised that the baggage would be delivered to the Berlin address. We put the tickets and papers in the document pockets of the two suitcases. I watched them bump along the conveyor belt and disappear through a rubber curtain into the belly of the airport.

That evening I sat on the terrace with a bottle of wine and read Jola's diary straight through. In the end, I knew the meaning of fear. I lay awake in bed for hours, waiting for the roar of engines and the slamming of car doors and the voices of broad-shouldered Spaniards, informing me that I was under arrest for the attempted murder of Theo Hast. At last, in the early morning hours, it occurred to me that three days had already passed and nobody had come to my house.

Around noon I drove back to the airport to pick up my new clients. Not out of a sense of duty, but because I had no earthly idea what else to do with myself. While we were still in the van, I informed Nancy and Martin that my assistant, who normally helped me run the diving school, had suddenly been taken ill, and that therefore there would probably be organizational issues. Nancy and Martin looked unperturbed by this warning. Like most tourists, they were in a holiday mood, and it didn't seem to them that anything in the world could spoil their diving enjoyment. They found the Casa Raya enchanting.

The following Tuesday we were joined by Ralph, a regular client and experienced diver who'd been coming to me for years. Starting Friday, I also had a family of first-time divers, including children, so that I had to work in two shifts. I warned everybody about organizational problems. There weren't any. In the evenings, I'd drive home as early as possible to fill diving cylinders and wash out equipment. I answered e-mails and did the bookkeeping. I worked late into the night. Sometime after the weekend, I went to my bank's website and found that a payment in the amount of fourteen thousand euros had been credited to my account. In re: "Diving instruction for casting Lotte Hass." I stared so long at this entry that my online session was ended for security reasons.

I thought constantly about Jola and her plan. I kept looking in her diary. As long as I could admire Jola, I wasn't afraid of her. On one occasion, I dialed her cell phone number. It no longer existed. After making that effort, I was soaked with sweat, like a marathon runner. From Jola's Facebook page I learned that a new season of *Up and Down* was in the works. About Theo I learned nothing.

*

Christmas passed without anything happening. On New Year's Eve, I had clients and went to bed before midnight. The New Year was 2012. A number like any other. After breakfast on New Year's morning, I sat around for a while. Exactly fourteen years had passed since the day I left Germany and began my new life on the island. Fourteen years. An unimaginable span of time. I thought about the day of the murder attempt, or more precisely, about a very specific moment in that day, and an instantaneous feeling of gratitude flooded through me. All at once, that second appeared to me as the most important moment of my life. I had hesitated, looked at Theo's unconscious face, and thought about Jola. And then I had decided. I hadn't let Theo sink to the bottom of the sea; instead, I'd saved his life. Gratitude for that decision drove tears into my eyes. I sat there with my empty coffee cup in front of me and wept. Afterward I could breathe, freely and deeply. Something had changed. I needed only to think back on that hesitation to feel that I'd become someone else. I no longer understood why I'd found "Stay out of it" such an appealing motto fourteen years before. Now it repelled me. When I climbed into the van to go diving, I felt better. In a fundamental way.

❋

January was, as always, a slow time. Who goes on vacation right after New Year's? Only a few retirees, singles, and freelancers. On the first Saturday of the year, a single new client arrived. Her name was Katja, and she was a criminal defense lawyer, a specialist in such major felonies as murder, homicide, and rape. We hit it off from the start. On the first evening, I invited her to dinner. On the second evening, we made love. She was over forty and correspondingly avid. She sucked my cock for a long time. In the end, she straddled me and rode me like an experienced jockey to the finish line. On the third evening, we signed a contract that bound her to secrecy and stipulated her consultation fee as equivalent to the costs of completing an Advanced Open Water Diver course and obtaining nitrox certification.

I told her the whole story. As I spoke, I had to control myself to keep from blubbering. Only then did I realize how much the previous weeks had exhausted me. The silence. The waiting. The questions. I couldn't take any more. I described to Katja how Jola's plan kept turning through my mind in an endless loop, how I couldn't stop questioning what had happened, how my obsession was eating me up inside. She said she was a lawyer, not a psychiatrist, and I should pull myself together. I gave her the diary. She read it so fast that it looked as though she was just superficially flipping through the pages.

When she finished, she raised her eyes and asked, "So how much of this is true?"

"In the beginning a lot, in the middle not much, and in the end nothing at all."

She smiled. "One of you is brilliant."

"What's that supposed to mean?" I asked. "Don't you believe me?"

"You haven't hired me to believe you. You've hired me to tell you what you should do."

Katja advised me to write this account. Because you never know what's coming. Why has Theo kept his trap shut so far about what happened on the *Aberdeen*? Maybe he and Jola have reconciled. Maybe he's blackmailing her. Or he's afraid of a public scandal. But there's no statute of limitations for attempted murder. Some factor or other completely beyond my control could induce Theo to bring charges after all. And then Jola will defend herself with the oldest of all human sentences: *It wasn't me.* She'll declare that Theo's only purpose is to destroy her with accusations of murder, while the actual guilty party is Sven Fiedler, the perpetrator of the failed attack aboard the *Aberdeen.*

After that, Katja said, it would be testimony against testimony. Jola's word against Theo's. Jola would probably have the public's sympathies, and perhaps the judge's as well, on her side. There were no witnesses to the murder attempt, and it would be too late to gather forensic evidence. At this point, the diary would come into play, just as Jola planned. The added weight, calculated to tip the final balance. Of course, I could destroy the notebook and claim it never existed. But if Jola had been cunning enough to make a copy, I could forget about trying to defend myself. Being caught in such a lie would mean a free ticket to the slammer.

Katja's observations precisely summarized my fears. She recommended that I start composing my account as soon as possible. She said that I should proceed section by section, setting my version of events against Jola's diary entries. Otherwise, she told me, my memory would soon start writing its own story. In her view, there was nothing more corrupt than human memory. First the details of incidents would become blurred, and then the incidents themselves.

"Maybe someday," Katja said, "you'll even come to believe that Jola's telling the truth and not you."

She gave me an ironic smile when she said that. As a defense attorney, she's probably all too accustomed to being lied to by her clients. I slept with her twice more, out of gratitude. Then she flew back to Nuremberg, where she's attached to the district court.

The very next day, I got on the telephone and canceled all the clients on my schedule. I took my home page down from the Internet and set up an automatic e-mail reply informing all inquiring parties that the diving school was closed. It took only a few days to sell my complete inventory of equipment. A colleague in Thailand knew someone who was planning on setting up his own business. I arranged for everything to be loaded into containers. Since then, I've been sitting around in half-empty rooms, and I have time. Outside there's a delicate green covering on the slopes of the volcanoes. It's the island spring. The talk in the news revolves around the euro crisis, the presidential crisis, and the Syrian crisis. As though time's been standing still. As though nothing, absolutely nothing, has changed.

I occasionally see Antje while we're both out shopping. She's looking good. She and Ricardo are considering buying a little house in Tinajo. Todd waits outside, tied up next to the shopping carts, and pretends not to know me. Not long ago, I ran into Bernie in the entrance of the Wunder Bar café. He congratulated me on Antje's pregnancy and laughed when I looked bewildered. And then we broke records. He delivered the longest coherent speech of his life, and I understood more English words per minute than ever before.

He said I shouldn't imagine I was getting away with anything, because everybody, but everybody, knew what had happened, and no one believed it was an accident. And therefore I could count on getting what was coming to me, one way or another, sooner or later, and it made no difference if I packed my things and pissed off like a cowardly dog. People had contacts, people were connected, and they'd make sure I couldn't work anywhere in the world. At least, not as a diving instructor. I was a danger to the clients, he said, and a disgrace to the sport. In other words, he was looking forward to the day I'd leave the island, and he wasn't the only one who felt that way. Just to let me know, he said.

The expulsion from paradise. There could be no response to such a rant. And so I left him standing there, a stocky fellow with a five-day beard and a pleasant, weather-beaten Scottish face. I didn't care about any of that. I didn't care about *him.* I should have seen what an asshole he was a long time ago.

That evening I called Antje and congratulated her. She started to cry. She said she'd always wanted us to have a child together. Ricardo was a nice guy, but she'd loved only one man in her life, namely me. I took care to sound as cheerful as possible. I told her how well pregnancy became her. I said everything had turned out all right in the end. I suggested we could see each other in Germany when she went home to visit her family. Antje was still sobbing a little, and she kept repeating, "Ah, Sven." But she sounded more wistful than desperate.

Now that I've finished writing, waiting is hard. I often spend a whole day not knowing what to do with myself. I've decided against flying. Instead I'm going to put my few belongings on a cargo ship and accompany them back to Germany. The voyage to Hamburg takes fourteen days, departure is early next week. I'm looking forward to the journey. I no longer understand how I could have taken this island for something special. It's a place like any other. War isn't a geographical phenomenon.

This morning I googled Jola's name and wound up looking at a gossip magazine's website. The headline read, "Jola Pahlen: Dream Wedding with Writer!" Below, a photograph of her and Theo. They looked reciprocally radiant. Jola had her dark hair done the same way as she had that evening on the *Dorset,* braided into a crown. A pair of spectacles I'd never seen before was perched on Theo's nose. The brief article reports that "Bella Schweig" has announced her engagement to the writer Theodor Hast. Rumor has it that the pair will go on an Arctic expedition in order to be married at the North Pole.

Right after reading that, I went to the web page of a real estate agency that specializes in vacation homes and listed the Casa Raya and the Residencia at a bargain price. I don't know why, but I can't bear the sound of the surf anymore.

ALSO BY

JULI ZEH

IN FREE FALL

In

is an unforgettable ride through a world where

Fiction

Printed in the United States
by Baker & Taylor Publisher Services